I THO YOU SAID THIS WOULD WORK

a novel

ANN GARVIN

LAKE UNION
PUBLISHING

Text copyright © 2021 by Ann Garvin
All rights reserved.

No part of this book may be reproduced, or stored in a retrieval system, or transmitted in any form or by any means, electronic, mechanical, photocopying, recording, or otherwise, without express written permission of the publisher.

Published by Lake Union Publishing, Seattle

www.apub.com

Amazon, the Amazon logo, and Lake Union Publishing are trademarks of Amazon.com, Inc., or its affiliates.

ISBN-13: 9781542022330
ISBN-10: 1542022339

Cover design by Kimberly Glyder

Printed in the United States of America

For all my friends who are my family, and vice versa.

Happiness is a place between too little
and too much.
—Finnish proverb

CHAPTER ONE

IF KATIE CALLED HOLLY

What I did at my house when I got the call about my best friend Katie's cancer: I inhaled through my nose, like my relaxation app told me to do when my body was deep into the whole fight-or-flight fiasco. As humid air rushed into my lungs, I asked myself, *Are you safe? Do you need to slap something or run away? Is this a good time for a drop of RumChata in your morning coffee?*

I exhaled and answered in the most grown-up way possible while trying not to hyperventilate. *Yes, I'm safe. No, I don't need to punch anything or, God forbid, exercise. And no, Samantha, no alcohol for breakfast—even just this one time.* So instead, I threw a plate that hit the drapes and slid into a full laundry basket with a muffled thump, in the least satisfying dish-tantrum of all time.

I steeled myself and dialed the number I hadn't pulled from my phone since Katie's first cancer battle. And before that, maybe once or twice after a couple of glasses of wine and some college reminiscing. But I always hung up before the connection was made, knowing how Holly's voice would sound. Terse, distant, unwelcoming.

Today, I had to see if Holly had heard from Katie. If she had gotten the news that our college roommate and mutual best friend might be deathly sick again. I put my head against the cool stainless steel of the refrigerator. I'd lived through the death of my husband, Jeff, and both of my parents, effectively leaving me alone to raise my daughter—I couldn't lose my best friend too. Holly's voice mail kicked in: "You've reached Holly Dunfee's phone." I hung up quickly and felt my brain go, *Whew!*

At first I didn't know why I had such an urge to call Holly. The person who used to mean so much to me but who hadn't acknowledged my existence in years.

I shuffled in my Birkenstocks to my bedroom, where I slid off my pajama bottoms and grabbed the jeans I'd been wearing all week while helping Maddie, my daughter, pack to leave for the summer.

In the mirror over my dresser, my hair looked like I'd been stored upside down and in a tube all night. With a drop of gel and water, I reconstituted my flattened fine and frizzy hair and wiped the remnants of mascara from under my eyes. Embarrassing confession: partly why I called Holly was because I wanted to know which best friend Katie had on speed dial when life was about to get hard. Was it Holly my best friend wanted, or me?

You'd think that I'd have been so devastated by the cancer news that I wouldn't have been wrapped up in such ugly, competitive mean-girl things. I pulled on a wool cardigan because despite it being a warm June in Wisconsin, I was shivering.

I needed to be Katie's emergency contact, her first call. We joked that we were each other's life partners, but it wasn't a joke. We *were* life partners by now, after twenty-some years as besties. After sliding my feet into a pair of unlaced tennis shoes, I hopped on one foot, then the other, so I could yank them over my heels.

It wasn't enough for me to be Maddie's point person—that was a given, at least while my daughter was still at home. Who knew what would happen when she was free of me, on her own. I could only dip my toe into the feelings of emptiness I'd experience without Maddie in the house. So, until I could face that, I needed to know that the other person that I loved so much, my Katie, would call me first when she needed help. I told myself that most widows probably felt the same when life was about to dramatically change, like a solitary helium balloon with no one to hold on to my string.

That was some of it, of course. But not the whole Samantha, Katie, and Holly story. Not even close.

———

I grabbed my keys, pushed my way out the front door, and started my durable Subaru. Katie and I had already defeated cancer once. Like a good Wisconsin native, I had organized the call tree, collected casseroles, and returned the washed dishes with ovarian-cancer-peach thank-you notes. I had made spreadsheets of her treatments, composed Facebook posts, and shared Instagram stories of Katie's plucky progress as she recovered. Katie sometimes credited me for saving her life, but I didn't. She was my dearest friend, and being command central kept me too busy to consider what it might mean to be without her. What that cold and lonely tundra would feel like. I was happy to manage the details of life while she managed to stay alive.

My tires squealed at the familiar corner on the way to Saint Mary's Hospital, and I made a mental note to check the air pressure, one I would no doubt quickly forget.

When my husband, Jeff, died before Maddie was born, an aneurism having burst in his brain, Katie moved into my house. At midnight and four a.m., she picked up fatherless baby Maddie and nestled her in my arms to nurse. Katie fed me broccoli and made me walk so my muscles didn't turn into the cheese I ate on so many delivery pizzas. I gave her all my computer passwords, and she kept the mortgage paid, the heat on, and teenagers coming to shovel snow.

When Katie got sick, I had my chance to repay her love and care. I would have traded places with her if I could have. Every time she threw up, I wished I were the one retching into the basin instead of the one holding a cool washcloth to the back of her neck. Honestly, that was saying something because anyone who knew me knew I was a huge emo-barfer. I tended to cry and bargain with God and get barf up in my nose and hair. Then, for days, it was all I talked about. Like barfing was news.

I'd have done so much more than organize things and barf for Katie. I'd have taken the chemo for her, if I could have. But that wasn't the way cancer worked. Cancer accepted no substitutes. That was why we all shuddered when the word was uttered. Cancer was synonymous with loss of control for everyone involved.

I squinted into the rearview mirror and swiped one of those three-in-one makeup sticks over my lips, cheeks, and eyelids so I didn't look as terrible as I felt. In the reflection I saw the hopeful reason that I had called Holly and that it wasn't because of misguided competition, pride, and fear.

If Katie had called Holly first, maybe she wouldn't need the over-the-top *Full Radical Healing Experience-for-Katie*. I had nicknamed my brand of caregiving FRHEK to make fun of myself, to lighten the load. I was proud of the friendship Katie and I shared and that I could go the distance with someone who I hadn't created, with help, in my womb. It proved I could be the kind of person, friend, you didn't just walk away from for no reason. That my presence mattered in a life.

On impulse, I swerved into Walgreens to pick up a few essentials and still made it to the hospital in a respectable time. As I stepped into the hallway, I was reminded that the cleaning crew used a citrus-scented solvent. It smelled like Orange Crush, which reminded me of skating at a roller rink as a teen, but now it made me nauseous.

I tried to call Holly again on the way to the Oncology floor. But as I walked into room 425, iPhone to my ear, the first thing I saw was Holly in a chair next to the bed. A frosty fatigue slid through me, my body urging me to duck and cover. It was as if Holly's presence were saying, *I'm here now. You aren't needed.* Then I saw Katie's smile, filled with ambiguity in the way smiles could be—happy to see me, stiff with resignation, sorry for what she was about to ask us to do.

Katie had called Holly first. I had to face it. Deep down, there was only one real reason for that. If my darling friend, the woman who was more sister than separate, had called Holly first, then Katie didn't need casseroles and Facebook posts and someone to keep her life on track so it was in good shape when she returned to it.

Nope, if she had called Holly, she needed the kind of person who could smite a rapidly dividing cell with a look, wrangle an arrogant doctor to her knees, and throttle an insurance company with clever legalese. She needed a sanctimonious, irreverent, inappropriate-humor-filled bitch.

And Holly was the woman for the job.

CHAPTER TWO

FUN, FUN, FUN. DONE.

The shock of seeing Holly looking the same plus better, sleeker but still distant, threw me. I'd been reminiscing about her on the drive over. Once, on the way to some college class, we'd been singing along to Hootie and the Blowfish. I only ever sang in the car with Holly and was deep into shouting the lyrics "I wanna love you, the bear said, the bear said I can." With hilarious outrage she said, "That's not right! Who is the bear? What bear? How do you get 'bear said' out of 'best that I can'?" I didn't believe her, and we laughed until she had to pull the car over. She'd hit the horn three times, and I'd clutched my stomach and gasped for breath. I never laughed with abandon with anyone like I did with Holly. She had a way of pointing out foolishness without making me the fool.

For a moment I'd had the ridiculous notion that maybe Holly was past the misery of whatever had ended us. Maybe we could laugh again. But now, in the room with her, I saw that Holly was neck deep in discomfort. A spotty flush crept up her jaw, something that despite her polish she couldn't hide. This was not how Holly greeted a friend, and I knew it. Shame, guilt, and my old, dear companion conflict avoidance reared up and muted those memories of our friendship long gone.

The nurse taking Katie's blood pressure bent her head, and Holly put her finger to her lips to keep me quiet. As if I didn't know to be silent during procedures. As if I hadn't been by Katie's side during hundreds of blood pressure measurements. The sudden urge to go somewhere quiet and slip into a quick, dreamless sleep would have swamped me if not for a competing urge to slap Holly.

In a way, that urge to fight and nap characterized my life in general and any difficult relationship I had. If someone—my father, or my husband—made me mad, I got stressed and then lethargic, in that order. That was how my sleep disorder worked.

My hypersomnia began in my high school economics class, a subject my taskmaster of a father excelled in. He'd make me work after dinner and into the night, angrily saying, "Clear the fluff out of your head."

If I made a mistake and tried to explain why I was confused, he'd tap my forehead hard and say, "Stop talking."

My mother would notice my eyelids drooping and rescue me by sending me to bed. Maybe my body got the message: *Once you get to the end of your rope, sleep is next.* She'd smooth the spot on my forehead where I could still feel my father's finger.

"You're lucky, Sam. If I could play dead around your dad, I'd roll like a possum into my pajamas and never take them off." She'd switch the light off and say, "It's okay to give up some ground to keep the peace."

Even when my doctor prescribed different medications during my sleepiest of semesters at college, my mom would say over long distance, "It's not a terrible thing to have a shutoff switch. Don't drug a gift horse in the nap." I realized later that she was battling learned helplessness and depression that came from living with a mean control freak. My mom would sigh her own resigned sigh and say, "Oh, Sam. Just take a nap. Not everything is worth fighting for." She was both right and wrong about that.

I'd remind my mom that a sleep disorder was serious, and I was having trouble in all my classes. She'd sigh and say, "Who's to know?" And I saw that was the stunning truth. After years of negating yourself, in the end there *was* no self. No knowing.

Holly, my roommate and best friend, took care of me. She'd set alarms so I wouldn't miss class, watched for stress, made excuses to friends when I needed a quick sleep.

My abrupt sleeping continued to roll like a determined fog through to the present, and just seeing Holly after all these years kicked off my fatigue.

"You have great blood pressure, 120/70," the nurse said.

"Is it?" Holly asked. "Maybe you should take it again to make sure."

The nurse didn't engage. Instead, she said to Katie, "Anything you need?"

Katie shook her head and reached out to me.

I shoved my phone into my pocket. "Sorry, you guys. I would have been here sooner, but I stopped to get some things."

I held my collection of recycled bags with Goodwill, IKEA, and Trader Joe's logos and knocked into an off-white wall with my funny bone trying to get to the other side of the bed. The side Holly was not on. I was late to the party and feeling all the knotty feelings I experienced when all three of us were together, which hadn't been since the night Maddie was born, eighteen years ago.

I took Katie's petite hand. Her cool fingers gave me a squeeze. I tried humor borrowed from my eighteen-year-old daughter's vocabulary. "What's the tea, bitches?" but it came out, "What's the bee, bitches?" I corrected. "The tea. What's the tea?" I tried to explain. "Maddie says that's like, 'What's happening? What's the news? The 911.' And *bitch* isn't bitchy, it's a compliment."

"411?" said Holly.

"What?"

"I love you so much, Sam," Katie said in a way that meant, *You're so cute, like an idiot is cute.*

"411 is for information. 911 is for emergencies," said Holly.

"Okay, then. What's the 411? What's going on?" I dropped the bags and tried to shove them under the bed. I was such a "Try Hard." When your friend might be out of remission, you didn't come with essential oils and fancy slang from another generation. You came with a fully charged phone and your big know-it-all brain, like Holly.

"My blood counts are wonky, and they've admitted me for a workup," said Katie.

"Oh, okay." I bent and kissed Katie on the cheek. From that angle I saw she wore a pulse oximeter, and an intravenous port had been inserted and taped onto the back of her hand. Katie hated that spot for an IV. I should have been there to advocate. Her wristband lay under the tubing, and I read her name, *Kate Martin.* The same birthday as mine.

"All this for a few tests?" I asked.

Holly's phone buzzed, and she picked it up. "Ralph. Great. What do you have for me?" She stood, high-powered lawyer Holly, and moved to the doorway.

"Thank you so much for coming, Sam," Katie said.

"Of course. I mean, seriously, Katie. Of course, you know I always come."

"I know." She pulled my hand to her cheek and snuggled my knuckles.

"What's Holly doing?"

"There's some weird thing in my insurance she's checking on. If I have to go through everything all over again, I need to be covered."

I heard Holly in the hall. "Don't screw with me here. Just find out what we need to do."

"It's good you called her, then. I mean, if you need someone yelled at, call Holly. If you need an in-hospital manicure, I'm your

9

gal." So I didn't sound completely pathetic, I added, "We make a good team."

Holly reentered the room and said, "Out of pocket." A phrase I knew sometimes meant unavailable and sometimes meant a form of payment. That was Holly, though: if she could use a buzzword instead of a full sentence, she was all over it. The fewer words spoken, the greater your personal value. I had loved it when we'd lived together. We'd had our own language that was flexible and clear only to us. For example, the word *skirt* could mean we were ready to leave a party or a bar or that we liked what someone was wearing. "Those pants are skirt!" she'd say, and I'd feel stylish all day. *Nugget* meant the boy in front of us in class or at the bar was delish, but it could also be used as a pet name for each other. "Hey, Nugget," I'd say, and we'd toss each other a kiss. Holly had created the vocabulary. We deciphered and expanded the meanings, and no one but the three of us were in on the game.

Katie scooted over an inch and patted the bed for me to sit, and when she motioned for Holly to get closer, I took another second-long assessment. The natural blush in Katie's cheeks sat high, as if she'd stepped in from a walk in the spring air. The chicken pox scar on her temple was present and accounted for, and her beautiful head of hair fell to her shoulders. We saved her chestnut locks the first time around with a cold-cap system: an icy hat that patients wore during their chemotherapy infusions that helped keep hair on heads rather than falling out in hairbrushes. By all outward accounts, she looked better than I did after a full makeover at Sephora.

"Okay, you two. We gotta talk. Bradley and Bebe will be here soon," said Katie.

"Your parents are coming? From Arizona?" If they were coming, Katie might be really sick. Bebe had such travel anxiety that they drove a maximum two hours a day, and only if Bebe sat in the back seat chain-smoking unfiltered Pall Malls. Bradley feared that any trip, even to a nearby Costco, might kill them both, given the smoke-filled hotbox of a car they drove around in. So they had moved to a community that had everything within walking distance and almost never left it.

The one time they flew to visit Katie, Bebe lit up in the bathroom, got in a fight with the flight attendant, and the YouTube video almost went viral. Bradley had coaxed her back to her seat with red licorice and a cocktail of lorazepam and beta blockers. When they reached their destination, Bebe's blood sugar was sky high, and the woman was so uncharacteristically chill, Katie saw her and started to cry.

"So this isn't a simple checkup?" I said.

"At ease, Sammie," Holly said.

Ugh, the name I hated, but only when she said it. When others called me Sammie, to be sweet or give me a nickname, it was fine. Holly knew my dad had called me Sammie to be condescending, not endearing. The authority in Holly's tone and the flush of frustration that filled my throat choked the witty retort I was sure to later say into the rearview mirror in my car.

"I'm trying to catch up. I only just got here, and already Katie's parents are on the way."

"There's no catching up. We don't know anything yet," Holly said with the royal *we* that Katie knew would annoy me.

"My parents are coming for a reason. I need you two to do something for me." Katie said, "Misty called last night."

"Misty? Tom's new wife, Misty?" As I said this, I could almost hear Holly biting her tongue. *How many Mistys do we know, Sammie?*

Instead, Holly said, "What could she possibly want that she didn't already get? Or did Tom get his johnson caught in someone again?"

"Is it bad to say I hoped for that?" said Katie sheepishly. "Or better yet, that Misty left Tom for her personal trainer or masseuse."

"Hope is a thing with lady parts," said Holly. "Rosie and I will get T-shirts made for the next Gay Pride parade. Or is *lady parts* too obtuse?"

"I think *lady parts* is self-explanatory," Katie said reasonably.

I glanced between Katie and Holly. Wondered if it was safe to laugh, if this joking was meant for me too.

Katie giggled. She knew Holly's partner, Rosie. Holly had moved back to town a year ago, but I had yet to meet her wife. Ten years after college, Katie had called me and said, "Holly has a girlfriend. She's gay." I had felt a sharp pang, the dimples and creases of the dried-up peach pit that I imagined lived in my stomach filled with the acidic loss of Holly. I had so many questions, and Katie and I tried to answer them together over many phone calls, coffee dates, wine bar outings. *When did Holly know? In college? Had she wanted to tell me but didn't? Was that why she got so mad at the Mike thing?*

"Do you care if she's gay?" Katie had asked.

"Only inasmuch as she didn't tell me. I mean, I know we're not friends anymore, but still."

But still what, Sammie? I questioned myself. *She didn't like you as much as you thought? Once she didn't live with you, you were no longer important? Your perception of your own value, admittedly low, is even lower than you know?*

I knew that Katie, Rosie, and Holly met for dinner occasionally or for beers on the Memorial Union overlooking the lake. I'd figured out that the few times Katie didn't immediately reply to my texts were when she was with Holly. Then it was as if Holly's twenty-some years of living in Manhattan hadn't happened, and everybody was friends but me. I was the awkward girl who had a mean dad, an opaque mom, and a liar husband. I was the woman with one friend and her daughter leaving the nest. And somehow this was all my doing.

When Katie said, "Hope is a thing with a muff," I tuned back in to the conversation.

Holly said, "I'm partial to muff."

"Obviously," I said, because, well, *obviously*. I wanted to join in the fun, remind Holly that we once thought the same things were funny, but it slipped out sounding sour, and so to sweeten things I said, "Hope is a thing with ovaries."

And with the word *ovaries*, we were all reminded why we were having a crappy and uncomfortable reunion in a hospital room.

"That would be a great slogan for a fundraiser," Katie said in her kind voice.

Fun, fun, fun, done. This was what we always said when something we were doing went from funny to unfunny in a flash. It was like being roommates in college again before that night we started as besties and ended as stunned and separated graduates. Unable to move back and unsure how to move forward without each other. A night that started with a party, boys, and drinking and ended with something none of us knew how to talk about.

"Focus, you guys," Katie said. "Tom dropped Peanut off at a dog pound, I mean a shelter, where they live in LA. Misty thinks it's one of those places that kills unadoptable dogs. Nobody wants a diabetic Great Pyrenees, especially one Peanut's extralarge size." She glanced at the wall clock. "It's nine a.m. here, and I'm going to start calling every single shelter until I find him. If they let me, I'll put down whatever money they need to keep him there. Then I'm going to go get him. I hate Tom."

It was clear to anyone looking at Katie that she didn't hate Tom. She inexplicably loved Tom, and Tom, for some reason, blamed Katie for his affair, her inability to conceive, her preoccupation with infertility, and her selfish cancer needs. All this and more justified, in Tom's mind, his search for happiness elsewhere. Whenever I thought of this, my anger rattled through me like a tornado, tossing my emotions like a chair through a window.

Holly closed her hand over Katie's. "You can't go get that dog."

She didn't understand people and their pets. In 2013, Katie and I had driven to Colorado Springs after the flooding and rescued the white puff of puppy that was Peanut. When we arrived on scene and saw the pup filthy with floodwaters and with too much skin for his body, we both fell in love. He'd been huddled against a worker's boot, shivering, until he saw Katie. One look at her with his old-man eyes and it was over for both of them.

Peanut's and Katie's devotion to each other only increased as the dog grew, and Tom was the kind of man who exploited that kind of love. He hadn't been part of the rescue effort, even though he and Katie had been married six years by then. Two years later, during their divorce, Tom had the time and money, and fought Katie for Peanut until she ran out of both. When Tom and Misty moved cross-country last year with Peanut, I thought Katie would never get out of bed from the grief.

"Yes, I *can* go get him," Katie said, her jaw set, her pale face determined. "I'm well enough right now to travel. I did not save him after all that flooding and shoot him with insulin every damn day, and train him to pee in Tom's shoes, to let him go." She took in a shuddering breath and said, "I should have gone right away. I can't believe I didn't. I've just been so tired."

For the first time, I noticed that Katie clutched a Kleenex with traces of what looked like mascara in her hand. The thought of Katie putting on makeup before coming to the hospital, dressing up for a possible date with cancer, made my heart turn into a tight fist.

I said, "Holly's right; you can't go anywhere right now. But . . ."

"Can you even imagine what is going through Peanut's big head?" said Katie.

"Someone will adopt him," said Holly.

Katie gasped. Suggesting that someone other than Katie would end up with Peanut was blasphemy. I wasn't proud to admit it, but I was almost relieved that the perfect Holly had made such a stupendous mistake.

In one quick movement, Katie swung her legs over the side of the bed, stretching the IV tubing in the process. "Tell my parents I had to go. Tell them whatever. I'm going."

I placed my hands on her shoulders before the IV ripped out of her vein. "No, *I'll* go. I'll go get him. I'll find him and fly him home."

I suddenly wanted to sip the words back into my mouth like loose spaghetti noodles. Who was I kidding? I was a fluff-pillows and nod-at-nurses kind of person, not a swoop-cross-country, get-into-a-fight-with-a-friend's-ex-husband-and-emancipate-a-Great-Pyrenees person. The breed alone evoked the moving of a mountain. I had a sleep disorder, and if this interaction with Holly proved anything, I was a coward. What would I say to Tom if I ran into him in LA? I pictured it, me trying to get the leash from Tom as he held me at arm's length, his big meaty hand on my forehead, my arms swiping in the wind.

"He can't be flown. He's way too big for the seats, and he would die under the plane in a crate without someone monitoring his blood sugar and keeping him calm. I have to drive him. We bought that old VW camper bus for this reason. Peanut can't even look at a compact car, let alone fly, without getting hypoglycemic. Remember that one time I test-drove a MINI Cooper and Peanut passed out when I pulled into the driveway? He took one look at the car through the window, flopped onto the carpet, and didn't move until I drove it back to the dealership."

"Tom spent thousands to get that dog. Why get rid of him now?" asked Holly.

"Misty is allergic."

"How did that conversation go?" With a whiny voice, Holly mimicked Misty. "I'm sorry we racked up tons of lawyer bills fighting you, and I got both your dog and husband, but boo-hoo, he makes my eyes itchy."

Katie had a way of looking at you when she was truly taxed, like the cartoon Belle from *Beauty and the Beast* come alive, but weary, oh so weary of the falling rose petals in the bell jar. Holly and I both knew that tears were coming from the girl who rarely cried. In college we would go into a comedy routine and make Katie laugh while we aggressively hugged her so we didn't have to see the weird smile before she sobbed. We always protected Katie, not because she was weak, but because she was so strong. If she was crying, something terrible was happening.

An urgent feeling flooded my chest. I was at an auction with a paddle, and I was competing against Holly and death. So I raised my hand and said, "I'll drive him back. No problem. I'll do it."

Holly laughed at me. "You can't drive that dog back. It would take you a year. You'll have to stop and nap at every McDonald's, rest stop, and national monument along the way. There isn't enough caffeine in the world to keep you awake, driving, and monitoring that dog."

I opened my mouth to object, but it hurt so much to know how well she knew me, and we weren't even friends anymore. Besides, I was conflict avoidant, not a liar. She was right.

After her closing argument, Holly turned to Katie and said, "Why doesn't Misty take an allergy pill if she's so sorry?"

Katie closed her eyes. "It messed with her sex drive."

"That's not true. Is that even true? I'm going to google that." Holly picked up her phone, and with her flawless gel-manicured nails, her blown-out bob swinging forward, she typed ferociously onto her screen.

"I can do it. I can," I insisted. I needed to do something to show everyone in the room that I was the kind of friend that could go the distance. That if you weren't my friend it was your own damn fault.

"Can Maddie go with you?" Katie looked hopeful.

"No, she's leaving for Colorado for her internship."

Katie touched my arm, knowing how the words *she's leaving* filled me with dismay. To Holly she said, "Maddie has a prestigious internship in Boulder and is going to live with my cousin and watch her kids at night."

"It's perfect timing. I'll need something to do this summer. You guys can keep me updated. It'll be an adventure," I said instead of saying, *I can't bear to be in my home, accidently wandering into my daughter's empty room while waiting to visit my sick best friend all summer long.*

To everyone's credit and my shame, no one fought me on that one. When your nest was emptying and you were a widow, no one needed you at home. I stifled a yawn. The stress was getting to me, snuffing out my lit-up neurons like candles after a Catholic Christmas Mass. That was how I always thought about it. Stress ignited my hypersomnia, and the call to sleep was irresistible. But not like the people on YouTube who had the kind of narcolepsy where they flopped to the ground like discarded dolls. I felt it coming on.

I knew if I was going to persuade them that I could drive across country, I couldn't take a speed nap on the corner of Katie's bed. I made a show of looking at my phone and said, "Hang on. I have to take this. It's Maddie."

I knocked my way out of the room, bumping against the bed and the metal doorframe, and felt slightly better in the hall. A man with a gauzy hairnet pushed a large silver cabinet past me; it rattled with discarded dishes. A woman in a lab coat rushed in the opposite direction, and I followed her with my eyes. I didn't need to lie down for a nap. If I could sit and sleep for ten minutes, I could give my brain what it needed and return to make my case.

I ran my hand against the cool wall and ducked into the room next to Katie's. A stripped hospital bed with an exposed mattress took up a large portion of the room. I dropped into a small cushioned chair and felt the grip of sleep envelop me at the same time as I heard a man's voice, confusingly close: "Don't even think about it."

CHAPTER THREE

NEVER TOGETHER AGAIN

I felt something on my forearm. A shake. A voice I didn't recognize said, "Ma'am? Are you all right?"

A piercing beep sounded somewhere above me, and I opened my eyes. Tried to focus. I was used to this, if you could be used to something as jarring as waking up to a stranger standing too close. I pushed back in my chair and said, in a voice that I knew sounded very, very sleepy, "I'm fine. I'm okay. I was resting." And then ridiculously, "I don't live here."

A scratchy voice with radio-like feedback came from over my shoulder. A woman. "Can I help you?"

The man's voice, too loudly, as if I might be hard of hearing, repeated, "Can we help you?"

I shook my head and focused on the person crouching in front of me. The thing about a hypersomnia-reset nap was that when I—as much as I hated to use the phrase—*came to*, my first impressions were the most honest ones in my day. I "saw" everything without bias or censure. All the guilt, chronic niceness, and fear of conflict that made me second-guess everything woke up a minute or two after I did.

Say I was taking a snooze in a friend's bathroom, one with tiny glitter pineapple wallpaper I was unsure about before the nap. Postnap,

I would see it as truly terrible. The shirt I wondered about earlier in the day was as dumpy as I'd feared. *And this man in front of me,* I thought, *with his full lips, flawless complexion, and long, lush eyelashes, would make a lovely girl.*

But he made a beautiful, stunning man.

I touched my hair, the universal sign for *You're cute; I hope I don't look like I usually do,* and sat up.

"I'm fine," I said loudly. "I don't need help."

The voice on the speaker said, "Oka—" and logged off so quickly it sounded like the speaker had the hiccups.

The man stood. He was taller and older than I had first thought. He slipped on a pair of glasses. "I was on the phone in the bathroom," he said, looking sheepish.

"In the bathroom?"

"It's private."

"That's why I was napping in here."

He nodded and said, "Aren't we a pair."

"Are we? A pair of what?"

"Weirdos, maybe? Introverts? I fight on the phone in empty bathrooms, and you sleep in deserted rooms."

"If I'm honest, it doesn't have to be a room. I can sleep anywhere. When I'm stressed, I get sleepy." The sun cut an angle off the foot of the bed, and the roar of a hectic hospital increased as my sleepiness dissipated. "Do you fight on the phone everywhere?"

"I have to think about that." He paused, dropped his phone into his lab coat pocket, and said, "Lately, I guess I do."

"Who are you fighting?"

"My wife."

The champagne bubble of interest that had floated into my chest popped and dropped into my tummy. This was how it went for women like me, those who didn't get out much, those who'd already had something like love once. The only men I garnered any interest from were thirty-five years my senior, had one unfocused eyeball, and weighed a solid three hundred pounds. At least that described my mailman, who seemed legitimately in love with me, even though he knew I ordered way too many things from Amazon. The men with the full lower lip and Cupid's bow, the men with hair and tight laugh lines when they smiled kindly down at you while you tried to straighten your sweater over your soft belly, they were taken.

"What are you guys fighting about?" I asked.

"What are you napping about?" he asked.

The biggest surprise about this chance encounter was that I noticed him in *that way*. The sight of his undeniable good looks must have elbowed some long-dormant lobe in my brain and said, "Eh? Eh? Check him out." My brain sat right up and did some assertive checking, as if it hadn't been sleeping for twenty years. I felt myself smile but quickly remembered why I was in the hospital in the first place, and my smile dissolved.

"My friend's cancer might be back, and her other best friend is in charge this time around."

"You want to be in charge of the cancer?"

"No. It's just, my friend called my other friend first. My other friend is fierce and good at everything, and I'm not as"—I cleared my throat and gestured at myself—"as alert as I'd like to be. I know it's not a competition, but if it was, my other friend would win."

I was certain he was going to say something that made me sound pathetic, like *Oh, I'm sure that's not true*. Instead, he said, "My wife said I didn't call her when I said I would. I don't remember saying I would. It's stupid."

"But that's not what you're fighting about."

"I think it is. I mean, that's what she keeps saying."

My neck felt tight, so I stood, looked him in the eye. He was at least four inches taller than I was. "No. She wants to know if you love her." I wobbled with postshutdown dizziness, and he steadied me, his fingers on my shoulder.

"There now," he said. "You want to sit back down?"

I bobbled forward, swiped my head against his shoulder, and caught a whiff of clean shirt. "I'm so sorry. After I wake up, I have no filter or balance. It's part of this weird sleep disorder I have."

"You might be right. About my wife. We're separated. We're divorcing." He looked like he was going to say more, but what? This last statement was very personal, considering our two-minute history. I felt that bubble of interest again, and if I could have, I would have watched what it was going to do next.

His phone buzzed, and he said, "I've gotta take this. You okay?"

I nodded, and he bolted from the room, and I realized I couldn't hide any longer either.

———

Thanks to being awakened by Beautiful Man, as I had dubbed him, I returned to Katie's room in under twenty minutes. I tried to act like an attentive friend who had taken a crucial break to e-parent. I gestured to my phone with a loving and exasperated *kids these days* expression. Katie's and Holly's heads were bowed in conversation, and they missed my improvisational theater. I added dialogue.

"Maddie wants to study abroad during spring semester." This was not a lie. Maddie did want to go to Ireland starting in January. It rolled off my tongue easily, as the worry of how alone I would soon be was ever present.

"How was the nap?" Holly said.

I knew this trick. My next move would either expose me as a liar and an unstable napper, giving Holly the edge. Or, if I was careful, I could reframe myself as an efficient snoozer and ever-present problem solver.

"It was good. Thanks. You know me. Stop, drop, and drool, then good as new. Don't you think Maddie should study abroad after her freshman year? Second semester seems too soon."

Kind, supportive Katie considered the pedagogical benefits of the early abroad experience. She thought that this was a real conversation and not a red herring for Holly to keep her from co-opting and controlling everything, but Holly saw right through my subterfuge.

"California is *two thousand miles*, Samantha. It'll take days. You'll have to stop and sleep everywhere. I'll go. I've done long road trips before. I can fly out and drive back in a few days."

"Would Rosie go with you?" Katie asked.

I felt this whole thing sliding too quickly through my fingers. The world extolled the value of sleep, but the cost of missing key conversations where decisions were made was a tax levied only on the well rested. I felt like I was in the middle of a coup. I heard my voice go up and shake, betraying my fear of being edged out of this mission to help Katie. To prove myself. "You guys, I can do it."

"No, Rosie can't go. She's too close to her due date," said Holly as if I hadn't said a thing.

I saw myself as one of those wind socks outside a car dealership getting whipped around by air. Katie stole a quick glance at me, then dropped her eyes to her lap.

"Pregnant?" Even in my shock at the news and how much I had missed, I knew not to ask how or why or by whom or anything even close to something that might sound too personal or judgmental or clueless.

There was a time when we three knew everything about each other's lives, but that was ages ago. I knew Katie got yeast infections when she was stressed, and Holly hiccupped when she ate too fast. I knew that Holly's left eye fluttered when she tried to lie, and Katie always saw that flutter first. It was like that when you lived, almost literally, on top of each other in college. We had been a triangle of friendship. After graduation we lost our geometry of connection. We became Katie and Holly. Katie and Samantha. But, Holly and Samantha, quoth the raven, nevermore.

Over time I stopped asking about Holly's life, and I assumed she, mine. Of course, Katie and I had speculated about what had truly ruined our friendship. Sure, there was that huge misunderstanding. The blowup. But we'd talked about it. Sorted it out. I knew Katie had asked Holly at least once, but when Holly had snapped back with the response "Ask Samantha," Katie had left it alone.

After college it was easy to avoid addressing the elephant in the room between us because we no longer shared a room, or a college, or even a state. Holly went directly to law school in Texas and afterward practiced in a huge firm in New York. One of those fearsome places that consumed their lawyers. Even for good friends it was easy to drift apart. Add our life inexperience to the fraying thread of our friendship; we didn't know how lucky we were, and we let it go, like it was a bit of fluff and not a lifeline.

"A baby." I pulled a chair under me.

Katie grabbed Holly's hand and said, "I lost track! It seemed to go so fast."

"Don't say that to Rosie. The wait has been excruciating."

My whole life I'd planned on having two children. Two babies with hardworking, sturdy, mousey-brown-hair DNA. I knew how lucky I was to have Maddie, but I'd wanted a sister for my solitary girl. I'd always longed for a sibling, especially to join arms against my dad when he went on the warpath—or at least to commiserate with. Living with Katie and Holly was like finally having people under the same roof who actively had my back. It was better than having sisters because there was no controlling father, no passive mother, only us.

Holly looked at me and interpreted my wet eyes as kindness, and her face softened. But I wanted to grab underneath her toned and tan arm and pinch her. I'd handled a lot of baby news from both friends and strangers. I should have said Katie and I handled other people's reproduction news together—both of us wanting, yearning for a child. When I got pregnant, it felt like a betrayal, and I'd made Katie Maddie's godmother.

I searched for Katie's hand and thought, *My God, Holly got everything she wanted.* A lucrative career, a life partner, a complete family, friendship, and her outrage at me.

"We're keeping Rosie's stress to a minimum. Since she's older they say she's high risk. But I can go alone, do it quickly."

"How are you going to manage Peanut's insulin?" I knew this was a low blow, but I wasn't going to sit there and be shoved out of the dog-rescue bus.

"Oh, I'll figure it out."

"Is that right?" I lifted Katie's hand. The one with the IV, the tiny spot of blood on the tape and in the tubing, and moved it to Holly's face. "Don't think I haven't seen you averting your eyes from this right here." I waved the IV tubing in Holly's face.

Holly closed her eyes and turned her head like a nasty scent had wafted up from the intravenous line. "Don't."

Katie giggled.

"You forget that we were all together in college when you woke up from your appendectomy," I said, without adding how I'd called the ambulance and insisted that I ride in the back. How I'd lied and told the driver that I was her sister, and how it had felt when Holly squeezed my hand as if to say, *You are.*

"When you saw your IV, you turned the color of a paper cup, and then your eyes rolled back." Katie stifled another giggle, but I could see this was as fun for her as it was for me.

I held Katie's arm aloft, felt the soft suede underbelly of her wrist where the fortune-teller, our senior year, had counted the creases just under the meaty heel of her hand. *See these three lines?* the too-young crystal gazer said. *The folds predict three children will come from your belly.* We'd paid five dollars at the Blues Festival for three lies and no truth, and we weren't even playing the game. I would have a long, happy marriage, Katie would have three children, and we all would be friends for life.

Holly pushed Katie's arm away, keeping her eyes on the dotted ceiling tile.

"She's got you," Katie said. It was fun for everyone when Holly had to admit defeat.

"Can't the dog eat insulin? Isn't there medicine for that? My grandma takes a pill," said Holly.

"Peanut needs shots. The pills don't work for him," said Katie.

Holly's phone pinged, and she put her finger up. That long-ass finger she used when making a point, holding court, admonishing. Her finger was a minimodel of Holly herself. Everything about her was long and high handed. She'd been like that in college too: long, correct, but funnier. When Holly stood, it was like a yardstick unfolding to make a point. She answered her phone, "Ralph. Yeah. Go on," and with one step she moved out of the room.

Katie glanced at the hall and whispered, "You have to take Holly with you."

I recoiled. "Oh my God. No. I can't imagine. She clearly can't stand me, and the stress of it would keep me asleep, which would piss her off all the more. Also, she would *never* go with me."

"You have to, Sam. I can't have her here fighting with everyone when she knows nothing about medicine and turns green at every finger stick. You haven't seen her. Every time someone walks in the room, she's like, 'Why are you feeding her Jell-O? Jell-O isn't food.' Or, 'Stop waking her up—she doesn't need her vitals checked; you have this thing here.' Then she points to the IV machine like it's taking my blood pressure. She hasn't been sick in twenty years, and all her information comes from *Grey's Anatomy.* When anyone comes through my door, she asks if they're the chief resident."

"Then why did you call her first?" I frowned even though I tried to keep my delight in check.

"I didn't call her first. We were having coffee when the blood work came in, and I asked her to come with me. Holly is different with me. She is irritated at everyone else, and we may never know what the deal is with you, but she's so cool in emergencies. Not medical ones, though. It took them two sticks to get my IV in, and I thought she was going to call security from the bathroom where she was gagging."

A giggle of unadulterated ecstasy bubbled up from somewhere. "I thought you called her because you were dying, and she had to write your will or be your POA or something. I thought if you called her first, it was because you needed Scary Holly."

Katie dropped her head into her pillow, but I could hear her laughing. "Don't. Don't let her hear you call her that. Oh my God, she will stab you with her finger."

"She bruises." I grabbed my shoulder, remembering all those years ago when Holly woke me up during graduation. Jabbing me with that finger all the time when I would nod off next to her, which made me feel oddly cared for. Like she'd never let me sleep myself into trouble.

"Did you tell her the same thing?" I asked. "When I walked in here, you were whispering to her. Did you tell Holly to get me out of your hair, to go with me because I'm pathetic and bothersome?"

"No, Katie. I would never. We were talking about my parents. That's another reason she has to get out of here. You know how Mom is. She still thinks if Holly finds the right man, she could have a 'traditional' life. The pregnancy news—you know Holly will *have* to tell her—Mom will haul out all her crystals. Dad is going to have anxiety-hives this entire visit, and I don't know how he's going to get Mom to stop smoking long enough to even get her in the building."

Katie had said *Mom* and *Dad*, like she was *our* mom, and I almost crawled right into bed with her and cuddled her. Katie put her hand to her head, and the pulse oximeter glowed red, measuring the blood and oxygen that flowed through my darling friend.

It hit me what Katie was asking for. She didn't need my Excel spreadsheets or Holly as a crabby ombudsman at the hospital. She needed her two feuding best friends to get along for one week, get out of her way, and, most of all, go get her dog. The dog that lay on top of her during the chills of chemotherapy. The dog who knew Katie was going to throw up before Katie did. The dog that had sniffed out Katie's cancer the first time by burying his big nose in her lap and refusing to move. When Katie's fatigue hit, she paid attention and made a doctor's appointment. Peanut was a cancer-sniffing dog before that was a thing. Katie's ovaries were in her lap, and they were sick, and Peanut knew something was not right.

I tried to picture the trip. Holly, her bony, highly groomed self, driving with a pony-size dog drooling pints of saliva, a dog that might go into insulin shock at the very sight of a MINI Cooper. Then there would be sleeping-me avoiding conflict and any conversation that might illuminate what happened between us so many years ago.

When Katie pulled her hand away from her forehead, I could see a small depression where her finger had been. The hinge on the oximeter pulled a haystack of hair from her head.

"You're dehydrated, sweetie. How did you get so dry?" I stroked her forehead like my mother did when I had a fever.

"I don't know. I drink and pee constantly."

"Holly will never go if I go."

"She will if you ask her to," said Katie.

"She will if *you* ask her to."

"No, she won't, Sam. She'll think I'm being strong or noble or something. She'll think I'm trying to act like I don't need her here. *You* have to ask her to come with you. There's no way around it. Besides, say what you want, but you can't do this trip alone. It would take you a year. I might not have that long."

"Don't joke about that. There is nothing funny about that." A couple lights went out in my brain, and I thought about my bed, and then I remembered how alone I would be if I escaped to it.

Katie pushed her hospital gown back, showed me the tops of her thighs. "The red dots are back."

I couldn't help it. I touched one. It blanched like my face must have, quickly turning white and back to an anxious red. Before Katie had gone into the hospital for a checkup, the first go-round with ovarian cancer, she'd noticed small red dots, like freckles on her thighs and shins. Petechiae is what the doctor called them. All the specialists said those red dots were nothing. Just an odd coincidence, probably due to stress. Before the doctors announced that Katie was in remission, those red dots cleared up, and that's when Katie knew she was going to be okay. I covered a few spots with my fingers, hoping that when I pulled my hand away they would be gone.

"But the doctors said," I tried to remind her.

"We both know what they said. I know what they are."

I stared at my friend, caught in my own racing heartbeat. The noise of the hospital suddenly amplified around us. Someone called a code; a television commercial for allergy medicine blared, then quieted.

"I need Peanut, Sam. I need to see that he's okay. I need to have his big boulder of a head in my lap. I checked with the hospital administration. If we make him a service dog, he can be here with me for as long as I need him. I can fight this disease again if he is with me." Katie said this, but this is what I heard: *The cancer will go away when I get to hold Peanut again.*

"Maybe you'll be out and fine by the time we get back." And there it was; by using *we*, my brain had decided rescuing Peanut was going to be a trip for two.

The second I said it I was sorry. This trip would be the first significant time Holly and I spent together without Katie since college. Over the years there had been no strained dinners, no odd celebration that the two of us attended with Katie as our glue. Holly had come to Maddie's birth at Katie's request, but I didn't remember her being there. Katie thought if Holly saw me during my epic vulnerability, she might defrost. That was not what happened. Apparently Holly dropped off food just as Maddie entered the world. The end. I was hopped up on baby-bonding chemicals, so I didn't fully see this at the time. Later, when I pictured Holly turning away from me and Maddie in all our glory, I cried Holly-tears I didn't even know were still hanging around waiting to be shed.

If I didn't get Peanut to reduce Katie's stress, to help her turn this wonky blood work into nothing, there would never be any combination of *us* again. Without Katie, the *us* of us was gone, and it was just Sam and Holly, absolutely never together. This thought made me feel like a tree with shallow roots ready to topple in the first storm.

"Maybe you and Holly can talk about what really happened to your friendship." Katie stroked the back of my hand and added, "This trip might be something you need."

Before I could respond with outrage, *Need? I do not need Holly,* she blew back into the room, pulling the heavy door behind her. It hushed shut, and she said, "Ralph has your insurance thing figured out. I'll bring the papers tomorrow to sign, and we will fax them in time for the deadline."

"What would I do without you, Holly?"

That was when I accepted that Katie needed me to do this—to drive, stop fighting with Holly, get her dog—and my outrage and resistance collapsed.

"No worries. I'm not going anywhere."

"Um, about that," I said. "I think you're right. I'll never be able to drive that many miles without stopping a million times. Do you think we could do this trip together?"

Holly looked between Katie and me. "What have you two been cooking up in here?"

"Nothing. Katie pointed out that it might be too much for me to drive all the way drugged up on stimulants and assessing Peanut's every mood. If we did this trip together, I could do all the blood stuff, and we could share the driving. You said yourself you could do it faster. Katie could have Peanut all that much sooner."

Holly narrowed her eyes at me, then she looked at Katie. "Did you get news? Did a doctor come in here and give you some information I missed?"

"No," Katie said. She closed her eyes for a second longer than a blink. Her trembling lids seemed to communicate both fatigue and resignation.

"I don't think I can do this on my own," I said.

"Now you want me?" said Holly to me. It was like being glared at by a fearsome principal who'd just caught me vandalizing lockers.

I hesitated; the only answer seemed to be *Yes*. But, another response could have been, *When didn't I want you? Why are you asking me that?* I knew pausing to think was death with Holly, so I said, "I can't do this without you."

"That's true."

At that moment, the IV machine beeped as if to remind everyone within earshot that there was a sick person in the bed who needed her dog.

CHAPTER FOUR
NOT LIKELY

Holly bolted to the door and yanked it open. "Hey. Nurse. Are you a nurse? This machine is going off in here. Somebody should check it, right?" She moved into the hall, and I heard her authoritative voice asking for help. "Nurse!"

"See?" Katie said. "It's like having a dog that barks at every leaf."

"Remember that night back in college when that guy had you pinned at the bar? She walked up to him and said, 'What you're doing is both abusive and illegal. I've called the police. They told me to wait patiently to give a statement.' He scurried off, she had two drinks, and went from laughing to crying like a sorority girl about how much she loved the law and living with us and tequila. After that she threw up in a red Solo cup, and we drove her home." I felt myself smile despite the stark difference between past Holly and current Holly.

"She acts so tough," said Katie.

"She is tough. She's tough on me."

As a thousand times before, my thoughts returned to the night of our college graduation. Holly and I had lain on the floor in the spinning living room, both of us too sloshed to make it up the stairs to our beds. We were steps from the bathroom in case Holly, the most nauseous drunkard in the land, needed a toilet.

I'd left Holly's side to get a wet dishtowel for her face, and Katie's boyfriend, Mike, had been in the kitchen, downing a bag of stale taco chips. When I returned to the living room with the towel and a glass of water for me, Holly was upright, an ugly brown-and-gold afghan around her shoulders with a pissed-off look on her face.

"What's wrong?" I slumped to my knees trying not to spill the water.

"I heard you, Sam. I heard you say I was disgusting." She looked pale, sweaty, and furious.

"What are you talking about?" My heartbeat surged; the sugary wine I'd swallowed along with Angry Hammered Holly left me woozy. All I wanted was to close my eyes.

"Just now. I was in the bathroom, I heard you two." She burped and imitated Mike's voice, "'She wants you.' I heard you slap him and say, 'Disgusting. Don't be disgusting.'" This last part she sneered.

I was so confused. I took a sip from the water glass, forced my eyes to stay open. "Yeah, he said that, and then he made a V with his fingers and slurped his tongue through it. I hit him. You know how gross he is. I don't know why Katie likes him."

"You should have stood up for me."

I put my head on the pillow we shared, pulled my own quilt over my shoulders, tried to lighten things like my mother used to. "You are a bit disgusting when you throw up in the sink."

"Sam!" she said, her voice going up an octave.

I only remembered falling asleep after that. The next morning she had gone without saying goodbye. In retrospect, once I knew she was gay, I realized that maybe Mike's comment made her so self-conscious, so aware of the world's homophobia, she had to get out of there. But, that almost made it worse in some ways. How could she have, to use today's language, callously ghosted me?

"She was tough on me for a while too." Katie repositioned herself in the bed, pulled the sheet up an inch. "Remember she went to Europe instead of being in my wedding, but eventually I think my divorce and cancer brought her around."

"I had a husband die!" I said like we were in a tragedy competition—the winner getting Holly's testy friendship. I'd never forgotten the funeral, me pregnant, feeling overwhelmed in every way possible, and even in my confusion and grief, who was I waiting to see at the grave site? Holly. She didn't call or write, let alone come to the ceremony. In some ways that hurt most of all. What could I have possibly done that merited this kind of rejection?

"Maybe Jeff's death happened too long ago. She was completely wrapped up in her career. It was just a coincidence she was in town for Maddie's birth. I tried, Sam."

"I know. I know you did."

From the hall, Holly's loud, bossy voice shot into the room ahead of her. "It's here. This thing is beeping," she said. I glanced at Katie, and she shook her head.

The thing about Holly was that you always knew when she was near. She talked as she entered a room as a time management technique. If you were the one she was talking to, you had to catch up or miss everything.

I sighed loudly sitting next to Katie, and she touched my arm.

"Is her blood pressure up or something?"

Katie and I waited to see who Holly was speaking to.

"People come in here all the time and push buttons without proper assessment. Could you come and take a look? A real look."

"Oh God," I said, just as Holly and Beautiful Man walked into the room.

He stopped a few feet from the foot of Katie's bed. "Oh, hi." He looked genuinely happy to see me. But who wouldn't be happy to see a friendly face when Holly was in cross-examination mode?

"Hi," I said, and I pointed to Katie. "This is my friend." I realized my mistake a second too late and swung my finger in an arc and pointed to Holly and said, "This is my friend too. Both of these people are my friends. I'm visiting this one. That one is also here."

I could feel Katie and Holly staring at me. Beautiful Man was staring at me too. Not for good reasons, though.

"Yes," Holly said, "I'm here too."

Beautiful Man pushed a button on the IV machine, and it shut down.

"Don't do that without looking at her," Holly said. "How do you know she isn't having a heart attack or something?"

"Do you feel like you're having a heart attack?" Beautiful Man asked Katie.

"No. My heart feels fine, thank you. I'm not supersure about my ovaries, though. Does that machine say anything about my ovaries?"

"No, we haven't hooked up the ovary ultrasound yet."

That's when I realized that Beautiful Man was no dummy. He had judged the Holly situation and knew how to join in the fun like a girl on the playground jumping into a double Dutch competition.

"Why haven't you hooked up the ovary ultrasound? Why are we waiting on that?" Holly looked outraged, and I felt a twinge of guilt.

"We only have one in-house. And there are ovaries down the hall that need some sonar."

"How much is an ovary ultrasound machine? Can we buy our own?"

As much as I wanted to keep going with this line of questioning, I couldn't do it. It looked like Holly and I were going to be driving together across the country, and I didn't want another line checked on a long document of slights between us. "The IV bag is empty. That's why it's beeping, Holly."

"Get a new bag," she said, pivoting like a champ.

I said, "Get a new bag" to Beautiful Man, and he smiled. He offered his hand to Holly. "I'm a resident working with Dr. Chopra, but I'm rotating off this service, and so, am sorry to say, I won't be working with . . ."

"Katie Martin. Ovary difficulties," Katie said.

I have spent years watching men meet Katie and fall in love with her. Beautiful Man was not immune to Katie's innocent mantrap essence. To a certain kind of man I thought she must smell like sugar cookies and home-baked bread. Online dating didn't get the same response. She was just an attractive woman in a sea of other attractive women, but in person she was irresistible to men. Asshat Tom notwithstanding.

"Are you the chief resident?" Holly interrupted.

"As much as I am an expert-in-training on ovary difficulties, no, I am not the chief resident. I am qualified to find someone to change this IV bag, though, and I'll do that right away.

"Drew Lewis," he said to Holly and shook her hand, and then he turned to me. "This is the situation you needed to sleep for?"

"Yes." Ugh, he just exposed me.

"And this one is the one who is good at everything?"

The look of surprise and delight on Holly's face was worth every odd moment I'd had with Dr. Drew Lewis, Beautiful Man. I felt like he'd opened the doghouse door and I could stroll out at my leisure. But then he said, "And this is your best friend?" He pointed to Katie.

This guy might know how to read a situation, but he didn't know a thing about female friendship dynamics.

I stuttered, "They are both my best friends. We are all besties. We've been friends for nearly thirty years."

"Okay, listen, Dr. Dreamboat," Holly said. "You gotta go get a new bag. Isn't this an emergency? The bag is dry. Also, could you price out an ovary detector? Because I'd like to look into purchasing one for Katie. We'll donate it after Katie gets discharged."

To his credit, he did not seem offended by Holly and her power plays; instead, he smiled at me and gave me the lightest of winks. Not the smarmy wink of the cruise ship captain hoping to entertain a girl on the lido deck. No, a kind of tiny flick of his long lashes that felt like a tip of his hat rather than an *I'll see you in my cabin later.*

Men typically did not notice me. I must emit the smell of *meh* and a second-favorite childhood shoe. I tried to wink back, managing only to squeeze both my eyes shut.

What a fun, dumb interaction, I thought, but something dawned on me, and I followed Dr. Beautiful Man out of the room. When I got to the hall, I didn't see him. I scanned both directions, but then I heard a laugh and saw a hair flip.

Behind a large desk-like partition that separated the medical staff from the hallway and the patients stood Dr. Lewis. He was talking to a young woman with a white coat. He pointed over his shoulder in the direction of Katie's room, and the woman nodded but didn't move.

I rested my arms on the cool laminate desk and watched. She looked up at him through her eyelashes, a big smile on her lips. She nodded and slid her hand down a long strand of blonde hair, pulling it through her fingers while gazing at Drew's face. Watching two attractive people interact in the wild was so very *National Geographic.* The preening, the eyelash batting, everything but the dung beetles and dirt were present right here in the middle of Saint Mary's Hospital. I looked closer and saw one other thing missing: Dr. Lewis didn't seem to know that mating moves were happening right in front of him.

"Thanks," he said, turning away, and he missed a second hair flip, this one more pronounced than the first.

Then he saw me and because I was staring, I saw him see me. When he did, his face turned from ice cap to sunshine. It reminded me of everything I'd lost when my husband died years ago: the recognition that you are visible and welcome. This was the kind of greeting that occurred between two people who were not a threat or in debt or in any way tormenting each other.

"Hey," he said. "Looking for a place for nap number two?"

"Soon, maybe. If things don't calm down in that room over there, I might need to spend the night."

"Your friend is intense," he said.

"Yes, she is. I have a question for you. A favor and I'm not sure why you would even consider doing it. It might be illegal. But I feel desperate."

"You had me at desperate and illegal."

That sentence alone gave me courage. "My intense friend and I have to get my sick friend's dog from her shitty ex-husband in California. It's going to take some time; we have to drive. I know you aren't working with Katie, but could you check in on her occasionally and text me how she's doing?"

My words and the look on his face made me realize what I was asking of a relative stranger.

I said, "She's single" at the same time he said, "Sure." I laughed.

"You didn't need to add that last bit."

"That was gross of me," I said.

"You're doing me a favor."

"How so?"

"My mentor says I have to work on my communication skills. Apparently I rush things. I'll need her permission to talk with you. I can't give you medical information, but I can check in as a friend."

The pretty white-coated woman appeared at Drew's shoulder and said, "Excuse me—when you're done talking to your mom, could you sign off on something for me?" The woman stood there, confident in her beauty and in her history with all things male.

I felt my face go from an expression of curiosity to annoyance. "Hey . . ."

"I'll be with you in a minute," Drew said.

With no hair flip this time, she strolled away.

"Wow. How old do I look?" I touched my face.

"Not old enough to be my mom. Give me your phone."

He gestured for me to put my pass code in, then deftly typed in his contact information. It felt wildly intimate to have his hands on my phone, which made me consider the last time someone other than my daughter had touched me. That made me think about Beautiful Man touching me, which made me feel like shutting my eyes and napping, maybe on his shoulder, on a gurney in the hall. The thought of being with a man, any man, and my neurons started to tap out one by one. If a man looked at me like the blonde had looked at Drew, I swear I might feel attractive enough to consider romance again. This was what Katie said anyway, that I'd feel different if it came my way. I knew attractiveness was part of the reason, but it was bigger than that, and we all knew it.

I concentrated on Beautiful Man's hands. He had short nails that he clearly bit to keep trim, and he hit the round call circle, and almost immediately I heard a buzzing.

"There," he said. "I'll text you."

"You don't have to text me all the time. Just let me know how she's doing. Her spirits, that kind of thing."

"Yeah. Okay."

"I'll remind you to brush your teeth and eat green leafy vegetables."

"I'll send you pictures of my artwork."

"If you call me Mom, I'm going to report your number to AARP and tell them you want a long-term care insurance assessment." I noticed his quick smile and tapped the phone to write *Beautiful Man* in the contact information.

"I have to do a bunch of stuff, but I'll stop in before I leave and get the okay from your friend to convey information to you in case of an emergency." He peered at my phone and said, "Who is Beau? I'm Drew."

Startled, I said, "I don't know what I was thinking," and I hit the delete button. "I'm Samantha Arias. Katie will report nothing but hearts and flowers so we won't worry. I need to know how she's really doing—not necessarily medically."

"Got it," he said. "See ya." He turned, stopped, and over his shoulder he said, "But what if I want to text you all the time?" and strolled off without waiting for an answer.

With a hit of pure pleasure, I typed *Beautiful Drew* into my phone and gently placed it into my back pocket.

———

Something had happened in Katie's room while I was in the hall collecting Drew's contact numbers and staring at his nice hands. Holly was frantically trying to lower the head of the bed, and Katie looked as pale as I had ever seen her.

"What's going on?"

"Bebe was admitted to the hospital in Arizona. They aren't coming." She hit the remote control of the bed, and Katie's legs started to rise and bend at the knee. "Ugh," Holly said. "Which button do I push?"

I rushed to Katie's side and said, "There," and I pointed to the cartoon stick person next to the upside-down triangle on the control paddle.

"I got it," Holly said, irritated, and Katie shot me a look that said, *You gotta get her out of here.*

"Is Bebe going to be okay?" I asked.

"Something about her oxygen needing to be monitored. They're keeping her a couple of days for observation." Holly hit another button, and the whole bed lifted like it was levitating. Holly said, "Christ, this thing is confusing. I'm trying to put her legs down."

Katie sipped water from a waxy paper cup and swallowed, looking almost too tired to say anything.

The only way to get Holly off the puzzle of the bed mechanics was to give her something else to fight.

"Okay, you guys, it's official. We're going on a road trip."

"I'm going," said Holly, finally getting the bed moving in the right direction.

"We're going, Holly. You and I will share the driving. When I get tired, I'll sleep. I will manage all Peanut's injections and his poop. You will do all the planning and navigation, and we will be back in less than a week."

Holly eyed me as if there was some catch, and she said, "Maybe I should stay here now that Bradley and Bebe won't be making the drive."

Katie gave me an alarmed look.

"Here's how I see it, Hol. Katie has a lot of friends who will sit with her, bring her food, help her take notes when the doctors come in and start spouting medical jargon. But only you and I are the kinds of friends who will drive cross-country to get her dog."

Holly dropped the bed remote control and said, "I'll have to check with Rosie."

Katie's face relaxed, and I said, "I'll stop my mail," as if calling the post office were the same thing as checking in with a loved one.

"Maddie leaves tomorrow?" said Katie.

I pushed away my disquiet and thought about what else I would have to rearrange to leave my life for the week. I'd notify the clinic, let them know I couldn't work. They'd been bugging me to use up my vacation time, and I was up to date on my charting.

Nobody cared at book club if anyone missed a meeting. We were discussing *Feng Shui Your Fridge for Better Digestion*, and there was no way I was reading that book. With Maddie gone, there were fewer things on my schedule. I'd been sprinting toward her graduation from high school for so long. Volleyball season had merged into spring track meets, planning a graduation party, attending awards ceremonies, completing scholarship applications. Now that it was all over, I could see how I'd lived Maddie's life and not mine. I knew that was what parents did, especially single parents. I also knew it wasn't advisable if you wanted your empty nest not to be your desolate nest.

"So, that doctor. How do you know him?" Katie said while Holly seemed preoccupied with her phone.

"I don't. I just ran into him in the hall."

"He seemed kind of into you."

I simultaneously rejected and enjoyed this. "It's a constant problem. So many married Prince Charmings finding me asleep and falling in love with me."

"They would fall in love with you if you let them."

I threw my head back and laughed. "Look at me. I'm not exactly the kind of woman people think of when they think of a dream girl. A bit long in the tooth for that."

"Is that what you think of me? Too old for love?"

I sat up straight as if I'd been zapped by an electrical spark. "Katie, no. No, I didn't mean that. You are so adorable. Everything about you is dateable. I just let myself go."

Katie had always been the girl everyone wanted. She had a sweetness about her but also a don't-screw-with-me temper. It was a great combination for attracting men. It served her well until Tom showed up. His dysfunction slipped under all our radars. I'm certain Holly would say she'd never liked Tom, but I had to admit I'd loved him.

When we first met, Maddie was three. I'd been the kind of mom who was invisible except for in her daughter's life, present at all parent-child activities, with no time for anything of her own. Tom had focused when he shook my hand. His smile—with its single dimple, his full lips—you had the feeling that they were all yours.

"The famous Samantha," he'd said, with nothing but delight in his tone. He took my hand and covered it with his and pulled me into a chaste peck on the cheek. He smelled like sandalwood, a scent I associated with creativity and hard work. He locked his eyes on mine and said, "Katie means the world to me," and I believed him.

There were flowers, love notes, invitations to moonlit picnics. His warmth was contagious. The gentle but unromantic Jeff, who had been utterly irresponsible, hadn't been anything like Tom, so I admit I encouraged Katie. No one was like Tom. It was as if he had studied every romantic comedy and lobbed every tool from them in Katie's direction. When we were in college, no one had used psychological terms to describe people, but during the divorce, we both became fluent in narcissist. Katie never had a chance.

In the stark light of the hospital room, where we should have been problem-solving cancer, we were talking about boys. It was college all over again, but without Holly's stinging take on the absurdity of relationships.

"I've had the great love of my life. If I got another great love, it would water down the whole soul-mate idea. Jeff was my soul mate," I said, flicking my gaze at Holly and wondering if she caught on to my lie. Wondering if she cared enough to tune in, knew enough from Katie to challenge me, cared if I told the truth.

Katie softened the moment. "You could have dinner with someone who was nice even if he didn't speak to your"—Katie paused, allowing my false characterization of my relationship with Jeff—"soul."

I shrugged. "You know me. I definitely want to leave my soul out of future relationships."

Holly looked up from concentrating on her phone and said, "Okay, done."

"What did you do?"

"We're booked on a flight out to LA on Thursday. Let's get this show on the road."

"We? You booked mine too? That's in two days," I said.

"I used miles. I have thousands. And you said we should go. What are we waiting for?"

I looked at Katie, and she had the same expression on her face that I imagined I did: as if we were at a bus stop and we had to hop on or we'd get left behind. So many years of this, running behind Holly to catch up, trying to understand what was in her head, how she kept up the pace and why.

I shook my head and squeezed Katie's hand. "Okay, then. I'd better pack a bag." My phone buzzed, and I pulled it from my back pocket and was astonished to see Beautiful Drew had written:

BDREW: Hey Mom. Sup?

ME: I wrote: 1-800-AARP Insurance

BDREW: Hahaha. Have a good trip.

ME: Not likely.

CHAPTER FIVE

I'LL BE FINE. WE'LL BE FINE.

Before I could untangle my shoulder bag from the electric cords at my feet, Holly was up and out the door.

Katie called after her, "Love you!"

"You too," she shouted, but you could hear she was already a room away.

It was startling how fast Holly moved; if she were a cartoon sketch, there would be swirling leaves and *zoom* written in Comic Sans font where her form should be. In adulthood she'd perfected the uncomplicated exit, which I assumed had started the day after graduation all those years ago.

After Holly had left our shared apartment without saying goodbye, Katie and I could talk of nothing else. We'd finished packing cardboard boxes, hauling milk crate bookshelves to the dumpster, and examined the night before from every angle imaginable.

"How mad was she? After Mike said that?" Katie asked.

"You know Holly, she gets outraged in one second, and then it's over. We were both drunk. She was sick. I told her to stop puking in the sink," I said.

"You always tell her that."

"I knew she had to leave early, but not before we woke up."

There was no Post-it on the bathroom mirror. No note on the microwave. Just half a container of mayonnaise in the fridge and a mascara tube in the trash in her room.

"She'll call us, right?" we both said again and again as we loaded our cars, cleaned the tub, vacuumed the carpet. My frantic anxiety fueled a kind of cleaning and packing never before seen in our apartment. Katie found me scrubbing the baseboards in the living room with a Q-tip, crying. She slid down the wall. "That Q-tip is worn out. Can I get you another?"

My eyes felt hot, and the dull ache in my forehead from crying, dehydration, and sleeplessness compounded my misery. Our college years were over, and that was enough to mourn. How would I . . . surely I wouldn't have to manage this without Holly? That was inconceivable.

In 1994, when we graduated, you couldn't text or call someone's cell phone. There was no Twitter or Instagram to browse to find someone, no Find My Friends app to track your lost relationship. In the nineties when people wanted to disappear, they could accomplish that pretty well.

"Should we call her aunt?" I wiped my nose.

"How would we do that? Doesn't she live in Italy?"

After Holly's mom and dad had died, her aunt had become her emergency contact person. We'd met her once during Parents' Weekend, but we didn't *know* her. Not well enough to take out our calling cards, figure out how to make an international call, and complain that Holly left without saying goodbye.

"She'll call you," said Katie. "Of course she will. She'll call you at your mom's house."

"She will," I said, but saying that was like sitting on a wobbly rock and hoping not to slide into the sea. Holly was unpredictable.

"She loves you." And that, I thought, was true.

Over the decades that passed between college and present day, many things had changed culturally. In the nineties we called our friends' parents Mister and Missus, never by their first names; they were not our friends. I couldn't imagine calling one of my friend's parents. That seemed like insanity. For parents, once a child left for college, it wasn't easy to talk on the phone. It was expensive, and you had to be home on a landline. Letters were a thing. Hard to believe now—Maddie and I talked and texted all day.

The other massive difference between then and now was the amount of stuff students owned and kept in their apartments. Pinterest created a dorm-room monster when it came on the scene, and twenty-first-century parents helped their children create a plush paradise with flat-screen televisions and full decor. When I left the apartment that day, I was able to move out with no help, shoving everything I owned in my orange Chevy Citation with the bike on the inside. I tossed my secondhand twin mattress to the curb, folded up my card table desk, and went to my occupational therapy internship at the same place where I'd completed my clinical hours. Holly could leave like a ghost in the night because she had packed her car the morning before graduation, and off she went to law school.

As I sat next to Katie in the hospital, everything felt both the same and different. Like we had jumped a time-and-space chasm. The three of us were together, and then, boom, Holly was gone.

Once Holly left the hospital room, all the noisy tension and static in the room left with her. The view out Katie's window was of an asphalt roof and a slice of blue sky. Sterile, ugly, institutional beige paint surrounded the small space. There was a large whiteboard on the wall with the information *Today is Tuesday, Your Nurse is Cheryl* written in blue ink.

As an occupational therapist, I was at home in hospital rooms. I could get people in and out of their beds for therapy, maneuver around the cramped spaces, get people ready for discharge. Being with Katie when she was sick made me see the place from a patient's point of view, and the familiar dread crept in.

I repositioned myself on Katie's bed and said, "Well, I guess I'm going on a trip with Holly."

Katie let out a nervous laugh. "Was that miserable for you?"

I rubbed Katie's legs under the hospital sheet. "No, sweetie. I mean, all things considered, it wasn't the worst reunion in the world."

Katie's shoulders dropped. "Oh, good. I'm sorry to spring her on you."

"Look, if you need to bring in the pope without consulting me, have at it. You never have to consult me."

"The pope would be a weird choice, but okay. I might call him."

"Be honest, Katie. Has she ever said anything to you?"

She knew exactly what I was asking. "She always says the same thing. She couldn't bear to say goodbye and had to start the long drive to Texas. Holly once said she isn't good at letters or maintaining long-distance friendships. I guess I believed her after she left."

"But that doesn't explain how she can be friends with you but is openly hostile to me."

"Something must have happened that you don't remember. That is all I can think of."

I looked closely at Katie's open face. She didn't seem to be holding anything back. We'd gone over this a thousand times. I didn't remember. The alcohol and the years. I remember taking care of her. It was all so unfair.

"Do you think it was because you didn't invite her to your wedding?" Katie asked.

"We hadn't spoken for years by then." I recalled the small guest list made for economic reasons. "I thought about inviting her, but if she didn't show? I would have been analyzing her absence as I walked down the aisle. That's just too much for one day. I'd have fallen asleep in the cake during the reception." Then I asked the question I'd already asked a thousand times, "You told her it was a small wedding, right?"

"Of course I told her."

We sat quietly with our own memories and theories, the constant symphony of beeping that makes up the background of a hospital. "She looks the same," I said. "Leaner."

"Meaner," Katie said, and we laughed.

"I know you see her, but this *was* very weird for me."

"You'd like Rosie. She's good for Holly. She wants a family in all the ways a family can exist, in and out of bloodlines. Rosie's sister goes with Holly for all their birthing classes."

"How's Holly with that?"

"Good for the most part, but only because it's Rosie's family. Holly wants a fortress with like two people in it surrounded by a big fence."

"She wasn't always like that. Maybe that's what being a lawyer does to you. Makes you feel exposed to elements beyond your control."

Katie yawned and said, "I'm going to close my eyes for a second."

"I'll go! I shouldn't have stayed so long."

"Please stay, if you can. Just lie down with me for a few minutes. I don't want to be alone."

I knew exactly how to do this. She lay under the thin hospital bedspread, me on top next to her. I expertly hit the bed controls, and the motor buzzed, positioning us so I was comfortable on my side while Katie lay on her back. She sighed.

I slipped my arm between us, sure I'd get pins and needles but knowing how to slide my arm out and shake it without waking her. Her breathing changed when she dropped off; her mouth popped open as she moved into another sleep stage. There was a small commotion of voices in the hall.

I knew how to do all this because before solid, kind, predictable Katie had gotten sick, there had been the three of us in college, which had introduced me to the devotion and family of friendship. To the fact that you could mold your body around someone else without getting both a cuddle and a swat, like with my own family and Jeff, for that matter.

The acoustic tile ceiling held my interest, the sprinkler system, the can lights. I felt my breathing regulate. I often listened to a podcast where therapists talked about therapy things. I guess it was my way of acknowledging that I could use some help without committing to any self-disclosure. One of the therapists had gone on a long jag about what you should expect from a primary relationship: spouse, partner, friend:

"At the very least, there should be a semblance of respect and predictability. You should know that you will be treated well, that you will get the same person every day with regard to personality, and for the most part mood, and you should never agree to walking on eggshells." That was Holly and then Katie for me.

That had not been my father; nor had it been Jeff. I glanced at the IV line, the steady blinking of the green light, and made a quick fist to make sure blood flowed into my fingers. Once a social worker who specialized in working with the grief stricken had said that I'd chosen Jeff because he was unpredictable like my father. Of course, this was only after I'd confessed that I was in therapy because I wasn't feeling enough grief after Jeff died. That I was overwhelmed by my pregnancy and a terrible kind of relief that I couldn't pinpoint the source of.

My father and Jeff had both had erratic moods that appeared at random times. One day Jeff would laugh and brush a wisp of hair away from my face, slide his hand to cup my jaw. The next he'd snap, "Jesus Christ, can you just stop talking for five minutes." My father would call up Judas Priest, a softer cuss, unaware that he was conjuring a rock band, and that knowledge, as a child, softened the fall on my ears.

Before we'd married, I'd seen Jeff's moods as deep sensitivity. He hadn't yet learned that he could direct his melancholy at me and feel better. Or maybe he knew enough to wait. After we were married, his angst leaked, then streamed, then shot out of him, as I was sure he saw there was no boundary for it. He started by shushing me, which turned to demanding *Quiet!* which became *Shut up!* if I was laughing on the phone with Katie in another room.

Katie twitched in her sleep as if she were saying, *I remember. Go on.*

I had turned into a divining rod for moods, quivering at the slightest change, shrinking from anything that wasn't steady. Anything, even joy, had signaled something that could turn to discord. I later learned that Jeff's moods, unlike my father's, vacillated depending on his gambling wins and losses, which I'd known nothing about. He'd left us almost bankrupt, and throughout the funeral, I'd thought, *I'll be fine. We'll be fine.* Only thinking of the loss of funds and not the loss of Jeff.

There had been times at the post office or gas station, months after Jeff's death, when someone would come up to me and say, "I'm so sorry to hear of your loss," and I'd think, *Oh yeah. The money.* Then I'd have to remind myself, *No, she means* Jeff. *Jeff is dead.* I'd feel an extremely intricate crisscross of emotions. Charismatic, sensitive, mean Jeff, who knew I wasn't going anywhere, because you couldn't leave your marriage with a baby without the kind of agency your parents should have taught you.

I repositioned a bit in the bed, watched Katie breathe. Her eyelids fluttered, and I remembered her asking me, after she'd heard Jeff shouting at me through the phone when I was pregnant, "Was he always like this, and you didn't tell me?"

And I'd said, "No." But maybe he was, and it was just beneath the surface, something my subconscious detected as familiar and attached to Jeff while my conscious mind focused on his lips and his sense of humor.

When I'd checked our savings to pay for Jeff's casket and had seen our money was gone, when a collection service had come for a staggering credit card debt and I'd discovered his gambling addiction, I'd felt shock, disbelief, and a swift liberation. People would not question my ability to go back to work without missing a beat. I had to! We were broke. But to me it meant no guilt. I wouldn't have to get my baby out of a miserable family, the type of family I had already survived once and had been anxiously problem-solving an exit from. We were out! We'd paid the price. Brutal yes, but there it was.

If people wondered about my ability to carry on, I often said, "We miss him terribly," which had some truth in it. I wasn't a monster. I would add, "It's good I have to keep very busy to make up what was lost gambling." I leaked information about Jeff's gambling as a way to explain not totally falling apart. And it had worked for the most part.

Inch by inch I pulled my arm out from under Katie's shoulder. If I pushed against the mattress, a channel for my arm could be made. I slipped off the bed and wriggled my fingers, then stretched. Quietly, I moved the side rail up and snapped it into place, made sure the call light was where Katie could reach it.

What I'd come to understand was that I wasn't the greatest judge when bringing people into my life. I'd been wrong about Jeff. I'd been wrong about Holly. Maddie and Katie were my family; I kept the numbers small for this reason.

In that way, I guess Holly and I weren't that different. Holly had stayed angry, I had stayed fearful—two strong sisters in isolation.

CHAPTER SIX
I HAVE AN APP FOR THAT

Flying was heaven for the sleepiest people in the world: the hypersomniacs, the narcoleptics, and those of us plagued with what the medical community called excessive daytime sleepiness. Nothing more ironic than attaching the prefix *hyper* to *sleepiness* in my mind, but I was too tired to take on the medical terminology field.

When held in the clouds by a Delta Airlines jet, a person had no place to go and virtually nothing to do but sit, doze off, and not feel embarrassed or guilty about it. The airline provided Wi-Fi, but I didn't let wireless get in my way of my sleeping skills.

I wouldn't normally sleep for hours in the middle of the day, but I hadn't been sleeping much at night. Getting Maddie ready for Colorado, answering questions about internships and babysitting, Katie's hospitalization, googling *empty nest*. Advice ranged from what to do if you found a robin's nest (leave it alone) to a page on Mayo Clinic's website diagnosing a syndrome. Mayo said I should accept the timing of my child leaving, keep in touch, seek support, and stay positive. This seemed like good advice for, say, when your lawn guy moves to Arizona. Not for the syndrome where you lose your cellular equivalent, the person who fed off your breast for a year, the one person you could always call your own, my daughter. Even if it was to finish the sentence with "My daughter is annoyed by me."

Maddie had insisted that she would drive to Colorado and had her bags packed for a summer in the mountains. I'd stuffed a quilted cooler with Diet Pepsi and baggies of carrots, jicama, sugar peas, crackers, pretzels, cheese, and Swedish Fish. Her expression had resembled, I supposed, a sailor about to shove off for uncharted waters, buried treasure, and cute boys. I'd hugged her too hard and kissed her hair too many times, and stood too long in the driveway after her car had rounded the corner out of sight. Then I'd taken to my bed and cried like a high school girl who didn't get asked to prom.

I lay with my head resting against the hull of the plane even as the wheels bumped onto the runway. Someone peeled an orange, and the scent reminded me that I would soon be standing on California soil. I heard the woman in the middle seat to my left say, "She slept the entire flight."

People were so judgmental about slumber, like sleepers had vexing needs that more motivated people did not. I almost opened my eyes and said, *Sleep is the only thing we don't let ourselves do, even though we love to do it.* If I had any guts I'd add, *The difference between my body and yours is that my body is well rested, and yours is sleep deprived.* And if I was Holly, I'd say, *Shut up.*

I peered through my eyelashes at the woman in the seat next to me as she yanked a bag the size of a second grader out from under the seat. She'd been wrestling items from her carry-on like she was on a camping trip. Every time I woke to reposition, I'd watched her smooth various emollients over her face, neck, hands, and arms. She'd spritzed herself with mists, sipped from an elaborate water bottle with its own filtration system, and swallowed vitamins the size of Alka-Seltzer tablets, at least once with a white wine chaser. Now her focus was on me.

She had large, shiny lips that maybe she was born with, maybe not. Her thighs were the size of my calves, and, for perspective, my calves were proportional and within normal limits for my height and weight. This woman had a very extra-American look that seemed perfect for Movie Star California, but an odd showing in the economy class on Airbus A321. And, PS, there was no possible way her eyelashes were her own.

This woman said to whoever was listening, "Do you think she's sick?" She bumped my elbow and sprayed something that smelled like hand sanitizer.

"Maybe she worked a night shift somewhere," said another voice.

God bless her heroic display of empathy, I thought.

"Maybe," said California Girl.

I wasn't going to explain my hypersomnia to anyone this trip. I was going to remain quiet, invisible, justify nothing, and try to face Holly as equals.

We'd made plans to meet at the gate after I'd realized she'd booked herself in first class while placing me in economy. You'd think I'd be pissed by the slight, but I was so grateful to not be stuck next to her. It was a dick move, but I knew this was just the opening act; now that we had landed, the main event would start. My phone vibrated in my jacket pocket—no doubt Holly nudging me along.

I opened my eyes wide, and just like that I became visible.

"Wow," the woman said to me. "You must have been tired. You slept the whole way."

"I have the gift of sleep," I said.

"I never sleep," she said, and I believed her. She looked fat-free and wired. Like her internal motor burned on high all day long, leaving her skin looking like softly glazed, sculpted pottery. Her eyes were round with alertness or surgery. It was hard to tell.

Now that I was awake, it was time to take my medication. I fished inside my bag, a navy North Face backpack with a broken side zipper that had been Maddie's in middle school. It had multiple storage pouches filled with snacks, travel documents, personal items, and writing materials. An old, free Clinique bag held medication, a small sewing kit, a Tide pen, a lint brush, and enough tissues to wipe up a nuclear spill.

Except, after quite a lot of searching, I couldn't locate my sleep medication. I took 37.5 milligrams of Concerta extended-release formula to keep my sleep fog at bay during the day. I always carried the original amber pill bottle plus a backup smaller stash in case of emergencies. One by one, passengers moved to the center aisle while I frantically checked every single pouch, sack, bag, and purse, dumping each one into my lap. I found earplugs, hairpins, one hoop earring, and oddly a magnet, but no medication. I hoped I had slipped them into my luggage. Before panicking, mentioning it to Holly, or admitting my error, I would kneel on the floor in baggage claim and search for my amphetamines.

With a sinking feeling, I knew I wouldn't find my meds. I knew because I could see them in my mind's eye, right where I'd left them on the bathroom counter. I'd been counting out the pills needed for two weeks. I'd carefully placed each oblong red tablet into a small plastic box for my backpack; the larger bottle would go into my luggage. Katie had called, and I'd rushed to answer. I'd scribbled down Tom's address in California along with his phone number. She had called five shelters, and one of them had a Great Pyrenees. They would not let her pay to hold him—who knows why. We'd talked about how she was feeling; then I'd zipped my luggage and gotten into the car to go to the airport.

The medicine that kept me from passing out sat waiting to be called into action in my bathroom many, many, many miles away. I rubbed my eyes.

"Still tired?" said the woman next to me. "That's why I don't nap. I can't wake up even after just a short snooze."

I resisted saying, *Stop talking! Just because I'm sitting next to you doesn't mean I want to hear your opinions on sleep.* Instead, I raised my eyebrows hoping they communicated my disinterest.

"I always have an iced coffee before I get on the plane. Then I can work the whole four hours." The woman delivered this tip over her shoulder as she lifted a mammoth carry-on from an overhead bin, her upper-body strength on impressive display.

I motioned for the man across the aisle to proceed. He gestured with irritation and said, "Go with your friend."

I grabbed my pouches and backpack in a clumsy attempt to hurry while also allowing the California woman to move down the aisle, but instead she waited. "Maybe you need some vitamins. Do you eat carbs? Carbs make you sluggish. And milk. And wheat does too. I also firmly believe that humans are not meant to eat beans. Maybe you eat too many beans."

Earlier this year I had seen a sweatshirt on Instagram with the words, *I don't give a crap about your diet, Debbie.* I wanted that shirt right now. Then I could stay silent and yell at the same time.

"Maybe," I said. "I'll give up beans and see if I can stop napping on airplanes. Maybe then I'll have time to learn Spanish instead."

"I have a great app for that."

She stroked the screen of her phone with a pink fingernail. I looked over her shoulder to see what the holdup was exiting the plane. I anticipated seeing Holly at the end of the gangplank, and this California woman was like a warm-up criticism band. Suddenly I experienced a full-body perspire.

"You can learn any language in three weeks."

"Uh-huh." I needed some quiet to figure out what to do. Yes, I could call the clinic for a new prescription. Yes, I could have them send it to a Walgreens or CVS near me, but it was a controlled substance, and I'd just had all my meds refilled. Additionally, my doctor had retired, and the new doctor had made it clear that there would be no more sleep meds until I came in for a checkup. Considering the high street-market profit for this medication, essentially what I called "good-girl uppers," this new doctor did not cotton to the lackadaisical practices of the old doctor, who was burned out and too irreverent to pay attention to drug laws. In short, I hadn't been for a checkup for this particular problem for ten years. My doctor had always re-upped my prescription when I called him.

Maybe my neighbor would mail them. But where would she send them? Our plan was to be on the road, sleeping in the camper, driving without stopping. I was basically screwed, and that would be fine if I was alone on this trip, but I wasn't. I was with the intolerant Holly. The woman who never slept, didn't medicate, and needed nothing artificial to shore her up in any way.

My phone vibrated in my pocket, and I found two texts on the screen. One from Holly. **What's taking you so long?** And another text from Beautiful Drew. **Are you there?**

———

With a flash of irritation, I texted Holly that I was on my way. How could I possibly know why it was taking a long time for people to exit? And if she had wanted us to be synchronized and truly time efficient, why hadn't she splurged for me to join her in first class?

My annoyance turned into anticipation as I texted Beautiful Drew. A safe man who I expected would fall in love with my best friend. Then I could write a memoir and call it *The Vicarious Love Life of Samantha Arias*. If Katie was with me, I would have made this joke and we'd have laughed, but I didn't feel like laughing right now. I felt sad.

I slipped the backpack onto both of my shoulders as Maddie said I should. Apparently carrying it casually, with just one strap, was oh so very uncool.

ME: I'm here. Landed. In California. Experiencing minor irritations.
BDREW: How was your nap?
ME: You know me so well.
BDREW: Not yet.

Yet?

BDREW: Katie is in good spirits. Nothing to report.

ME: Anyone coming in to draw blood?

BDREW: Yes.

ME: THX

BDREW: NP

I knew NP was *No problem* from Maddie, and so I didn't have to look foolish and reply, *What?* Or *Nurse Practitioner? Needle Problem?* Thank God for hanging out with a teen who kept me young. Just another thing I would miss when my daughter left the house for good. There it was . . . a dull thread of loneliness slid through me. I already felt her absence with so many miles between us.

I'd inhaled her scent, hugging her close before letting her go.

"Mom, are you sniffing me?" she'd said, without pulling away.

"You know I am."

"I'm not leaving forever." She'd squeezed and released me, knowing how hard this was going to be on me, but wanting the freedom for herself.

"I'm so excited for you," I'd said, leaving off the next part of that sentence: *My God, what will I do without you?*

"I left you my shampoo in case you want to sniff me some more."

I tried to say something funny, empowering, parental, but instead I signed, *I Love You* with my right hand.

"I'll text you," she'd said, like she hadn't packed my heart in her suitcase and was going to be driving down the road with it.

Who would keep me from grocery shopping in my Birkenstocks and favorite soft sweater, the one with the unidentifiable stain on the sleeve and thread pulls from the neighbor's snaggletoothed hound named Radar? Who would tell me what music to listen to so I didn't use references from the nineties when joking with teen cashiers? Who would love me unconditionally? No one. That's who. And if something happened to Katie, then negative one.

It was good to have this mission even as I walked off the plane, led by my new walking, talking California girl doll.

I texted Katie.

ME: We're here all is well. Almost no cell service. Everything going as planned. Love you.

KATIE: Ok, talk to you when you get back. You have your hands full. Don't worry about me. Love you for this.

Observing my texting conversation had not slowed my new friend's zeal to make my life better. She had hacked my sleep issue, diagnosed it as diet related, and was set on Spanish being my second language. I wasn't fully listening as she talked over her shoulder. But I couldn't ignore her when she turned on her heel and proceeded to walk backward out of the plane and up the long aluminum hallway.

"I like to use a couple of different apps when I'm learning a language."

Reading my nonverbal lack of enthusiasm, she paused for a minute, assessed me, and said, "You're just visiting, aren't you? Let me guess. You're from Nebraska. No, Iowa."

"Wisconsin," I said, and she nodded like everything about me suddenly added up.

"Yes. I can see that now."

If I'd felt rumpled before, this made me feel drab and in need of a full-life exfoliation. Not to kick myself when I was down, but becoming a young widow and a single mom had buffed out most of my shine over the years.

The woman stopped, and I walked right up to her extended leg and almost barreled into her collarbone. She clutched my shoulder, her fingers like well-manicured spider legs. "You should get a blowout and some cupping. I have a shaman you should see too."

She might as well have said to me, "You should find a million dollars, eat haggis, and grow three feet." I'd never had a blowout, cupping sounded like a bra fitting, and a shaman? Well, that was just insanity.

She saw my bewilderment, shoved her arm shoulder deep into her bag, and withdrew a card. Apparently, shamans had cards. The two of us were planted like boulders in the middle of a stream of people exiting the plane. The pint-size woman owned the space, and I had to hand it to her: she did not care that people were huffing and pissed that they were forced to dodge us. I glanced at the card.

"Marvin Shamansky? Marvin? The Shaman Shamansky?"

"Don't judge a spiritual healer by his Marvin. He's amazing." At that she moved, and we joined the flow of passengers.

At the last steps up the ramp, I blinked in the bright light. I saw Holly. Tall, thin, looking as she always did, neat and pressed, while I felt frumpy and wrinkled. She spotted me, and I had to admit it was okay to see her standing there. I was about to say so when the woman said, "Is this your partner? That's awesome. I'm so glad you two found each other after so much loss in your life."

Holly had a complicated expression on her face. It was as if she wanted me to dispute this, but if I did, I'd offend her. Also, there was that offhanded comment about loss. I hadn't said two words to this woman. What was she talking about?

"You've got to look Marvin up," the walking doll said. "He's out of town, but he's worth it. He can talk to your husband or at least tell you what spirit you're carrying around on your back. The one that keeps you so tired."

Then she was gone. California Girl moved into the sea of people and was out of sight faster than I could process what had happened.

"She thinks we're partners," said Holly with a nasty smirk.

I couldn't speak after having my dead husband mentioned by a complete stranger.

"You want to run after her and set her straight? Tell her that we aren't a couple?" Holly's tone mocked me.

I considered going after her, but only to ask how she knew about my loss. Was she referring to Jeff, and was he in a place a shaman could reach?

CHAPTER SEVEN
NEVER CHANGE

"Well, it sounded like you spilled your guts."

"I didn't talk about anyone. I slept the whole way."

"Not the *whole* way it seems. You stayed awake long enough to tell her your life story." Holly said this with a jeering eyebrow lift.

"I didn't. I don't even know her name." Someone's luggage hit my ankle and set off a zip of pain up the side of my leg.

"Summer," said Holly, a silk scarf on her shoulder in the most casual, *this-old-thing* way.

"What?"

"That's Summer Silva, from *She Talk Live*. How do you not know that?"

"Summer Silva?" I sounded slow; I wasn't used to being with Holly yet. You couldn't be halfway with Holly; she required 100 percent, 1,000 percent of the time. "I used to watch that show. But are you sure? She was sitting next to me in economy," I finally managed to say.

"She's not on the show anymore. She got superweird, talked about tarot cards and being a Wiccan, then lost her money in that famous Ponzi scheme. God, Sammie. Get with the program."

"I am with the program, Holly. I'm with Maddie's program. That's the only program I watch. You'll see what it's like soon enough."

Holly snapped her luggage handle into the extended position and turned. "I guess people are always unloading on celebrities. They're in living rooms, and so people think they're friends."

"I do not think Summer Silva is my friend." I heard the annoyance in my voice, and I thought, *I'm not a moron.*

"Right now, Summer Silva appears to know more about your husband than I do. I'm going to the restroom. Get yourself a cup of coffee. You need one."

Rude as it was, she was right about my needing caffeine even as the rest of what she said was unfair. I schlepped my backpack and the carry-on bag I didn't remember collecting and stood in the caffeine line. I'd get a colossal cup of coffee, a legal, sloppy second to my missed amphetamine dose. Maybe then I'd remember the conversation I'd had with a D-list celebrity about my dead husband.

I wiggled my jaw, tight from clenching my teeth, and worried that my enamel was never going to make it cross-country.

Holly hadn't always been so difficult. We'd met at freshman orientation and had been paired off to play a mixer that involved the alphabet and our names. "I'm Sam and I'm Sappy. I'm Holly and I'm Happy." Everything Holly said was funny and sometimes a bit mean. Not mean like a bully, just sharp commentary about the students and the world around us.

"That boy there," she said as she pointed to an athletic guy with a neck the size of a ham, "hopes his high school football stats translate into college credit." She laughed. "Later we'll take a shot of tequila every time he says *running back*. We'll be drunk and asleep in under fifteen minutes at the rate he's going. But, that's perfect for our orientation games tomorrow; we'll be well rested and ready to rhyme." She said in a funny, irreverent way what I was thinking and feeling bad about. She put people in their places, which helped me to stop putting myself beneath others.

We were inseparable, except for classes; we met for dinner, studied in the library, shared clothes. When Holly's parents died in a snowmobiling crash sophomore year, her sharp tongue became a razor, and her theoretical drinking became real. I spent the spring semester taking Jägermeister shots away from her and driving her home while she swore at people and cried. I explained situations to professors, sometimes did her homework as well as mine, fed her when she got too thin. It was the only time in her life when she looked as disheveled as I felt. That was when things had started to change with Holly. Her tongue got sharper, and often she'd say, "What's the use of any of this. What's the point?"

To which I'd reply, "You're the point. I'm the point. We are the point." And sometimes that would help.

Meeting Katie at an off-campus housing seminar that put potential roommates together was pure luck. A transfer from another college, she helped both of us. Katie was a fresh squirt of friendship Febreze, and I needed the help. My grades were slipping, I couldn't get enough sleep, and I felt like staying in the library longer than I needed to avoid going home. Katie came, and her sunny disposition blew some of the dust off Holly's old happy personality. Helped Holly find her way to the other side of her grief.

I never worried that Katie would take my place with Holly. She was the kind of person who wanted her own place in a friendship, not someone else's. She moved in when we needed a third person to share the rent, and she did things Holly and I were terrible at. She cooked, cleaned, changed light bulbs, bought toilet paper, paid bills on time, and made us giggle with her kindness.

Another dimension of Holly's and my friendship was that we thoroughly entertained each other with our antics. We were each other's biggest fans, and when Katie joined our friendship, she became our audience. We did everything to entertain Katie, which only made Holly and me closer. That's why our party of three had worked.

In the airport, I took a hard look around me while I waited for other people's complicated coffee orders. Tall, decaf, soy latte at 120 degrees with cream. This specified by a man in flip-flops whose only luggage was a paper grocery bag. There were so many colors and sizes of people swarming between the large white walls and windows of LAX, so much variety. A thousand blondes. Double that number in tanned limbs. In Wisconsin I was an acceptable hazel-eyed girl. Occasionally someone would remark that I looked like a brown-haired sister of Jennifer Aniston before she'd had her nose done. Jeff used to say, "Jennifer wishes she looked like you," which I might have believed if he hadn't always said it after a night of apologies for his temper, tears, and okay makeup sex.

I checked my phone while I waited. I'd missed a text from Beautiful Drew. I was alarmed at first, thinking it was potentially bad news from Katie, but this quickly changed to delight when I saw it was not.

BDREW: Hey when you come back bring some Cali Sun. It's gloomy here.

Me: Will do. I'll bring some Botox too, I think it's in the bubblers.

BDREW: Water fountain, WI-girl. It's water fountain in California.

Me: Noted. I'll try to get it right.

BDREW: No. Never change.

The inscription on every high school yearbook sent me into a sweet, romantic nostalgia. I wanted to send him an emoji that relayed the cautious pleasure his texts brought me without turning it weird for both of us. I settled on the unicorn head thinking it the best, meaningless whimsy for the situation, but my shaky overexcited fingers slipped and sent the snail emoji instead.

BDREW: I love a good gastropod.

ME: Who doesn't.

I took a deep breath, calmed myself. My unsubstantiated romantic notions aside, it was fun to text a conversation with an adult. For one thing, he punctuated. Maddie barely used words, and our texts were janitorial. You forgot your lunch. Where are you? Do you need tampons? This texting with Drew was the kind of back-and-forth wordplay that I could manage. Even though texting was fast, it wasn't as fast as face-to-face. The added seconds to respond via text allowed for my sometimes syrupy brain to process faster. I liked *exciting* as long as it had a firm seat belt.

I placed my order, and the man blinked at its simplicity. I had to repeat it twice. "A large coffee, please. Whatever you have brewed."

Holly showed up at my shoulder and said, "You're like a white rhino sighting. Nobody just gets a coffee. I'm surprised they didn't make you pose for a photo."

"Just say it, Holly. I'm a relic. Then I don't have to endure a week of your jabs."

She put her arm around my shoulder, hugged me, and kissed me on the head. "Come on, sweetie, let's get this party started."

In that half a second I grew an inch, but when I saw her wink at the barista, I sagged back. She was playing off Summer Silva's mistake, that we were lovers, with a mean edge to her smile. I shrugged her arm off, and she said, "What's the matter, honey?"

Our first year together in college, Holly was approached by a smooth-haired beauty, one of the members of a campus sorority. She wanted Holly to rush. It was a big house with lots of perks, but Holly, with a beer in her hand, said, "Nope. Not interested." Out of the side of her mouth she said to me, "I have a strategy. Reject before rejected." I hadn't thought of that in years.

Today I pushed her away. I didn't want her to know how briefly wonderful it felt to have her, however artificially, be kind to me.

———

Finally we were outside in the kind of sun that felt like someone had slathered butter over everything. Reds were redder, greens were varied

I Thought You Said This Would Work

and succulent, yellows were the color God had intended to save the world from all malaise. I turned my head to the blue sky, and just holding the blistering hot coffee cup made me feel good.

"Let's do this," I said out loud.

"I think we should rent a van and go get the dog."

"Peanut. The dog, as you say, won't get into a van. He will only get into and out of the camper."

"We're in charge."

"He'll panic, his blood sugar will drop, and he'll start vomiting."

Holly paused, seemingly to picture the barf. "Right. We'll go get the camper. Do you want to call the Uber?" She saw my expression; I had no idea how to summon one. "Never mind, Sammie. I've got it." She punched a few things into her phone and then scanned the incoming traffic. "We are looking for a green Honda Accord driven by a Terri. If you see a moving edamame, that's our ride."

The nut of dread in the pit of my stomach calcified as I visualized a day (a week?) of her simmering scorn.

"We meet again!" Summer Silva appeared in front of us with the recognition energy of a long-lost best friend. I couldn't have been happier to see her, and before thinking I said, "An Uber is coming. Can we give you a ride?" From the corner of my eye, I saw Holly whip her head around with a deadly glare.

"You guys! I'll give *you* a ride. That's how I'll contribute."

She gestured to a black sedan with a driver standing ready holding the rear door open, a sign dangling from his side. I started to refuse, but Holly touched her phone and said, "That sounds great; just canceled the Uber. Come on, sweetie," with another malicious wink. It was my turn to glare. What was going on?

Summer clapped her hands, saying "Wonderful!" like this was the best thing that ever happened to her, and we settled into the back seat. "Give the driver the address."

In minutes we were engulfed in bumper-to-bumper traffic.

67

"So, Summer. How was it sitting next to Sam on the flight? Did she talk your ear off?"

"Her aura spoke to me." Summer stretched the seat belt and propped herself up against the side door. She trained her eyes on me and said, "Your aura speaks volumes when you're sleeping"; then she waved her arms. "So much love and sadness, confusion and empathy. Plus, so good at math and your home filing system is to die for. What a gift."

I can only imagine what my face looked like. Aura? What? But Summer was dead on about my filing system, and for once I was content to not have Holly's withering look targeting me.

Holly had half a smile on. The one that looked friendly but when you knew her meant, *Oh, shut the ef up.* "So what is my aura saying to you?"

"Oh, sweetie. You know what it says. A wall is not a door to good parenting."

Holly shot a killer look at me, but before she could get a word of outrage in edgewise, Summer said, "So, what's the plan?"

Holly said, "You and Samantha must have had quite the conversation on that plane."

Summer closed her warm, bony hand over mine and said, "Oh, we did. She can't stop talking when asleep."

"I do not talk in my sleep." If Holly thought I was revealing information about our history and her life to complete strangers, the rest of this trip was going to be absolute torture. "I slept the entire flight. Summer, tell her I slept the whole flight." I looked at Holly. "She told me I should cut beans from my diet."

Holly looked out her window, and Summer patted my hand. "You two have some work to do if you're going to take this relationship to the next level."

There was nothing I could say to that.

"Where are we going? What are we doing?" Summer asked.

"We have to go get a camper from our friend's ex-husband so we can pick up her dog at a shelter, transport him back to our friend, who is sick. The husband is a dick. His new wife hates us. We don't have keys, permission, or authority to do any of this," I said.

Summer nodded and said, "I thought it was something like that."

Holly scoffed, but Summer didn't seem annoyed in the least.

"Are we going to call Tom?" I said.

"No," Holly said. "This is going to be a surprise. I don't want him to prepare. Katie said the VW wasn't in the divorce papers. Peanut and the bus went together, but I think we can make a case that the vehicle still belongs to both of them."

"What if nobody's home?" I asked.

"We take the camper. He'll probably thank us."

"OMG! I love crime," said Summer like it was a danish at a buffet. I couldn't help but be drawn into the fiction and excitement of Summer's view. I was like a kid watching this all on television.

"Here we are, ladies. Time to go!" The limo driver pulled into a cul-de-sac with modest-looking homes, some with palm trees and others with massive yuccas spanning the property. I'd spent the night before the trip perusing online real estate listings, just to get an idea of what kind of terrain we would be riding into. Tom and Misty's house had a white stucco exterior and a big dormer window. It was not a large house and looked dated, but I knew that it had to be worth at least a million and a half in the Culver City zip code. I heard Holly talking to the driver, but my attention was on the old Volkswagen camper bus, which sat securely behind a black iron gate at the side of the house.

I wasn't sure what to do. I wanted to see if the gate was locked and if not, if the keys were indeed under the driver's-side mat, where Tom had always kept them. I was thinking about what Holly would say to Tom when Summer brushed past me, her monstrous bag bouncing on her hip.

"You and Holly stay out of sight." She strode right up the front path and knocked on the door. I hustled to the gate, and in seconds Holly crouched at my side. A déjà vu of another time, Holly, my friend, huddled next to me, watching a couple make out under our apartment balcony. The memory dissipated as her knee touched my leg, and she instantly pulled it away.

"Let's see what happens." Holly shrugged. "If I don't have to talk to that son of a bitch, all the better. I might take a swipe at him, and then we'll never get what we want."

"This isn't going to work."

"That limo wasn't there to pick her up at the airport. She stole someone else's limo. She told him while I was paying."

"That can't be right. You said she's famous."

Holly gestured, and I saw the taillights of the sedan leave the cul-de-sac, the driver's hand in a salute out the window, flipping us off until he was out of sight. "After this we'll get rid of Summer. But, I gotta admit she's got some skills."

This was all happening too fast. I did not have this kind of life, but Holly's expression was reminiscent of her undergraduate self when we stole from our favorite bar. She'd shove all kinds of things down her pants in bars: shot glasses, toilet paper, Tabasco sauce, Christmas decorations. She'd give me a wicked grin and I'd get the getaway car, my crappy Chevy with the missing gas tank cover. We were Bonnie and Bonnie, because nobody needed a Clyde when we were together. Today it was Bonnie and Bonnie's nervous, sleepy, and slightly disoriented sister.

From our spot at the side of the house, I could only see Summer, hands emphasizing whatever obscure thing she was saying. "Who is she talking to?"

"Sounds like Misty."

I heard snippets of conversation but nothing coherent. She reached into her bag and pulled something out. I heard a laugh; the tone changed. There were murmurs; they appeared to take a selfie.

Summer turned, and I heard her say, "Thank you so much, Misty. You are the high priestess your spirit is telling me you are." A clunking sound followed, and the large metal gates opened out with some unseen mechanical force. Summer waved to Misty and gestured for us to follow, and I did as if I were hypnotized.

"Get in! Get in, you guys, before she changes her mind, googles *She Talk Live*, and finds out I'm not on the show anymore."

We sprinted through the open gates, and Summer chucked the keys at Holly, who caught them in a one-handed, sporty catch I could never have managed. Holly slid behind the wheel, jammed the keys into the ignition, and the engine turned over. Summer sat cross-legged on the floor between the seats, and I slammed the passenger door shut, out of breath from excitement.

"My coffee! It's in the limo." There, I'd shown my cards. What I was truly concerned with was my own alertness and not what might be grand theft auto.

Summer said, "Well, it's gone now. Let's do this, squad."

CHAPTER EIGHT

THE TIRED GIRL, THE MAD GIRL,
OR THE CELEBRITY

The vehicle bounced out of the cul-de-sac and hit the curb, the glove compartment dropped open, and the horn beeped twice. The van sounded like it was held together by rusty hinges, and it stretched noisily with every roll of the tires in the quiet neighborhood. I felt my phone vibrate in my pocket.

"Jesus, don't hit the horn!" I said.

"I didn't! It beeped by itself!" Holly laughed her deep college laugh, and it made me remember all those nights we'd spent together dancing in our apartment with Katie and singing into our beer bottles. When girls were friends, it was like a beautiful bouquet of funny flowers eternally watered by their togetherness. When the friendship failed, it was an ice storm on a hothouse plant.

Holly peered through the rearview mirror and said, "Do you think Misty will regret this?"

"Nah," said Summer. "Her story isn't finished. I think she is going to surprise us. You'll see."

Holly and I exchanged glances.

"Why was she so willing to hand over the camper to us? Does she know we're all here to help Katie?" said Holly.

"Yes. Misty doesn't have anything against Katie, as it turns out. But she'd like not to think of her every time she looks out her window."

I was about to ask Summer what Misty said about Tom, but Holly interrupted me.

"Thanks so much for this, Summer. Where can we drop you?"

"Oh, I don't have anywhere to be."

"We're driving back to Wisconsin."

"I've never been there. This is exciting." Sun lit up the cab of the RV and landed squarely on Summer's face, filled with expectation, and I noted a fraying around her carefully curated edges. Her blonde hair stopped at her crown, showing a half inch of gray I hadn't noticed before. A line of makeup at her chin, a dark vein on the back of her hand showed through her paper-thin skin. I held my breath. I wanted her to stay with us.

Holly's tone had turned lawyerly, a tone I knew well and hated when she used it on me. "Summer, we appreciate your help. But this is going to be a big trip. No nonsense. We gotta go."

This was exactly the kind of conflict-filled conversation that I avoided. I would come to parent meetings late and leave early just to miss all the sideline bitching that happened there. In restaurants when the waiter asked how the meal was, I gave a cheerful thumbs-up and then spat my food into a napkin.

Summer dug around in her Mary Poppins bag and extracted a file folder. "Misty gave me the registration and proof of insurance. I also have a handwritten note from her that says she has lent the vehicle to me, Summer Silva, to return on the completion of our journey." As quickly as she pulled the documents out, she shoved them back in. "You're stuck with me."

Holly made a protest noise in her throat, and I enjoyed seeing her speechless.

Summer slid a sturdy plastic storage container from behind my seat and parked her tiny butt on it. To me, she said, "Does she smoke weed? She should. She would benefit."

I stifled a laugh.

"Or CBD oil on your stress points." She pulled out a brown bottle with a rubber dropper top and said, "I have medical grade CBD oil right here. Hand me your wrist."

"I'm not giving you my wrist." Holly sucked the corner of her bottom lip. "Why would you even want to go with us? We have to drive thousands of miles to the Midwest. We'll be sleeping in this crap bus. You're Summer Silva. Don't you have something better to do?"

Summer put her head back and squeezed a drop of the alleged CBD oil on her tongue and said, "No, I don't." She slipped into what I can only assume was LA lingo. "I've got a few projects in the works, but funding got held up with talk of the screenwriters' strike. My agent says there is a reality TV show looking for a host, and there's a sitcom a director likes me for, but it hasn't been green-lighted yet. So"—she put her hands together as if she were praying and dropped her head to her fingertips—"I'm at your service."

"No offense, Summer, but we don't need your services."

To her credit, Summer snapped back, "You don't know what you need, no offense."

"Shots fired," I said. I couldn't help myself; I had the feeling Summer was tossing me a lifeline.

Holly said, "You are not helping, Sammie."

"Look, you two," Summer said. "Consider me a benign stowaway rather than an interloper. I'm working on a memoir, and a road trip will help me clear my head. Plus, this one"—she gestured to me—"needs to meet with my shaman, and she can't get in without me. He owes me a favor too." I was about to protest, but Holly beat me to it.

"Too?" Holly had pulled over, and the bus idled at the curb. She looked at me. "Did you put her up to this so you weren't stuck in the car with me for days?"

"No! I'm telling you I slept the whole flight."

"Sam's a wreck. Leave her out of this."

"Hey!" I was a smidgen offended by that. I was on Team Summer, after all. Admittedly I wasn't thrilled about being alone with Holly, but I was holding up pretty well. I didn't feel too tired. I was game to be riding in a vehicle obtained under questionable circumstances, and we were about to pick up Peanut. I was on point.

"You guys," Summer said, "I can be a goby fish to your snapping shrimp."

"What are you talking about?" Holly had her phone out, and the glasses she never wore except for reading were perched on the end of her nose. She appeared to be looking for directions to the animal shelter.

"The goby fish helps the nearly blind snapping shrimp by alerting the shrimp to danger while they build burrows for them both to sleep."

Summer was kind of hilarious and definitely could read people. I thought about her assessment of me. A wreck. Instead of outrage I felt a pang of fondness for the skinny woman who didn't have it quite as together as it had first seemed.

"Let's go," I said. "It's almost five. We have to get to the shelter before it closes." My phone vibrated again, and I read the text.

BDREW: What's happening over there?

I thought of that old country-western song that was on jukeboxes in college. The one where the question is asked. Love? Friendship? Check the box yes or no. A wash of *Of course not, Samantha!*

ME: We just stole the camper and we either have a stowaway or we've been kidnapped. Unsure which.

BDREW: Do you need the police?

ME: God NO.

BDREW: All in hand then?

ME: All in hand. How's Katie?

The three dots rolled and I waited as the camper lurched forward. I anticipated getting a long, thorough assessment of how my friend was faring without us by her side.

The dots appeared again and words followed.

BDREW: She's good.

I thought about pressing him for more details, but this didn't feel like the time. I wanted to get to the shelter, figure out what was next, and to be honest, I was starting to feel fatigue drip like thick honey filling the ventricles of my brain.

ME: Can you write me a prescription for my sleep medication?

BDREW: No.

ME: Come on. What's some amphetamines between friends?

BDREW: No. I'm deleting this request.

———

She's good, Drew had said. Katie was good. Not much information but enough for now. I should have asked for more, but I wasn't sure I could handle more stress. If the information was not positive, I worried I wouldn't be awake to get Peanut.

I decided to text Katie; I knew she'd be waiting to hear from me.

ME: Hi Honey. On the way to get Peanut. Everything is good here.

KATIE: Hi! I was getting worried but then I remembered the time change.

ME: How are you?

KATIE: I feel good. Drew stopped in.

ME: I asked him to. OK?

KATIE: Sure. ☺

KATIE: He's kind of chatty honestly.

If I had been a dog, my ears would have perked up with anticipation—*He talks about you*—or cautiousness—*I think he likes me.*

ME: What about?

The dots scrolled, and I felt my mouth go dry.

KATIE: Nothing. I'm kind of tired. Holly okay?

I knew what she was asking. How was I doing with Holly?

ME: She's great! Rushing off. Go to sleep. xo

KATIE: xo

I tuned back in to what was going on around me just in time to see Summer pluck the phone from Holly's hand and say, "I'll navigate."

I would never, ever take Holly's phone out of her hand, and I waited for the explosion. When none came, I thought about the Group Dynamics class I took in college where the professor had said, "However large or small a group is, the addition of one person will forever change interactions, and preexisting ground rules no longer apply." Just like Katie had added a new dimension to our lives, I saw Summer was causing some shifting as well.

Katie was the ghost leader for this expedition. The three of us had our historic dynamics. Katie was the glue, I was the puppy, and Holly was our motor. With Katie's physical absence but her illness hanging over our heads, she had become the motor, which left Holly, Summer, and me jockeying for position. Who was in charge? The tired girl, the mad girl, or the celebrity? It was a low-stakes Hunger Games in the camper.

Summer looked at the address of the animal shelter. "I know right where this is. Okay, Hol, we're not far at all."

I glanced at Holly. She always told me and Katie, "There are two syllables in my name. If you don't have the time or energy to enunciate both, then you need a stress management class." Yet here she was, driving this dusty barn of a camper through the streets of LA letting a D-list celebrity, who we just met, hold her phone and call her Hol. I'd never been more interested in life than at that very moment.

"Take a left up here. There's a Juice Bar and a real hippy-dippy market on the left. Sometimes Gwyneth herself sells her Goop stuff there. Everyone shows up for Gwynnie," she said with a snide tone. "The perfect Gwyn Gwyn." She exhaled and squinted at the phone. "We're just going to make it. While you guys go in and get Peanut, I'll air this camper out, try to clean it up."

The camper smelled of damp dog, balls of white fur rolled with every bump in the road, and an old fleece blanket I recognized as Katie's lay in a lump in a grimy corner. The cracked caramel-colored seats spoke of a different era, and every surface had a fine layer of dust. It may have been the height of modern in the seventies, but the bus had seen better days.

I remembered when Katie and Tom bought it for Peanut. They'd searched for an inexpensive vehicle for carting the nervous dog around, and they'd found someone on Craigslist who was willing to give it to them for hauling it away. Tom hated the thing, but Katie had insisted. The vehicle had to be big enough so that Peanut would voluntarily walk into it without falling into a heap of anxiety, but not so big Katie couldn't parallel park it. She had anticipated needing it for small trips like the vet and dog park but never a cross-country drive without her. For a second I was flooded with sadness for Katie, her broken marriage, her bitter divorce, the loss of her darling dog, and now more cancer. All this happening in the last few years. As if she knew what I was feeling, Summer touched my knee and squeezed.

"Turn here!" Summer hollered, and we skidded to a stop in front of a one-story storefront decorated with an enormous mural of cats and dogs. "Let's get Peanut, team!"

"Let's go get the dog," Holly said like a bookworm forced onto a cheerleading squad who would rather thumb through her Kindle.

"Here we come, Peanut!" I said with enthusiasm that fell below Summer's but was several notches above Holly's. I noticed that Holly rarely called Peanut by name, and I didn't know if it was a thing or just a Holly-ism.

Summer wiped her hand over the dashboard and grimaced. "This chariot is not worthy of this noble mission."

Holly ignored her as we pushed our way through the heavy glass doors of the Found Animals Stop and Shop. A short woman in a T-shirt that read *My dog is smarter than you* lifted her head and said, "Are you looking for a furry buddy today?"

Still jazzed from Summer's enthusiasm I shouted, "Yes!"

Holly scowled at me. To the woman at the desk she said, "We are looking for a Great Pyrenees with diabetes that was dropped here a few days ago."

"Peanut. His name is Peanut." I tucked myself in next to Holly and the wall. A tabby cat, curled in a plaid fleece bed on the desk, stared unblinking at me.

A startled woman with overplucked eyebrows was ready for our energy. "I know exactly who you mean. A darling doggo. He left earlier today for the Best Friends Sanctuary." She reached into the neck of her royal-blue T-shirt and gave her bra strap a yank as if she were just getting started. "His size and diabetic status make him a low adoption choice."

"What do you mean 'left'?" I said so abruptly that the cat stood, lifted her back, and resettled away from my drama.

"We are a *no-kill* shelter, and when the Best Friends Sanctuary people are making a pickup, we hand over hard-to-adopt dogs, and they go to the sanctuary." The woman pushed her black plastic glasses up her nose. "No offense to Peanut, but big dogs with diabetes are super hard to find homes for. Plus, he's not a puppy. People want puppies."

"That's fine. What's the address? We'll go get him," Holly said.

I was grateful for Holly's determination. I couldn't see myself texting Beautiful Drew or Katie to say that we didn't have Peanut.

"Hang on." The woman clicked through computer screens. "Okay. I've got it. Five hundred Angel Canyon Drive, Kanab, Utah."

"Utah?" I blurted. "We'll never make it by five."

Holly gave me another unfriendly look.

The woman hesitated. "Um. No. It's far. But, it's an amazing place. I went there earlier this year and volunteered in the Bunny House. It was life changing. I adored Mr. Piddles and Catmando." She pointed to the grumpy tabby on the desk. "When you go to get your dog, be careful. Almost no one comes out without a few best friends."

My screen lit up with a text from Beautiful Drew: Is Peanut in hand?

I cringed and closed my phone. "How far is Utah?" I asked the woman.

"Past Vegas, on top of Arizona. I think it took me something like six hours to get there. That's why I've only been the one time."

Holly seemed to kick into gear. "Six hours?" She turned to the receptionist. "You sent a big ol' dog that wasn't yours six hours into the desert?"

The woman frowned and said, "Hey now. That dog was abandoned, and we took care of it."

"You got rid of it, you mean."

"No. It's, *he's*, in a better place. He'll love it out there. So many other dogs and open spaces to run."

Holly slammed her flat hand on the counter and said, "We came for the dog, and now he's not here." The tabby on the counter lifted her tail like a big middle finger and turned her butt around to face Holly.

"Easy, tiger." I'd seen Holly mad before, but I was surprised at this outburst. I smiled apologetically to the woman and said, "Come on, Holly. We have to make a plan B."

"Can't we go in the back and get another dog? You know Katie—she'll fall in love with any dog."

The woman behind the counter gasped.

I yanked Holly toward the door and said, "Are you kidding me right now? Asking a dog owner if their dog is interchangeable is like asking a mother if she could take a different kid home from day care."

"Don't be dramatic. That's not the same thing."

"It is to dog owners. What is your deal with Peanut anyway?"

"It's not just Peanut. It's people with pets in general. We spend so much time and money on animals: rescuing them, saving them with expensive surgery and meds. What's the point?"

The woman behind the desk called out, "We don't save them. They save us!"

The second we stepped out of the glass doors, I heard the dead bolt slide into place behind us. With Holly, you either made friends or enemies quickly.

I looked over my shoulder, sending the woman apology-eyebrows, when I heard Holly say, "Where is the camper?"

CHAPTER NINE
PEACE-OUT GIRL

A navy Ford Fiesta sat at the curb outside of the animal shelter where our shitty camper should have been. No ugly bus took up two spaces anywhere on the block, and my mind was doing that squirrel thing: *What should I do? Where should I go? Who should I call? Holly's going to be mad.* I sat with a slap onto a metal bench just outside the shelter. Even though Holly had been in favor of getting into the limo with Summer, it was I who'd sat next to her on the plane. Ultimately Holly would fault me.

"I left my phone in the camper. She has my phone!" Holly paced, training her neck right and left.

Oh God. Holly would not tolerate being separated from her phone. If I could slip into a micro-sleep I would be able to process this. I closed my eyes.

"Don't you dare fall asleep on me."

Holly's voice was so loud and so close, I shrank away from the force of her frustration. With a calm I didn't feel, I said, "Holly, sometimes people other than you need things. I need a minute."

"This is a ridiculous thing we're doing. It's like this whole mission has changed into an episode of *Game of Thrones*."

"That's dramatic."

"She's got our camper, our luggage, my phone, and your purse. This seems like a high-drama situation. Call 911."

"And say what, Holly? 'Hello, Officer, we think a TV star drove off with our camper.'" I shook myself and took three deep breaths—sometimes hyperventilation brought me clarity. "I'll call your phone."

Holly didn't sneer at me, so I felt a spark of triumph. I dialed and waited. When Holly's voice mail answered, without thinking I said, "Summer, please come back with the camper, no questions asked."

"No questions asked," Holly said with disgust. "I have some questions for her." She paced, and a semitruck whizzed by and coughed up a cloud of dust that floated toward us on the sidewalk. Holly said, "She can't get into my phone. It's password protected."

I switched to texting, knowing the texts would show up on the locked screen.

ME: Summer. Please come back. Or call me. 608-554-4242

I was about to write, *You can't leave me here with Holly* but stopped myself in time, remembering that I was texting Holly's phone and that if she returned, Holly would see my incriminating plea for help.

ME: If you needed transportation you could have just asked. We need our stuff. Please. The prospect of failure so soon on the tails of starting this adventure brought tears to my eyes. I blinked them back.

"If we sit here for a while, she's bound to come back. Right? She wouldn't just leave us," I said, wondering if that was true.

"You would know. She's your friend."

"Whatever, Holly."

I watched her race-walk to the corner and peer around the block, then do the same thing at the other corner. It was like observing a sleek cat in a cage. A cat I did not want to step in front of. A cat I did not want to be stuck in a car with. Disbelief washed over me as the realization of this moment came into focus. The fatigue started, and I knew I wouldn't be able to function if I let myself get overwhelmed.

I hit Google on my phone. "Holly, there is a Travelodge just an eight-minute walk from here. Let's get a room. We'll text Summer where we are and regroup. She will come back. She's not the kind of person who steals crap campers from women. Also, I know you hate this, but I need to close my eyes." I got up and started walking, and with nothing left to do but follow me, Holly complied, but not without cleaning house on her list of bitchy complaints.

"Can't you get ahold of this sleep thing?"

I was going to let it go, take the high road, but I just couldn't. I had my phone, Apple Pay for things, and could finish this trip on my own if I had to. I didn't need Holly and her shitty moods. I kept walking and shouted as if I was giving a lesson to a group of kids.

"You know how your aunt has MS? Ask her if she can get ahold of it. You go ahead and ask her. Say, 'Hey, Aunt Kathy, I think if you were strong enough you could get ahold of this MS thing. All physiological difficulties are just a matter of mental weakness. I should know. I don't have any weaknesses. I am the queen of my body and will live forever because I think it so. I am Holly Dunfee, the queen of physiology.'" Anger blew through me.

Holly, to her credit, said, "Okay. Whatever." Just like a kid who had been chastised.

And, honestly? That felt like a big win for ol' Sammie.

We were at the corner of Washington Boulevard and Sepulveda, right in front of Starbucks, and I knew at that moment there was a God. "I'm going to buy a Nitro Cold Brew, then I'm getting a room. I'll drink my coffee after my ten-minute nap." I pulled open the door, and a blast of cool air hit my face. "When I come out, I want you to consider that this is happening to me too. That you and I are on the same side."

Inside the cool, dark cave of Starbucks, music from an indie band crooned from the overhead speakers, and I put my hands on the counter to steady myself. I was tremulous. A woman with a slim silver nose ring said, "Can I help you?"

"Yes." But my mind was on what I'd just said to Holly. I recognized that voice of mine, the straight-up, no-nonsense reasoning tone. It was my parenting voice. I used it when Maddie was being a snotty teen about her curfew or that one time she wanted to stay in a hotel room after prom with her date and a bunch of friends. I'd get so tired of being pushed that I'd *go off*. Which is what Maddie would say: "Wow, go off, Mom."

I did it with Maddie but no one else. I was impressed that I'd used it on Holly.

"Would you like a coffee?" The woman had pretty almond-shaped eyes and blonde braids on either side of her face.

I nodded. "Nitro Cold Brew. Iced." I went through the motions of paying, but I was searching around for my fatigue, and for once, it didn't seem to be present.

This is how cults get people to do stuff. You take people out of their normal circumstances, screw with their sense of time, add bossy people with strong ideologies to the mix, and the next thing you know, you are doing things you normally wouldn't do, like steal campers and yell at the person you are most afraid of. I picked up my coffee and said to myself, *Samantha, you are on new ground. Take it slowly,* which was different from what I usually said to myself which was, *Just shut up.*

Without speaking, Holly and I checked into the Travelodge, booked a room with two double beds, and I crawled into one of them. I texted the address to Summer, hoping she would come back. The sheets were cool, and I barely noticed the dampness in the room, the two straggly palm trees that grew outside our window, or the steady stream of cars outside our door. I did hear Holly say, just as I nodded off, "I bet you're a good mom."

"I am," I said, and I was gone.

———

I woke to Holly's voice, at least a version of Holly's voice I hadn't heard for decades.

"Okay, sweetie. It's okay. I'm sure it's nothing. Lie down. Are you drinking enough water?"

I knew immediately she was talking to her wife, Rosie. I'd heard that voice so many years ago when we were friends, if I wasn't feeling well or needed a tiny snooze. It kicked off a feel-good molecule in my brain, and I sighed.

She waited, and in even softer tones said, "I'll be home soon. Call your sister. Ask her to come. I love you."

I wondered if Rosie knew how lucky she was to have Holly. When Holly was your friend, it was like having a superhero on your side. I could only imagine if she was your spouse. When Jeff died, I'd hoped she'd come to the funeral, and when she hadn't, I'd curled up with baby Maddie and poured all the love I had in a holding cell waiting for Holly into my daughter. I drip, drip, dripped it into Maddie's ears, saying, "I'll always love you. I'll never leave you when you need me. You can do anything. You are the world." Like a song before bedtime, I assured her of love everlasting.

Still on the phone, Holly said, "What do you mean, it's good for me to be away? No, it's not." She had none of the bristly irritation in her voice that she used with me. She was listening and responding not as the imperious Holly but as the soft Holly I knew from so many years ago, the one who would say just before I'd go to sit for an exam: "Sam, you are good at math. You've done this before. You can do it again."

"I don't need more people. I like the few I do have." She paused and added, "I like our tiny village, and I'm coming back to it as soon as I can." There was another silence, and then she said, "I know. I wouldn't have met you. I know, honey. Now stop worrying about me and go to bed. Always."

I opened my eyes and saw Holly's straight shoulders, slumped. She faced the wide window that opened to the street, in the same position as when I'd fallen asleep. I rolled onto my elbow. "Everything all right, Holly? Is Rosie okay?"

Holly startled and cleared her throat. "Yes. Fine. I used your phone. You should put a password on this. Some beautiful person is texting you."

Annoyed, I swung my legs off the bed. I'd slept for an hour, according to the digital clock at the bedside. I reached for my blessed cup of coffee and took a sip.

"I didn't know you had a guy."

"I don't."

"Beautiful Drew says, 'You up?' Nothing says booty like *you up?*"

"It's a joke. He's joking." I know I was smiling like it was much more. I couldn't help the pleasure that each ding of my phone sent through me. I was going to explain that Drew was the physician we'd talked to in Katie's hospital room to fill her in on what he was doing for us. Did I want to say this while hoping it was something else? Would Holly confront me later if I didn't get it exactly right now?

"Now what?" said Holly.

"She'll come back. I'm sure of it." Holly walked my phone over, dropped it on the bed next to me. "I think you know she will."

We were unused to conversation. Chatting seemed like the simplest of things, but it was a gateway drug to friendship, and if you were working backward like Holly and I, that gate had to be unlocked. We needed a prompt that wasn't a gauntlet.

I opened my phone and googled the Best Friends Animal Sanctuary. "Let's see where we're going." The page loaded, and I read, "The sanctuary has been open for thirty years. The nation's largest no-kill sanctuary."

"No-kill?"

"*No-kill* means they want to care for or find homes for all animals."

"How big is it?"

"Geez. It says here there are three thousand seven hundred acres where we're going, and they lease another seventeen thousand acres of state and federal land."

"Really." Holly sounded impressed and mystified.

"They have dogs, cats, bunnies, birds, pigs, horses, and other animals. One thousand six hundred animals."

"Running around? Are we going to have to walk around and find him?"

I thought of Peanut, galloping with a stately mustang or kicking it up with other big dogs, ears flapping in the dry heat. The image made me wish for that for myself.

I said, "I hope so," at the same time as Holly said, "That sounds like chaos."

We both smirked. Unsurprised at our different reactions.

"It looks organized, though. Here's a map. Check it out."

Holly put on glasses.

"I have readers too. All of a sudden I couldn't see anything close up."

She ignored that commonality and peered at the map. "People like animals."

I didn't remember that Holly didn't like animals, wanted to understand. Years ago, I would have asked her straight out, but every question that I came up with sounded like recrimination, even to me. Maybe if I pretended we were friends, spoke like I used to when she liked me. I unlocked my jaw, searched for something other than acres and numbers to talk about, to try to explain Peanut and Katie without explaining anything to know-it-all Holly.

I had barely completed the thought when the camper slid into view directly outside the window and stopped. "Summer's back!" I shouted. I felt like a suspenseful movie had ended unsatisfactorily even while being happy the tension line had been cut. *Oof,* my brain said.

"Son of a bitch, you were right."

We raced out the door just as Summer hit the sidewalk. "You guys! Wait until you see what I did!" She'd pulled her hair into a ponytail, and the expression on her face gave her the look of a hopeful grade-schooler excited about a floppy art project.

"What the heck, Summer? You can't just take our crap and leave us!" said Holly.

Summer did a stutter step of indecision, like she'd never for a second considered she'd done something wrong. "I didn't leave you. I'm here. That is the definition of not leaving you. Sam texted me the address." She shifted her annoyed gaze between us and said, "Where's Peanut?"

"They moved him to Utah," I said, so relieved that Summer had returned, so ready to forgive and reduce the friction of the moment.

"Utah? Huh. Random, but okay."

Holly yanked the front door of the bus open and, without looking at anything, grabbed my bag and her phone. She shoved my purse at me, and I embraced my nondescript belongings. As much as I had believed Summer would return, I'd missed the security of having my small comforts. I pulled out my ChapStick and swiped it onto my lips.

I had learned a couple of things already about traveling with Holly. Even though we had the same assignment, the same higher mission, and a celebrity guest, no less, she wasn't going to ease up on her Holly-ness. On the other hand, Holly would always be Bad Cop in our threesome, so if not Good Cop, I could be cease-fire girl, peace-out girl. I could just observe with serenity the way that Summer lit Holly's irritation on fire and maybe even enjoy it.

"Thanks for the texts, Sam. I found you guys super easily," Summer said to me. "But, remember, when you're lost, you should always stay put." She wagged her finger with a smile on her face.

"We weren't lost, you idiot," said Holly.

Summer said, "Ouch, Hol. No name-calling." She counted off on her fingers. "No garbage dumping. No bringing up past grievances. 'No' is a complete sentence. That's *Crucial Conversations 101*. I think that last one might be from *The Gift of Fear: How to Spot a Predator*. Both books I think you should read, Holly. You could use interpersonal help."

Holly sputtered. I loved that I didn't have to say a thing, but Summer may have gone too far.

"This is not working out, Summer," Holly said, rubbing her eyes. "Enough is enough."

Summer moved to the side of the camper, and I followed. I'd have followed her anywhere at this point. When she opened the side door, I gasped.

"Give us the insurance and registration. We'll drop you off," Holly said. "You pick a location."

"Holly. Check this out," I said, unable to tear my eyes away from the inside of the camper.

She sighed that beleaguered Holly-sigh and peeked around the door.

The inside of the camper had been transformed from a grubby, ugly, 1970s disaster to an updated, chic glamper. I'd seen the pictures on Pinterest and Instagram-people renovating small spaces—dorms, tiny houses, and Airstreams—in luxurious ways. I'd never seen one in real life.

Summer's hundred-watt smile and jazz hands were unnecessary as I stepped up and into the camper that smelled of paint and something fresh. Everything had been whitewashed, the walls, ceilings, and floors.

"Don't touch the edges quite yet—we used quick-dry paint, but we don't want to smudge the sheen," said Summer from behind me.

The windows had natural roman blinds, and the upholstery looked straight out like a design studio for small spaces. Summer saw me examining it and said, "It's anchored in there. You can pull it out, and it becomes a bed. Lift the mattress; the linens are stored there. Even the throw pillows are Velcroed into place so they don't fly around when we're driving."

The ceiling had been draped with a white filmy fabric that gave the entire space an Arabian tent feeling. The small cabinet had been covered with something that looked like shiplap but on closer examination was wallpaper.

"I picked white because Peanut is a Pyrenees, and they're usually white, right? When he sheds, we won't even notice."

"This is amazing," I said.

"We're not paying for this," said Holly, ready to litigate.

"How did you do this so fast? How is this even possible?" I said.

Summer shook her head, disappointed. "You guys. Obviously neither of you uses the internet extensively, so fine, okay. But, didn't you even google me while I was gone?"

"You stole my phone, Summer."

"Oh, Holly. I didn't steal your phone. I borrowed your camper. But a good lesson for you. Don't leave your purse and phone behind. You never know." She tsked. "Midwest women. So trusting."

I had to admit she was right: we should have done research on her.

"I have a YouTube show called *Trick Out My Tent*. The goal is to create luxurious spaces for vacationing in the wild. We do it all in my friend's backyard a couple of blocks from here. The show is on hold until we find another sponsor or we make nice with IKEA. They got mad when we spelled their EKTORP sofa with a *c* in the *Buy* links. Said we were unreliable. Can you imagine?" She rolled her big eyes. "I mean, nobody knows Swedish here—who cares?" Summer stepped into the camper with me and said, "Apparently, IKEA cares, and if we want them to keep donating their stuff, we have to spell things right."

Holly looked like she was trying to focus on a hummingbird but didn't have her glasses on.

"Anyway, my friend and his wife are the fastest reno-geeks in the business."

I said, "Reno-geeks?"

"Renovation geeks. You know, like Geek Squad, but not for computers. She can trick out a space and have it camera ready in a couple of hours. Honestly, Sam. I'm disappointed in you. Didn't you check out my IMDb page?"

"I guess I just trust you, Summer," I said with a grin.

In the front of the camper, through a narrow opening just big enough for a person to sit, I noticed that the dated control panel shone. Somehow it looked charming against the rest of the renovations in the cab. The cracked seats were covered in taupe linen, each layered with a bright-white sheepskin throw. The dashboard was a trimmed version of the fur on the seats, and it should have looked tacky and thrown together, but it didn't.

I touched the soft fur, and Summer said, "It's vegan. Don't worry. We're going to an animal sanctuary. How would that look if I'd used leather?" She laughed and covered her mouth with her hand, and the mission took on a new sparkle.

"I could do so much more with this thing, but I knew you guys wanted to hit the road. Smell that? There's an aromatherapy diffuser in the cigarette lighter. I have lavender in there now, but I have peppermint for you, Sam. It'll keep you awake."

Right or wrong, I loved what Summer had done with the camper, but I waited for Holly's next move.

She surprised me: "All right, you two. Wheels up." She clapped her hands like a very stern, very organized kindergarten teacher. "Since we never unloaded the camper, it's ready; we're ready. Let's hit the road."

"What about our room?" I said.

"What about it? We paid for it already. The money's gone if we stay in it or don't stay in it."

I didn't want to mention that I was hungry, but my girl Summer had me covered.

"I stocked up." She opened a tiny, vintage-looking fridge. Inside I spotted raspberries, ready-made salads, and predictably, sushi.

Holly stared, then slowly shook her head as if defeated. "Fine, Summer. I don't know what you're up to or why you're so into this, but you can come with us. But no more disappearing. No more"—Holly waved her arms around the camper—"magic tricks."

I leaned in and whispered to Summer, hoping to create an ally while making fun of Holly, "Yeah, no more magic tricks."

Holly took two steps to the side door and slammed it shut. The window rattled in the frame, and the light in the trailer dimmed. "Sammie, you're rested and caffeinated. You take the first leg. If we drive all night, we'll get to Utah by the morning."

"You want a snack?" Summer said. I studied her, amazed at how unaffected she was while being treated like a misbehaving seven-year-old.

"I ate a Power Bar. I'm fine." Holly rummaged through her purse for a phone charger. I settled into the driver's seat with Summer as my navigator. My fatigue abated, I was more awake than I expected. I started the engine, looked at the GPS on my phone, and pulled into traffic.

"So, what's the deal with you and Holly anyway? Why is she so crabby?"

Holly called from the back, "I can hear you, Summer. At least wait until I'm asleep to talk about me." I tried to suppress a tiny wicked smile; for once Holly was the one on the hot seat.

CHAPTER TEN
THE BEST THING IN THE WORLD

I pulled onto the I-10/Santa Monica Freeway following the directions on my phone. I'd never driven a camper before, and if the beeping horns were any indication, there were several massive blind spots. I lost a fuel tanker in one of them, and one outraged driver swerved onto the shoulder to get around us, in an exaggerated, dare I say, Hollywood display of irritation. Their MINI Cooper tires sprayed gravel like a tiny hissing cockroach, and the driver threw his middle finger out the window in case we didn't catch the first screw-you signs.

From the back Holly said, "Jesus, Sam. Alive, okay? Get us there alive?"

"I thought California drivers would be more laid back."

"They don't have rifles in the back windows of their trucks like they do in Texas, so this is laid back," Summer said.

"In Wisconsin we cuss you out quietly and then send a casserole in apology," I said.

"I had a casserole once. Delish. All that cheese and soup. It was for the release party for the movie *Twister* in Oklahoma back in 1996. We all had to dress like we'd been in a tornado and bring a dish to pass. I'd never heard that expression before, a dish to pass. I brought an empty bowl." Summer laughed.

"You were in *Twister*?" I asked. I marveled at the ease and diffi-culty of her life. The flexibility, the uncertainty, the struggle. I couldn't fathom getting through a day not knowing what was next, scrabbling for every job, fighting for exposure. I did peaceful invisibility pretty well as an occupational therapist. People who needed me focused on their deficits and not mine.

"Could you two keep it down? I'm going to sleep so I can be fresh to drive when Sleeping Beauty falls apart."

Summer giggled and mimed a cranky face, pointing her thumb to the back, where Holly sat examining her phone. I caught a glimpse of Holly's face in the rearview mirror, concentrating, her fingers scrolling.

We were on our way, and I felt pretty good driving. After a compli-cated bunch of turns, I realized that you had to give the bus more time to adjust to changes in direction. The steering wheel had a bit of slack to it, and the brakes needed a couple of pumps if you were serious about stopping. The sun dropped to the horizon, and before long, darkness fell. Summer had fallen asleep like a child, open mouthed and imme-diately. Back in Wisconsin, Katie was no doubt under the thin covers in her stiff hospital bed, awaiting answers from us, her doctors, her parents. She slept on her side, her fine hair in a tangle, one arm around her own waist. I'd rubbed her back often during past chemotherapy visits, still recalling her slight shoulders, the feel of her ribs under my hands. I would call her the minute I had some privacy to tell her what was happening, to talk about the results of the blood work, see how she was feeling. I wanted to have Peanut in hand before I did.

I rarely went a day without talking to Katie. We weren't big texters and, against all modern trends, liked talking to each other on the phone. We told each other everything, but since her remission, I'd tried to keep her stress to a minimum. I didn't complain about my job, didn't take on irritating committees at Maddie's school or talk about how sometimes I was so very lonely. The cancer made me much more careful, and in some ways, it made me miss our less-careful conversations. Talks that emotionally took care of both of us. I cracked the window, and a stream of cool, dry air hit my forehead.

As the miles unfolded, I decided driving at night might be the way to survive this trip. The traffic was manageable, the white lines straight and steady. We were on I-15 North and making good time. I was now eagerly waiting for a text from Beautiful Drew. When the ding came, I lifted my phone, trying to keep a handle on my delight.

BDREW: Katie is resting. Bebe has been discharged with oxygen. No need to reply.

Here I was, wondering about Katie, and Drew reassured me. I'd often wondered at the electricity of thought and its long-reaching connection between people. Had Drew and I established that?

I breathed; for now, the chaos of the last few days felt handled.

Men like Drew. What could their lives be like? Handsome, smart, a head full of hair. Generous, too, it seemed. I wondered if he would fall for Katie like so many had before. Maybe that would be nice . . . a romantic interest, something fresh among the rot of cancer. I blinked at a feeling that seemed to seep from a crack in my heart somewhere. Jealousy, was it? I chased it, tapped it on the shoulder, tried to get a look at it. It said, *Finders keepers* in the most childish of tones.

Every so often I lamented being single to Maddie's friends' parents. They reliably replied, *Nothing wrong with being single,* or some other semisupportive crap. I found it curious and frankly annoying that this reassurance came from people who were not single. It was as if they were saying, *I'm not single, so it's not okay for me, but it's totally acceptable for you to settle for it.* Sometimes it came with a sage head tilt and condescending arm rub. As if my singleness were a bad case of acne that wasn't going away.

Honestly, I tried not to overthink my quiet single life. I focused on my job, which, like most health-care jobs, was arduous. After and before work, it was all Maddie, her activities and all that was required of families like driving, fundraising, and feeding teams. Organizers rarely acknowledged a single-parent home, so I had to do all the things kids with both parents had to do. In the quiet evening, though, I'd catch an old Meg Ryan or Julia Roberts rom-com on the television. And I can tell you this: no one in the world wants to be single during a rom-com. No one in the world says, *Thank God nobody looks at me that way. Thank God nobody sprints through an airport and shouts "I love you" just before going through security.* Every time I thought about doing something about being alone, dating someone, that old terror of conflict would root me to my seat.

I thought about the ease with which Drew gave me his number. Could it be he was interested in me? Maybe I was such an obvious non-romantic option that just by looking at my sleepy, drab self, he knew he was safe to hand out his number to me. Like if his soon to be ex-wife saw me, she'd think, *That old chestnut?* Maybe he had a love interest, and she'd probably say, *Sure, give her your number. Hell, have her over for a sleepover. I'm not worried.*

A few fat raindrops hit the windshield. This was travel for you; it provided the time and enough out-of-context living that allowed for movement down untraveled highways, both real and metaphorical. It had been a long, long time since a reasonably young single man had been interested in me, as far as I knew. It was no wonder I didn't have the map to all the social cues.

I let people think that I didn't date because of my love for Jeff, but only Katie and I knew that wasn't the reason for my singledom after being widowed. It kept me safe and conflict-free. What if I got into another relationship that I didn't know how to get out of? It served me well to be the brokenhearted widow, and I played the part. The message of an epic, lost love stopped people in their matchmaking tracks. I only wished for one thing: that Jeff had lived long enough to give Maddie a sibling. I'd been an only child with a tyrant of a father. Once I was gone, Maddie would be alone; she'd need someone on her side, and the thought made my throat close up.

I turned the radio on, kept the volume low, heard the strains of an old country ballad. I thought of Holly and Rosie—their obvious adoration. Holly's voice speaking softly to Rosie, "I'll be home soon," the kindness there. The courage it must have taken to admit that you were not like the majority; that you were part of the people of the world who could be furiously hated for the act of loving.

In fourth grade, I asked my mother what she would say if I came home with a boyfriend, like Mr. Bronson. I didn't mean *like* Mr. Bronson; I meant actually Mr. Bronson. He was the student teacher, from Jamaica, in my fourth-grade classroom, and for some reason he didn't look over my head like most teachers did. Naturally, I loved him.

My mother took a moment to consider my question, and she said, "I'd be worried that your life might be harder with Mr. Bronson. People are not always kind to . . ." and she hesitated. Even at age eight, I could see she was choosing her words carefully. "Differences." She paused, I remembered, and she said, "Race is still something America hasn't figured out."

I went to school the next day knowing my future with Mr. Bronson was doomed. It made me sad. If we'd married, he could have helped me with fractions forever. The end of the year was coming, and I knew that without my mother on board, I probably wouldn't be seeing Mr. Bronson again. I wanted something to remember him by, so I asked to touch his hair during quiet reading time.

"Samantha, that is a question that sometimes makes black people angry." This surprised me. I just couldn't imagine why this would be so.

"Why? You can touch my hair if you want."

"No, thank you," he said. He had dark-brown eyes with a tinge of yellow in the sclera. "It's complicated. You have to know someone pretty well before asking to touch anything. Good for you for asking first, Sam." He thought for a moment and offered the top of his head to me. I flattened my hand and patted his tight, dark, wiry hair. It felt exactly like I thought it would; springy and dry. I got a good look at the skin on his dark forehead, and I almost asked to touch it as well.

Maybe three years later, I'd heard from my mother that Mr. Bronson had gone jogging and died suddenly on the side of the road. He had a heart anomaly, but I thought she'd said *heart anemone*, and forever after I pictured a spindly sponge in the center of his chest that wilted, the tendrils closing in on themselves.

When I cried, my mom said in a matter-of-fact but not unkind voice I've carried in my brain throughout my life, "People die, Sam. That you can count on." My mother had a way of simultaneously talking to me as both a child and an adult. It could be harsh sometimes, but there was a stickiness to her lessons.

"We're odd, we humans," she would say. "We know people die, but we act astonished when it happens. What *is* astonishing about death is our certainty that it isn't going to happen to us or anyone we know without some kind of warning. And, we live our life doing stupid things like gossiping, when we should spend all our days planting flowers."

If I asked for clarification on any of these points, she'd wave me off and say, "Ignore me. I'm irritated today."

Now, here we were on the road, and though I'd done everything right, my measured responses were doing little for me. I'd planted flowers. I'd not gossiped. I'd married after the first positive pregnancy test. Stayed in my lane. Kept quiet, safe. More raindrops fell on the windshield.

Not Holly, though. She acted in whatever way she wanted. If her cells said, *You love women,* she went in that direction. If she wanted a child, she pursued it. Her fearlessness in college I'd found exhilarating. But now I snapped off the radio and settled into my outrage. The unfairness. How could recklessness be rewarded?

Summer stirred and without lifting her head said, "Stop thinking. You're waking me up."

I thought she was sleep-talking, and so I didn't say anything. I was enjoying this snit I was having.

"Ugh. If you insist." Summer sat up and rubbed her eyes with her knuckles. "Let's talk it out."

"What out?"

"This thing you've got going in your head that's making so much aura noise that I can't sleep."

"That's not a thing, Summer."

"Okay, Holly." Summer had only been with us for less than a day, and she knew it was a slight to call me Holly. I looked at Summer in the dark, crossed over the fog line to the part of the shoulder that had the rumble strips. The noise and vibration caused Holly to grumble, and I gently guided the camper back into the lane. "You could feel my negative energy?"

"Anyone could. It gushes from you."

"No, it doesn't."

"Okay, then." Summer plucked the aromatherapy reservoir out of the lighter. She rummaged in her bag and exchanged the lavender scent for peppermint. The cab smelled immediately of candy canes. It made me think of Christmas, after-dinner sweets, and my garden.

"Is that how you knew about my husband? My noisy aura?" I said with curious disbelief.

"Sometimes I get things right, but I definitely had you and Holly wrong. You guys are the antipartners."

I had a surprising urge to defend Holly's and my friendship—it must have been a leftover defense mechanism from a long time ago. I let the moment pass. "Why are you here?"

A semitruck bore down on us in the passing lane, so close that the driver's-side mirror looked at risk. I flinched and gripped the steering wheel. Once the truck passed, I glanced at Summer, who had placed a sheet mask on her face. She was pressing the edges down over her knife-sharp jawline and smooth, wrinkle-free forehead. "These are amazing. I get them online from China. They have placenta in them."

This was the kind of thing Holly and I would joke about back in the day. I pictured what I'd say to Holly if we still had that kind of friendship. *She said her mask had placenta! Only a Californian would think that is not dreadful.* I'd save this for Katie. Or maybe text it to Drew, someone new who could laugh with me. The thought made me feel unusually happy and not anxious for a change.

"Actual placenta? Like baby placenta?"

"Gross. No. Soybean placenta."

"I don't think that's a thing either."

Summer repositioned her body, yanking the seat belt wide, so her back was pressed against the passenger door. "Tell me about yourself, Samantha. Why so flat?"

"Flat?"

She squinted at me in the darkness. I didn't dare look in her direction. I didn't want to be read. I didn't want to be enlightened. I liked living on a somewhat stable surface where I could see, hear, and touch everything. If there were alternative planes of existence, where auras could talk to each other and spirits chatted, it would add a dimension of worry to parenting that I couldn't cope with. Would I have to start warning Maddie about predators that could read her aura and manipulate her while she had a couple of shots at the college bar? I shoved that anxiety into a closet to deal with later. Much, much later.

"Tell me about your daughter."

I swiveled my head in her direction. "Why did you ask me about my daughter?"

She shrugged. I couldn't see her expression with that silly mask on her face, but I felt entirely exposed to her. "Give me one of those masks," I said, wanting to cover my face, feel less vulnerable to this woman who seemed to be tuned into me.

Summer laughed. "Now we're talking."

Her floral bag must have been alphabetized because she reached right in, pulled out a thin packet, and tore into it in seconds. Her manicured nails slid between the damp folds, and with her dainty fingers, she placed the mask expertly on my face. The cold, wet material clung to my cheeks and provided some cover for a conversation that I couldn't seem to stop.

"You're going to love how your face feels after this. I promise you."

I poked my finger into the left eyehole to make sure it didn't obstruct my vision, and Summer said, "What do you want, Sam?"

"I'm fine right now. I could eat in maybe an hour."

"No. I mean for your life. For you?"

"Oh. Easy. I want Maddie to be safe and happy. I want our friend Katie to not have cancer."

"But, what do you want for you? For Sam?"

"That is for me." Why was I getting frustrated? I could feel it crawling into my chest, rising up my sternum. "I want good things for the people I love. That will make me happy, and I get to keep them in my life." I didn't have an answer, and I wanted to stop thinking.

"It's fine if you're not ready for this conversation. Lots of people are blocked."

"I'm not blocked. I'm a simple person. I like my people happy. What could possibly be wrong with that?"

"I think we can do something about that block. It's not a permanent situation."

I shook my head, pressed the wet mask around my forehead where I felt it coming loose. "Summer. I'm from Wisconsin." I wanted to turn the radio up and feel the breeze on my newly moisturized skin. I wanted to keep driving and not think about anything but the directions on the GPS—which took its cues from satellites and Google and the mystical internet. That was all the woo-woo I could handle.

Then I yawned.

I'd tried to stifle it, but Summer said, "You should let me drive. I'll get us to Vegas, and then you or Holly can drive."

"I'm fine. I've had quite enough sleep for today."

"Maybe so, but I think you need it. Being the only person taking care of the world is hard work."

I could have protested, annoyed as I was. I could have acted tough, and insisted on driving, but if I stayed behind the wheel, Summer was sure to keep trying to analyze me. I didn't like being seen before I had a better view of myself. It made me itch with discomfort. I peeled the mask off my face, stuffed it into my empty paper coffee cup, and rubbed the rest of the lotion into my skin.

We were just outside of Baker, California, so the transition was an easy one. Holly grumbled but didn't fully wake. Once Summer was settled behind the wheel and had produced a blow-up travel pillow for my comfort, we were off again. "You do have a driver's license, don't you, Summer?"

"Of course I do."

"And no detours or funny business. No pit stop at some friends who can give us better shock absorbers or anything. I don't want to wake up in Death Valley and have to drink my shampoo or something."

Summer didn't reply, and I said, "Summer. I'm serious."

"I promise not to deviate from the route in any way. Except for a potty break at a rest stop."

Satisfied, I tucked my neck into the pillow and closed my eyes, but I didn't fall asleep. Sometimes my disorder was stubborn during appropriate sleep times. That's what made it a disorder, I guess.

Summer's question was like a pea in a mattress keeping me awake. *What do you want?*

I remembered when Maddie was a baby, not even a year old. I'd been so unprepared to keep a human alive by myself. I knew I'd be exhausted from a lack of sleep, but I didn't know I'd spend my days smelling of spoiled breast milk and trying to heal a yeast infection that endlessly transferred between Maddie's mouth and my nipples.

I'd had Maddie on my shoulder and was hauling the ungainly plastic recycling bin to the curb when my neighbor Mrs. Langdon offered to babysit for a day. She took Maddie as I stood next to a dandelion weed in my front yard that had a spiky prehistoric quality to it. I didn't even consider pulling it out. I just hoped it flowered. Mrs. Langdon said, "What would you like to do with a full day off?" I stood in the sunshine, arms free at my sides, trying to think of something to say.

Mrs. Langdon looked at me expectantly, her purse of a mouth in a smile. My brain raced, struggling for an answer; acid rose in my throat. What activity would be *good enough*, knowing a handful of hours was all I was going to get? Should I shower, go to the grocery store, nap? Put a vegetable in the fridge? Sleep with a book on my chest and call it reading? What could possibly be good enough for a day of freedom, knowing I would be going right back to the gulag of baby care hours later? Wouldn't it be better to just keep my head down and keep going?

My arms, light without Maddie in them, lifted almost of their own accord. I took my child from Mrs. Langdon's arms and said, not unkindly, "How could I possibly know what I want? I don't even exist anymore."

I turned from her and trudged up the driveway. I heard her alarmed "Oh" and imagined the sound puffed out of her like a smoke ring from a cigarette.

She must have said something to Katie, because my cherished friend insisted I go to the doctor, where I heard myself say, "Joy? No, I don't feel joy."

Then there were peach pills that helped right away. Often, I thought, maybe too well. I definitely experienced more joy in Maddie's dimpled elbows, her sausage legs, but since I felt less numb, I was also introduced to the deep end of sorrow. Sorrow of being alone. Sorrow at giving myself away so quickly. Sorrow at losing the fairy tale by marrying too early and losing so much.

I'd had boyfriends in high school and college. Learned about deep soulful kisses and real boy-induced orgasms from a soccer player who had beautiful thighs. I was a normal girl, with an acceptable level of self-esteem, somewhat avoidant of conflict, but learning to trust myself as a woman. I'd had my heart bruised and had hurt a few lovers on the way to becoming a person. I was a plucky skiff, rushing with full sails into an ocean of romantic possibility, until losing Holly, marrying Jeff, and watching my mother fade away after my dad died.

These events made me realize you could sink with the weight of loss and I'd better rein myself, my wants, in or get further hurt.

"Focus," my dad would say when trying to get me to see everything as a fight. But I started to think that maybe not knowing what you wanted in the world was a safer way to go.

CHAPTER ELEVEN

A CYNICAL, DOUBTFUL CUPCAKE

"Why aren't we moving?"

Holly's voice boomed from the back, and I startled awake. Summer's travel pillow clung around my neck like a baby monkey. It was very early in the morning, but day or night, I always woke up guiltily, as if I were sleeping on the job of life.

Holly thrust her upper body between the driver and passenger seats, looking for answers. I searched for my phone to check the time and saw a list of notifications from Maddie and Drew. Unnerved, I felt my chest clutch with anxiety. I opened the messages from Maddie first.

MADDIE: Mom. I'm so overwhelmed

MADDIE: I can't sleep. My job is hard, and the kids I have to babysit don't like me

MADDIE: I know you're asleep. Text when you wake up

Summer stretched her arms in a languid display of anti-alarm. "I got tired, and I didn't want to wake anyone. These old bucket seats are surprisingly comfortable."

I sent a quick text to Maddie, wanting so much to soothe her, knowing how my daughter got when she was swamped with stress.

ME: I'm here. Sorry, I was asleep.

I remembered her full-body hives during ACT testing junior year, teaching her breathing exercises, and smoothing hydrocortisone cream to ease the itching. "Hardship makes you interesting," I told her, knowing that phrase hadn't helped me that much. I didn't feel more interesting.

ME: It can be overwhelming caring for kids. Especially kids who aren't your own. But they have short memories and are very durable. I'm sure they love you. A good rule is sleep when they are sleeping, if you can. That's what I did with you.

MADDIE: What?

I closed my eyes with frustration at myself. When would I learn? This was the cell phone generation. They felt a feeling. Offloaded it by texting their support person, usually a mother filled with guilt about not breastfeeding long enough or putting their child in day care so they could survive. The mother absorbed the anxiety and responded to the SOS text after the sender had already wandered off, unburdened.

ME: You're overwhelmed?

MADDIE: We're making a pillow fort. I can't talk now

My heart rate slowed in relief, but once again, there I was. The slow learner. On the other hand, there was Summer. Clearly in the wrong, not caring two shits that she'd gone rogue again. She had parked the van, and there she sat, stretching like she hadn't done anything wrong. Like she hadn't deviated from the plan of driving without stopping.

Holly's head disappeared from view, and I was vaguely aware that the side door of the camper opened. She was at the driver's-side window in seconds. "I'll drive."

I loved that Holly had no influence over her. By all accounts, Summer shouldn't have been traveling with us. We didn't know her, she'd done us several "favors" we didn't ask for, and yet she felt 100 percent entitled to be with us. She acted like we'd been friends for years, was part of the squad, and had equal voting rights in all things. Filled with admiration, I wanted to study her, see how Summer did it.

"My friend lives here. Let's pee and get coffee and then hit the road," said Summer.

"We're parked outside your friend's house? That's a coincidence," Holly said. But she said it like, *That's bullshit.*

"No, it's not. The GPS took us within five blocks, and I thought this was a fair give-and-take for staying on our route, like I promised Sam before she fell asleep. You can't park just anywhere and sleep, you know. We aren't gypsies."

"We weren't going to pull over anywhere, remember? We were going to keep moving until we got to Utah," said Holly.

"Well, I didn't agree to that," said Summer.

I respected the lunatic more and more. To have that kind of confidence, that brand of surety that you were wanted. This is what Holly had, and I laughed inwardly thinking how that conversation would go, the one where I pointed out how Summer and Holly were similar. I literally considered digging in my bag to take notes on this interaction for a future conversation with Katie.

"We're not on a college road trip. You're not twenty, Holly." Summer brushed her bangs out of her eyes. "We've all been flying, are probably dehydrated, any one of us could have fallen asleep driving. I made the safe decision and pulled over in a perfectly acceptable place."

Holly turned her Medusa gaze on me and said, "Sam?"

I opened the side door and slid off the seat. "I gotta pee."

Checking my texts from Drew, I misstepped and almost face-planted on the curb. He had me so distracted with mixed emotions. Every text from him could be concerning information about Katie, but hearing from him gave me a jolt of wonder.

BDREW: Katie is talking a lot about Peanut. How is the doggo?

Guilt dropped on my shoulders as if straight from the heavens. I thought about telling him the truth, but I couldn't stand thinking he might tell Katie that we not only didn't have Peanut, we weren't absolutely sure where he was.

ME: He's great. Good ol' Peanut. He's his usual jolly self.

I sounded like Mark Twain.

ME: Wait! I'm lying. We don't have him. We are on the way. Tell Katie I'll FaceTime her. Or can you stall.

BDREW: Be cool, Samantha. I have this covered.

He texted my name and my brain jumped on a trampoline and did a high kick.

ME: I am totally. Cool.

Which was ridiculous because my face felt hot, hot, hot.

"Grab your bag, Holly. My friend is super nice. We can shower here too. You look like you could use one," Summer said.

Holly's hand flew up, and I watched her self-consciously smooth her hair, rub her fingers under her eyes. Holly did not like to look unkempt.

"Fine," she said. "While you and Sam are screwing around, I'll clean up. Don't take too long."

"I'm not going to screw around," I said, defending myself. "I'll use the bathroom and we can go."

Before we knocked, the door opened, and a man with a gummy smile and close-cropped beard greeted us.

"Summer, Summer, Summer," he said so quickly and with such enthusiasm that I wanted to get in front of him and feel some of that radiant glee.

"Marvin!" Summer air-kissed the man near both cheeks like she was in Paris. "I want you to meet my new friends."

I shouldn't have been surprised that we were at Shamansky-the-Shaman's house.

If there were shamans in Wisconsin, I didn't know about them. I suspected they kept a low profile, to keep the scoffing to a minimum. Wisconsinites worked hard, drank hard, and most likely did not spend time considering their spirit animal, unless it was at a university football game where they were praying for their team mascot to make a field goal.

"Samantha," Marvin said, "Summer has told me so much about you."

That was startling. "She has?"

"Enough to know that you are welcome here anytime." He turned. "And this must be Holly. I hear you need a shower. Let's get you right back to the bathroom, so you can feel as fresh and lovely as you always do. The bathroom has the best Wi-Fi signal if you need to FaceTime anyone."

Summer walked through the door first, and that gave Holly the opportunity to grab my elbow and whisper, "Try to get the camper registration and insurance out of Summer's purse." I felt her warm breath on my ear. "If we can get our hands on it, we can leave her here." Holly walked ahead of me. "I won't be long freshening up. Then we can get back on the road."

Getting the file folder was a good idea, even if it involved pickpocketing. Summer could stay here, at her friend's house. We would have the official papers in case we needed them. It would win points for me with Holly—maybe put us on even footing. I watched Summer dump her bag on the floor and walk into the kitchen as if she owned the place.

My phone buzzed.

BDREW: You are such a nice person.

A butterfly of emotion loop-de-looped through my chest. A nice person would not steal from another nice person.

———

The light and airy interior was decorated in a spare Scandinavian style— blond wood, white walls, cream carpet. It was not what I would have predicted for a shaman. There were no dream catchers hanging from doorways, tapestries, or silk scarves covering a collection of hollow bones or animal skins. Marvin ushered Holly down a hall, and I was directed to a smaller half bath off a guest room. The house had a hushed quiet that smoothed my frayed, confused energy.

"There are towels in the basket. Feel free to wash your face. I might have a new toothbrush if you check out the bottom drawer of the vanity."

There was another text from Drew. In the half second it took me to read it, a shiver of pleasure and worry crept through me.

BDREW: Katie is tired. She's eating and seems cheerful. They are watching her pretty closely. I'll let her fill you in.

With one quick sentence my fear ratcheted up.

ME: Why? Is there something you can't tell me?

It was two hours later in Wisconsin. I hoped Drew would reply right away, and he did.

BDREW: Not medically. I'm being respectful and ethical.

I considered how to reply. I wanted to ask a question that would not challenge his ethics. I concentrated and texted.

ME: Does she seem any worse?

BDREW: No.

The answer came right back. No delay. An easy, honest response that reduced my anxiety. I saw this for what it was: a game of asking the right questions so my nerves might be calmed without asking too much from Drew.

ME: Is there anything you can't tell me?

BDREW: Excellent question. No.

Whew. Another text came through.

BDREW: Did you get some sleep?

Cautious pleasure.

ME: Yes. We slept on the road. Holly is grumpy. Our kidnapper is now traveling with us. We are at her shaman's house.

The three dots bounced as I waited for his response. I smiled in anticipation, knowing how crazy this all sounded.

BDREW: Is this code or is this happening?

ME: It's happening.

BDREW: Next time you go get a dog, I get to come.

Was he serious? If we were together, I would be wheezing a thready nervous laugh while trying to figure out if he was being flirty or if this was what he said to lots of people he barely knew. What would be a good noncommittal cool-girl answer? I typed.

ME: Deal. Gotta go. Getting coffee with the shaman.

BDREW: Of course you are.

ME: Of course I am.

I didn't move for a few seconds. Less anxiety, check. A gentle wonder? Check. I finished in the bathroom, feeling fresher after washing my face and hands. I could hear Summer and Marvin talking in the living room, and when I reached the doorway, Summer gestured me in and said, "Marvin can do a quick journey. We only have until Holly is out of the shower. Lie down."

My visceral reaction was a pretty big nope. "I just want a cup of coffee. Maybe a piece of toast if you have it."

Summer's disappointed look hearkened back to my second-grade teacher when she admonished me for using pen to do my worksheet on the layers of the earth. *Tsk, tsk, Samantha, pen is only for those who are sure of the right answers.* Then and now, I was loath to disappoint.

Marvin, with the warmest, unassuming smile, said, "You can trust me. Trust us. We will stop the second you are uncomfortable."

You know how it is when you meet someone and you immediately feel relaxed? It isn't something that happens often, that sudden friendship connection when your instinct says, *Go on. It's fine. No red flags here.* That's what being in Marvin's presence was like. His warmth was not like Drew's. There was no heat to it. His company was a weighted blanket, calming my frazzled worry. I didn't want to spend my whole day with him or give him all my money. It wasn't, I imagined, like being caught up in the thrall of a charismatic cult leader. No, Marvin's open face, like that of a teacher or a nurse, welcomed me in.

"You can sit or lie down. I'll do some quick work. Then get you back on the road."

Summer nodded and said, "I'm not going to watch you, Samantha. I'll be cleaning up." She scampered out of the room, and I knelt on a pillow next to a drum, a small circle of fabric with a couple of rocks, and what looked like a pair of maracas. "I don't believe any of this. I'm only doing this . . ." I faltered. "I don't know why I'm doing this. I just met Summer. We aren't even friends."

"I know," he said like a father would say after a child insisted at their bedtime, *I'm not even tired*. "There is much to learn from our spirit guides. Why not find out what they have to say?"

My reaction to this statement was 98 percent skepticism with a smidge of *Let's get this show on the road*, and a pinch of interest sprinkled on top. I was a cynical, doubtful, somewhat curious cupcake, if you will. Did I think something otherworldly was haunting me? Did I want to know if some weirdo-stalker-spirit was hanging around my aura? I already had someone in this world hanging around my neck, Holly with her incessant push, push, push. I absolutely did not want to know if my husband was pressing his big fat spirit thumb between my shoulder blades.

I had a choice: I could lie down for a few minutes and explore this odd situation, or I could wait until Holly stormed out of the bathroom and made the decision for me. My natural contrary reaction to Holly, either in the room or out, had me lying down and crossing my arms across my chest. But there was a wonder in all this as well. I was curious.

Summer's bag lay near Marvin's drum, deflated and vulnerable. The corner of the folder with the camper's permit and insurance was in clear view. If I grabbed it now, Holly and I would be free of Summer, her detours and unpredictable ways. Holly and me in the camper alone. Holly calling all the shots. Holly irritated at my every sigh and grumble.

Marvin frowned. "What just happened? Your aura darkened."

I looked over my shoulder in the direction of the bathroom and said, "Let's get to it."

It didn't take long before he was sweeping a feather fan over my body, placing a rock on my forehead, and drumming softly at my shoulder. If I had been watching this, I'd have rolled my eyes at the oddity of it all; instead, I consciously decided to close them and try to relax. The sun from a large picture window fell on my feet, and the warmth traveled up my legs. For once I wasn't tired; in fact, I felt alert—even without my morning coffee. I opened my eyes and saw Marvin concentrating his movements around my diaphragm. He swept and pulled something unseen, winding around his hand and letting it go into the air above me. I imagined cotton candy, not taffy, because it looked easily done, as if waving steam from a boiling pot. I tried to feel something. A lightness or closure of some sort.

I knew I should clear my mind, but I'm not the kind of person whose mind is a quiet place.

In college, before Jeff, I dated a boy named Mark. He was a non-talker. The silent Mark, we called him. I met him in a statistics class, and he was able to explain chi square analysis to me when neither the professor nor the textbook made sense. He drew a graph with shaded-in bars and explained it without jargon. For the first time ever, I understood statistics. I was so grateful, I dated him for a month.

When Katie asked me what we talked about, I couldn't tell her. Mark and I barely talked. I talked. I reported, I guess. He listened, or at least I thought he did. We kissed a lot; it was pretty chaste, when I think about it. He had deliciously soft lips. Once, when I asked him what he thought about when he was alone, he said, "Nothing." He had grown up in North Carolina, and the few things he said had an almost-feminine southern lilt to them.

I'd laughed and said, "That's impossible. You must be thinking something." I clarified, "Like when you're driving. Or mowing the lawn or something."

"Nothing," he said. When he saw that answer wasn't working for me he said, "Sports, I guess. I like baseball."

I stopped seeing him after he dropped me off that night. It wasn't that I wanted him to say he was thinking about me, although that would have been nice. I wanted to know what was going on in that brain that could so easily explain data analysis, false positives, and normal curves. I thought a brain like his must be filled with proving all kinds of things. Sifting ideas, analyzing information, coming to conclusions. When he said "nothing," I decided to believe him.

Often, if I wasn't careful, I made up a story about people in my head and didn't check it with the facts of that person. I absolutely did that with Jeff. I made a list in my head of all the good things, added to it characteristics I was sure would surface, and ignored anything else.

For example, what had looked like astute political interest was, in actuality, a place to put all his anger and make it look like it was for the good of all people. "Can you believe what our government is doing right now? Bailing out enormous corporations while we get our hands dirty, working all the time." Jeff was a landscape architect who did manual labor. He'd stop as if he wanted me to fill in the blanks. I didn't know he was in debt and on the verge of bankruptcy. I thought he was arguing for a fair wage for hardworking families, equality, and a government that cared for its people. But what he wanted was money, to be easily richer than others, and someone to absolve his losses and guilt.

Marvin shook the maracas over my body, and after a quiet moment, he spoke in a low voice. "Take your time. Sit up when you're ready. This was a very abbreviated session. I'm being mindful of the time." I glanced at a clock over Marvin's shoulder and was surprised to see thirty minutes had passed. I got to my knees, saw the folder almost waving to me in Summer's bag.

With Marvin's back to me, I could easily pluck the folder and slide it into my bag. If he asked me what I was doing, I could show him the camper registration. Shrug it off. But my mind was clear on the topic.

I didn't want to. I wanted Summer to ride with us, play the role of the human shield between Holly and me. She lightened our ride, seemed to provide a fairy-like contrast to our heavy energy, and I clasped my hands in front of me.

Softly Marvin said, "I was able to get rid of some energy just kind of hanging around. You were blocked around your digestive system. I moved some energy out of there. I know this all sounds pretty crazy, and I'd explain it to you if we had more time. In fact, we can talk on the phone if you like, do another session that way. I don't need to be in the same room with you."

"You don't?" I was skeptical.

"I can do this from anywhere. I believe it's more effective when I'm in the room with clients, but the phone is fine."

"Isn't that kind of shady?"

He smiled graciously. "I know what it sounds like. And I know what it all looks like. I don't expect everyone to be open to it." In that moment he looked like a kid in high school who didn't have a place to sit at lunch. "It was my grandmother who noticed I was different, could read people. I had vivid dreams that often came true in one aspect or another."

"Couldn't everyone say that?" I couldn't explain why I was questioning this man I'd never met before. It wasn't like me. I usually just let people have their own weirdness and went on my merry way.

He nodded. "Yes, there are other things. Things that can also be explained away by the placebo effect, suggestion, and other physiological measures. But I know there's a dimension that others don't seem connected to."

"Like?"

"Well, I wasn't going to mention this. I wasn't sure if you're ready, honestly. But your husband. He isn't dragging you down. I don't feel a sense of him. Another spirit communicated to me that he crossed over. Was your husband very invested in our culture's value system?"

"Yes. Isn't everyone?"

As if he didn't hear me he continued. "There is another voice. With a strong message. 'Speak.' I heard the word *speak* repeatedly."

I stood—too quickly because I felt dizzy—and staggered a step to the side.

Marvin steadied me. "Okay. There's a nerve there. Take a breath to center yourself."

I did what he said. I took a deep breath, waited until my head cleared.

"Sometimes I get a word or phrase that isn't quite right. I don't hear voices or even words. It's more like thoughts and feelings come to me and through me. I give them language, but I don't always get the words right."

I closed my eyes. "No. It's right. 'Speak,' but harsher." I'd thought I'd left my father's haranguing behind me so many years ago, after his death. I rubbed my forehead to clear my thoughts.

"There is a heaviness around you, and that word is in the center of it."

"I'm sorry. I'm just a meat-and-potatoes girl. You know? I deal with what's ahead of me. One thing at a time. I don't have layers and layers of hidden stuff to uncover." I moved a step away. Laughed nervously. "When my daughter was born, the doctors asked me if I wanted to cut the umbilical cord. I'm just not that kind of human. The person with the medical degree should cut the cord. I didn't want to have my baby in a swimming pool. I wanted as much pain medication as possible, and I didn't want to bury the placenta in the backyard. I'm not earthy. I'm plastic maybe. Or," I said and looked around the room for something that was better than plastic but not as earthy as earth, "I'm cotton. Functional, kind of versatile, not at all complicated."

"No, Samantha. You are telling yourself the wrong story." He let go of my elbow. "Don't get me wrong; there are people who are, as you say, cotton. But that's not you."

Where was Holly? Where was the noisy Holly who never missed a chance to interrupt and make a moment her own? I needed a minute, a week, a month to consider that I was something other than an easy one-dimensional person.

"You don't have to be a certain kind of person to accept the help of the earth, spirit animals, and the universe. They are here for organic farmers and investment bankers alike. In fact"—and he looked away—"my day job is as an accountant."

That struck me as funny. I laughed with relief, and so did he—but he didn't drop the subject.

"Is that what's keeping you so quiet in your life?"

"Quiet? Is that how you see me?"

"The spirit animal you called to you is the deer. It wants to work with you if you'll let it. It wants to help you deal with an upcoming challenge. To help you steer the compassion you have for everyone else inward to yourself."

The kindness in his voice almost undid me. I felt tears coming, and then, of course, there was Holly. I didn't know how long she'd been standing there watching. It would have been fine to have her interrupt the session with a loud "Let's go!" But to have her watch me, tearful, while I stood too close to a man clutching a chicken feather fan—ugh. I didn't know what I thought of it, but for certain I would never hear the end of this. Her unwavering belief was that thoughts alone created the kind of life you deserved, but I knew talk of a spirit animal was a bridge too far. If she didn't understand Katie's need for Peanut, she sure as Shinola wasn't going to understand a ghostly deer that wanted to help me stand up for myself. And maybe that was what I needed, but I wasn't going to have Holly bully my possibly fake spirit deer.

Then I saw it, the famous Holly smirk.

"Isn't Marvin amazing?" Summer flitted into the room, all blonde hair and shiny skin. All savior and sweetness.

I wiped my eyes. "Okay. Thanks," I mumbled to Marvin, hoping to slam my spirit door closed.

Summer hefted her bag onto her tiny shoulder, and the folder with all the camper documents slid out of view. My chance to be free from her over.

"It's normal to cry," he insisted. "Sometimes people laugh or feel anger. Everything is normal here."

I nodded, sneaking a look at Holly, who managed skepticism, impatience, and authority in one twitch of her eyebrow. Embarrassed by my need to be accepted by her while gifting her another reason to reject me, I sagged at the unfairness.

Marvin didn't see it. Maybe a man who dealt in phantoms didn't pay attention to the noisy human poltergeist in the room. He continued. "I'll tell you something people find clarifying. If you bury yourself in the sand, give your negative thoughts to the earth, you can uncover yourself with a new perspective."

"Sand? Like up to my neck?"

"You can lie flat. Wrap yourself in a sheet."

"Well, we won't have time for that," Holly interrupted.

Marvin didn't turn, but it was Holly he spoke to. "And that's a shame because you could use some release work so that your inner sun can shine. Who are you mad at, Holly? Do you even know?"

Me, I wanted to say. *She's mad at me, and I'm terrified to know what I did because what if I deserved it and I can't make it better?* If I could have, I would have added, *So I'm not going to address it.*

Marvin glanced at me, as if he heard my thoughts. He slipped his card into my hand and said, "Talk to your inner deer. You're going to need some help these next few days." The thought of help had me thinking, *What would that be like? To ask for help and have it come.*

I turned to follow Holly and Summer out to the car, but I stopped and said to Marvin, out of earshot of the others, "My father. He'd berate me and then say, 'Here's your chance, Sammie. Say whatever you want to say to me.' If I didn't have ready words, he'd shout, 'Speak!' My mother would touch my shoulder to remind me that speaking just made things worse."

Marvin, an empathetic pro, didn't project easy sympathy. Instead he said, "It sucks to have to think of your mom's loving coping as something you have to get over when it was your father who was the problem."

I was raised by a father who, when presented with an antagonist, reared up and attacked. He didn't smile or go silent like my mother did. He pushed back, intimidated, turned tables.

My father, in an uncharacteristic decision, had paid a contractor to lay a slate patio in our backyard. Day after day a haphazard crew my mother and I called the pirates showed up to do work. They arrived when their supervisor wasn't present—told stories, smoked cigarettes, kicked around a paver or two, and went to lunch. It was like having a bunch of mutinous sailors in the dry backyard fooling around with the yardarm.

After a week, the patio almost complete, my mother joked at dinner that she was going to go out with limes so no one got scurvy.

Later that night I heard my father on the phone with the owner of the company. "It's your business if you hire from Big Brothers of America, but the job had better be perfect." My father slammed the door to his office, and I pitied the guy he was on the phone with.

Days later, I stood back from an open window, a sheer polka-dot curtain hiding me from view.

"Unacceptable. Shoddy. How are you going to fix this?" my father interrupted as the man tried to explain, ask a question, defend the work. "You're a victim," he shouted, his words plowing over the man's attempts like a lawn mower killing a patch of my mother's black-eyed Susans. My dad twisted the other man's words around until the contractor's jaw went white, his temple pulsing, and even as a fifteen-year-old girl, I knew it contained anger.

My dad shook his head and said, "You just don't get it," in that way he'd said it to me when I tried to tell him I didn't want to take accounting or learn coding or how to play golf. That I was going to work with sick people, as a nurse maybe, and I didn't need to make business deals on the golf course. He would grit his teeth, push over my words, and with bitter scorn say, "You just don't get it, Samantha. You never do get it." That would be enough to wind him up for an hour. One sentence spoken in my own defense, and it was an hour reprimand that started with the word *idiot*.

The contractor made the ultimate mistake when he said, "I'm sorry you are unhappy with our work."

My dad looked at him square in the eye and said, "Sorry? What do I care? What does your apology do for me?"

My mother came behind me as I stood at the window watching. She put her lips to my ear and said, "No reason to watch your dad with that man outside. We have enough of that inside."

She rubbed my back. "Why is he so hard, Mom?"

"His dad was hard on him. Just very exacting. Your dad is so much better than his dad."

I gave my dad one more look. In that instant he saw me watching him bully that man. I froze. I tried to stay beneath his notice so as not to turn his wrath in my direction.

Instead of being embarrassed or feeling shame that his daughter was a witness to the manipulation going on just under her bedroom window, he gave me a sly grin like I was a coconspirator in his domination. Like I was his student in the art of bullying.

The contractor followed my father's gaze and saw me. His anger changed to pity. The man who was being yelled at by my father felt sorry for me.

Later that night, after tossing and turning, trying to sleep, I threw up. I'd shut my window, and it was stuffy in the room. My mother, by my side, brushed my hair back and said, "Maybe it was something you ate?"

I heaved the fried chicken and cherry ice cream I'd eaten for dinner. My favorite foods made by my mother as an apology for a difficult father. He had regaled us at the table with his tough business dealings.

"You have to show who is in charge. You have to explain to people what they can't see themselves." He looked at me and said, "Not everyone is as smart as we are. People are laborers because they can't do anything else."

My best friend's father had been a doctor in India but in Wisconsin was forced to work at the Oscar Mayer factory in maintenance. I thought about her kind dad, his dark skin, his soft hands that always had at least one black nail from getting it caught at the machine shop at work.

I gagged a final time into the toilet, watching the remnants of my dinner pool in the black circle at the bottom of the toilet; the yellow bile dribbled from my lower lip.

"There, there. Honey. Get it out. Let it all out."

After my mother tucked me in, I said, "How do you handle him, Mom?"

She had her hand on my forehead, and instead of feeling cool and comfortable, it felt like a sticky weight. I shifted, and she removed it.

"I listen and go somewhere else in my head. I think about how kind he can be. I think about how much I love you. I fix his favorite meals. I count days."

I remember wanting to ask what counting had to do with it.

"Roll over, honey. I'll rub your back and blow on your neck." She knew how much I loved a cool breeze on my neck. How much I wanted to sleep and shut out the hardness that lived both in the world and in our house. I pushed my face into my cool pillow, felt her lift my hair. A cool stream of air from her lips blew across the nape of my neck. I sighed.

I was on the verge of drifting off as I always did when I was comforted by my mom, but then my kitty cat of a mother whispered, "His dad died of a heart attack at fifty-one."

My dad was fifty at the time. He died the next year.

In the seconds it took for that memory to slide through my brain, I realized everyone was watching me. "Come on, Sam. We gotta go!" Holly called from the curb where she was already in the bus.

I wanted to defend my mother. "No. My mom. She was amazing." My mind scrambled to hang on to her loving touch, to keep her love untarnished.

"Consider this," Marvin said with kindness. "Speaking shows passion. Maybe you have to be passionate about *you*."

Being passionate about me seemed to be the very last thing this trip was about.

CHAPTER TWELVE

NOT ASKING FOR A FRIEND

Holly hissed in my ear, "What was that all about? Did you spend your time telling that guy how difficult I am?"

She grabbed my elbow, and I snatched it away. "Leave it," I said in the way that I'd heard Katie talk to Peanut when he jumped on a visitor.

"Why did he say that thing about me? Did you tell him I was closed off?"

"I know it's shocking that I might not spend my first-ever shaman visit talking about you, but I didn't. He must have picked up something from your energy," I said with barely concealed irritation. "It's not like you keep your disapproval to yourself."

"I never imagined you as someone believing in spirits," Holly scoffed.

"Why not? You think I can't come to California and get spiritual like everyone else?"

"What I want to know is, how can you gain insight if you're fixated on how difficult your friend Holly is?"

"News flash, Holly. I do not spend every interaction with people talking about you."

"News flash, Sammie. It seems like you do. First, Summer making all kinds of comments at the airport, then the two of you up front in the camper with your inside jokes that I can't hear in the back. And now this guy."

There was no point in denying anything. She had her mind made up. I wanted to hang on to the peaceful feeling I'd had moments before—but whatever serenity I had gained was lost. "Whatever, Holly. Believe whatever." I turned toward the camper.

"Do not walk away from me."

I put my hand up. "I do not have the energy for you. How about we just don't talk."

She mumbled something just as Summer zoomed past us and yelled, "Shotgun!" She jumped into the passenger seat, which meant it was my turn to travel in the back of the camper. Thank goodness. I needed some time alone.

"Summer," Holly said, "we're not slowing down for any more of your unsanctioned pit stops. You should stay here with your friend."

"And leave you two to kill each other? No way. I don't want that on my spiritual conscience. Get in," she said and thumbed in the direction of the driver's seat.

———

I settled myself in the back of the bus, the morning sun filtered through the gauzy blinds. I ran my hand over the soft sheepskin. I wanted to scroll through my phone, read the news, have a chat with my daughter to see how she was feeling. I did not want to listen to Holly and Summer talk. I did not want to think about where Holly and I had gone wrong. All I wanted to do was lie down, consider what Marvin had said about Jeff being gone but my father shouting instructions from the great beyond.

My phone buzzed.

BDREW: How was the Shaman?

Since texting Beautiful Drew, I'd begun to see the value of the low-stakes text conversations where no body language had to be interpreted and you could stop midsentence if you wanted to. Hell, you could type *be right back, brb,* and it was like freezing time. The other person couldn't yell at you, grab your arm, or demand attention. Sure, they could call you, but you didn't have to answer. There was an ignore button, right there on the screen. What was rude to one generation had become to another an appropriate, magical touch on a flat screen.

ME: Startling.

BDREW: How so? Are you free of all ailments?

ME: No. Holly is still here.

Something else that was great about texting. It was perfect for the person quick with a searing comeback who, during a spoken conversation, was just as quick to censor it and regret it later. The privacy of texting, with no chance of anyone overhearing, allowed me to speak.

Holly wasn't the only one whose mind worked in a flash when properly stimulated. The difference between the two of us wasn't that I didn't know what to say. The critical distinction was that Holly let herself say whatever popped into her head while I clamped my mouth shut. I knew that made me more likable than Holly in general. But after years of this practice, I felt like there might be a reservoir of unspoken retorts somewhere in my body, ready to burst. Perhaps sometime in the far future I'd go in to have brain surgery. The doctor would be concentrating and cut into a blob in my frontal lobe and a loud stream of saucy comebacks would scream from within. I pictured the doctor's hair blowing back, which was silly; they always wore a cap.

Texting Drew softened something inside me. Gave me a gentle outlet, something I hadn't had much of until now.

BDREW: Haha. But seriously. What did you find out?

Was he interested? Was he being polite? Making conversation? That was another thing about texting. You could interpret the flat emotion in whatever way you wanted. And afterward you could forget it ever happened because the conversation was vapor. It gave me courage in a way I never braved face-to-face. I decided Drew was sincere, and with new boldness, I started with some backstory.

ME: I was married. My husband died before my daughter was born, eighteen years ago.

BDREW: I'm so sorry.

The typical response to my history was first an apology followed by a myriad of tag-on comments ranging from *He's in a better place* to *man, that's a bummer*. I waited. When there was no follow up, I responded.

ME: Thank you.

BDREW: That must have been very hard. How did you cope with that?

Wow, textbook correct response. This means I get to decide what to say next. I could joke and write, *Wine*. Or be a bit more serious and text, *Therapy*. I could reply with a Hallmark Card version, *My daughter gave me purpose*. Any one of these responses would be fine and at least partially true, because I'd used all those things to survive.

My fingers touched the screen. I typed, *I built a wall*. Deleted it. He'd been so nice to keep track of Katie; didn't I owe him the truth? Did I know the truth? The truth was a puzzle that only made sense if all the pieces were on the table, the first piece shaped like my father. I stalled.

ME: How much time do you have? Haha.

BDREW: I have a lot of time. Just got off call. I'm hanging out with my best friend, coffee. Tell me everything.

The camper hit a pothole, mimicking the bounce of cautious delight I felt by his interest. I almost dropped my phone.

Summer shouted, "Weeee!"

ME: It's complicated.

BDREW: Go on.

Okay then. And I felt the distance of the internet and Drew's sincerity make it more comfortable to share.

ME: When Jeff died he left us almost entirely alone. No family to fall back on. No help financially or otherwise.

BDREW: Oh, damn.

His response made me smile because yeah, it was totally not good. Also, this was such a guy response.

ME: It took most of my daughter's life to dig us out. Not that many people know.

BDREW: I get that.

I wondered at his acceptance. I wanted to know more.

ME: Do you?

BDREW: People judge.

If Drew and I were going to be friends—more?—shouldn't I try honesty? Build this friendship on truth? But what was the truth? Should I tell him how Jeff broke my desire to trust anyone? How my notions of happily ever after were destroyed in such a way that I wasn't interested in even a risky coffee date with a new person? Or should I tell him the whole truth? I wasn't strong enough to get myself out of a bad situation. And I wasn't going to get rescued by death again.

ME: The truth is I married him too soon. I often felt trapped.

I hit send too quickly. The camper creaked. I waited, my pulse quickening. He could answer in so many ways. He could call me harsh or type *ouch!* He could disappear and quit talking to me altogether. Instead he wrote:

BDREW: People get married for a lot of reasons. I've started to wonder if any of them are good reasons.

I exhaled.

ME: Yes. Me too.

I would give him a second to elaborate. Then I thought WTF.

ME: You?

I thought that was enough. He could go with it or drop it. I held my breath again. Waiting for a text could be as thrilling as watching a movie where a hero has to save the world from aliens.

BDREW: I married my wife because she needed to stay in the country. She's Canadian. Long story.

I started to type *Wow*, but he sent another text.

BDREW: Phone call.

ME: No fair.

And he was gone.

I reread my texts. It was all true, but it was ancient history. Why couldn't I move past it? The thought of a relationship made me nervous, not excited—trapped, not hopeful—but something was happening. A door had cracked open, and new revelations were coming uncomfortably fast. But I had work to do, if I was going to make it through this trip without shutting the door, going home, and breathing the old stale air of sameness.

But now that I had fresh air in my lungs, I didn't think I could go back.

CHAPTER THIRTEEN

NO NAME-CALLING

Despite its newly upcycled insides, the camper's bones and joints were old. Uneven pavement or a break in the asphalt brought on a bouncing wheeze like the whole thing was made of rusty springs. If the camper's tires crossed the fog line and ran up against the edge of the highway, I'd hold my breath, fearing we'd tumble, top heavy, into the ditch.

I pictured the dozens of accidents I'd seen over the years, unbalanced trucks toppled and in the median, RVs lying sideways like fat, beached harbor seals, unable to roll back upright. Holly always drove faster than I did; she did everything like she was on a deadline.

I ventured a look in the front cab. Summer sat cross-legged with her wrists on her knees in a meditation pose: back straight, chin lifted, eyes closed. Holly stared through the windshield and said, "Uh-huh. Okay." I realized she was on the phone when I saw her earbuds.

"Darling," she said in her Nice Holly voice. "There's no cramping this time, right?" She paused.

I could see in the reflection of the rearview mirror that Holly looked fearful. Her expression, the tone of her voice made me hold my breath. I listened hard.

"What did the doctor say?" I wished I could hear Rosie's report. "We're making good time, sweetie. We'll be home soon." Holly touched her face, wiped her eyes.

I almost touched Holly's shoulder to offer a squeeze of reassurance. She'd scoff, brush me off, so I kept my comfort to myself. Besides, what did I know about the knife-edge Rosie and Holly lived on? I'd had an accidental conception with the easiest of pregnancies and deliveries. Holly would be sure to remind me of that, as if that was another blessing I didn't deserve. That my pregnancy was accidental, which somehow negated my love for my daughter, which ignited, once again, my indignation. However it was that my daughter came into my life, nothing had made me happier.

My phone buzzed, and as if my daughter knew I was having a mothering moment, she texted.

MADDIE: I've got a handle on the internship, Mom. But the baby-sitting! I'm supposed to make dinner for the kids. I don't know what to make. Also, I accidentally fed Lyddie milk chocolate, and she's had diarrhea all morning. I'm terrible at this job

I texted some ideas for an easy meal. I comforted her about her mistake and sent her an internet link with a list of foods with hidden milk in them. While I problem solved for Maddie, I was totally engaged with being her mother. But then she texted:

MADDIE: OK. Later mom. I love you

And she was gone, and I was once again alone with my thoughts, stuck in a camper in the middle of who knew where. There was no quid pro quo from kids. No *How's the trip going?* Or, *Are you having a good time?* That's not how the parenting contract went. For every ten times parents supported their child, their child might think to respond once in kind. Typically I didn't notice such things, but for some reason, listening to Holly talk to Rosie, watching the self-sure Summer in the passenger seat of this rolling rust kettle, I was feeling lonely. I realized this feeling was going to be my life, and my shoulders sagged.

My mind wandered to the moms of Maddie's friend circle. More often than not, they spoke with extreme irritation about their husbands.

There was Genevieve Post and her husband, Jim. After Jimbo forgot to bring the seven-layer bars that Genevieve had individually packaged and priced herself to the swim team bake sale, she said, "Well, what do you expect? Men are one chromosome away from a cricket." It was clear from that woman's expression she was not kidding.

And Melissa Trenton's exasperation was real when her husband's marketing position had been phased out, and he was on the job market for the third time. "Listen, if I could phase him out, I would phase him the ef out so fast and replace him with a drone. At least the drone moves if you push a button. It would be so satisfying to have something, anything, at my command."

As many times as I was conflicted about being a single parent, just as often I was relieved. When things went wrong when you were single, you had no one to blame but yourself—which cut the accusations in half because no one was looking at you disapprovingly. You were alone in blaming yourself for all the errors you made.

I remembered the shaman's words, wondered if there was any wisdom to be had there, and began googling down a speedy e–rabbit hole. And, after an hour of increasingly tense browsing, I reviewed my history.

Are shamans real
Spirit animals and you
Animals that saved people's lives
Six surprising animal and cancer facts
Health effects of letting your dog sleep in your bed
Nine things happy healthy people have in their bedrooms
The best summer sex toys
Why does everyone hate Gwyneth Paltrow?

I closed my eyes, let my disorder take over, and when I woke we were in Utah.

———

Outside the dusty camper windows lay a wide-open landscape. Cliffs in shades of pink and orange were punctuated by scruffy brush and layered stone. The geography looked like a colossal birthday cake that had been left in the searing sun to bake, dry, and petrify. An occasional off-kilter wooden shack dotted the vista just like in the westerns made here decades before.

Sometime between my googling, reading, and sleeping, Summer had taken over the driving, and Holly had curled up in the passenger seat. I could hear her congested inhale, still sleeping soundly despite the cramped space. I scooted between the two seats and spoke softly to Summer.

"Are we close?"

Summer blew a kiss over her shoulder. "Good morning, Princess Sleepy."

"I think I might be Sleepy the dwarf."

"I think his name is Sluggish. There's some kombucha in my bag. Take a sip."

Her sweet greeting and offer had me feeling cared for. I squeezed Summer's shoulder and said, "I'm glad you're with us."

Summer hugged my hand between her cheek and shoulder. "I know you are. Can't say the same for your soul mate over there."

"My soul mate?" I laughed.

Summer widened her eyes for emphasis. "You two may make each other insane, but there's no denying your connection. You are two peas in a pod."

"I don't think that expression means what you think it means."

"Oh, I know what it means, all right."

"How long has Holly been asleep?"

"See how much you care? You two are the best kind of women." She swallowed, and the tip of her nose went red.

"Summer?"

She waved me off. "She's been sleeping for a while. You'll both be fresh for our reunion with Peanut. Holly called the sanctuary. He's there and waiting for us."

"She's so practical. So prepared. I should have done that."

"You've got a lot going on. You're keeping track of your best friend, your daughter, and healing from the past. Also, this man you are texting." She caught my eye in the rearview mirror and wiggled her eyebrows suggestively. "What's that all about?"

"Is this part of your magical aura reading?" Her insight did seem magical.

"No, sweetie. I snooped your phone when you were sleeping. It should be password protected, hon. I can show you how to do it. We can pick a number even you won't forget."

"Hey!" But I didn't really care. What did I have to hide? "I can remember my passwords. I don't have it protected because I have nothing to hide."

"That's what everyone thinks, but when our privacy goes haywire and the fascists come to get us, you'll wish you had a password on your phone."

I squinted through the dirty windshield into the dry but colorful vista and said, "I don't know what to say to that."

"Take it from me. When that video of me and that Italian porn star surfaced at Coachella, I realized how fragile our privacy is. You have to get all your photos off the cloud." She air quoted "the cloud" as if it wasn't a real thing.

"You had a sex video on your phone?"

"No, someone filmed it from a hole in a hotel room in Vegas."

"So it wasn't stored in the cloud from your phone?"

"No. Why does that matter? Sam, you need to straighten some things out with your inner deer."

"What are we talking about?"

"Oh, Sam." She sighed like she'd been my parent for more years than she liked to admit.

Talking to Summer was like listening to the old Girl Scout song "The Song That Never Ends." There was a circularity on the surface that made sense but was also crazy making. I would have tried to sort out this conversation, but rising out of the desert, right at the foot of a bluff that looked like an erect head of a python, sat the sign for the Best Friends Animal Sanctuary. Summer yanked the steering wheel to the left and hit the edge of the asphalt. By some miracle we didn't tip over and skid into the ditch. The popping sound of pebbles and stones kicked up against the underbelly of the cab, and the combination of the swerving and the noise woke Holly.

I heard Holly grumble and say, "What tha?" It was nice that when Holly was asleep, I could relax, but this was the next stage, and I needed to be alert and not sleepy with avoidance.

There were a lot of things I was expecting to see when we arrived at the sanctuary, but the reality far outplayed my imagination. Even after seeing photos, I couldn't have been further off with my animal-camp fantasy. This place was not a hippie establishment with thrown-together lean-tos and food troughs scattered in the fields. Along the driveway to the center of the sanctuary were tidy cabins and a place to camp and park RVs. A wide green field corralled horses within white fences, all seemingly held in place by an umbrella of wide blue sky. A few hundred feet more, and our camper rolled to a stop at the bottom of a cliff where the Best Friends Animal Sanctuary Welcome Center was housed.

"This is not what I imagined," Holly said with a bit of wonder in her voice.

"Me either. It's stunning."

Summer said, "It's amazing, right?"

"Have you been here before?" I asked.

"No. I'd never heard of it until I met you guys."

I shook my head. "It's so orderly. So organized. I thought it was going to be a huge field of dogs, and we'd have to search for Peanut for hours."

Holly shrugged. "Honestly, me too."

"You guys, that's silly. They can't mix animals and let them run all over the place. They would kill each other. Transmit disease and generally reproduce."

"I thought you didn't know anything about this place." I glanced at Summer.

"I don't," Summer said. She put the camper in park, opened the door, and slid out of the seat.

Holly glanced at me and rolled her eyes.

My heart leaped. Was that an accident on Holly's part, a by-product of waking up and not having her irritated-antennae tuned in and focused on me? Or was this a bonding moment, like when people lived through a hardship and found an inside joke in the darkness, or when soldiers from the same platoon who otherwise hated each other came together to save the day?

"You two drive me crazy," Holly said, and my soldier's heart broke in two. I wanted to stop my feelings right there, get ahold of them, and say, *No, don't do it. You'll only be hurt in the end.* But being with Holly again had me feeling the freedom I'd felt in college, admiring her fierceness, wanting it for myself.

"Summer, I looked up your IMDb page like you suggested, and you did a whole special on the sanctuary two years ago. There's a photo of you with an enormous parrot on your head," said Holly.

"Oh yeah," Summer said, slamming the cab door. "I forgot about that. We hoped that would take the place of the porno."

I climbed from the back into the front seat and out of the passenger-side door right after Holly.

"Summer," I said, annoyed, "can you just try to be more honest with us? I mean, I think you owe us that."

"I'm an artist, you guys. Truth is a flexible concept."

"No, it is not."

"I got you here, didn't I? I think you owe *me* a thing or two. But you can pay me back another time. I'm going to the pig house. I have an old beau there who, if I remember right, knows how to treat a lady."

I watched her walk away. Sometime in the night, Summer had replaced her white jeans and platform shoes with a prairie skirt and flip-flops. She'd given herself two braids that hung on either side of her face. From behind she looked like an eighth grader who hadn't gone through puberty. It was endearing.

"Have you seen her eat yet?"

"I have not," said Holly, "but she must have eaten something from that giant bag of hers. I wouldn't be surprised if she had a month's worth of bento boxes in there."

"Maybe," I said, unsure. "I'm worried about her."

"Don't worry about her. Summer takes care of Summer."

It felt good to stand on the pea gravel and not feel the sway of the camper, the growl of the engine beneath the seats. The canyon had a photographic quality to it, as if we were standing in front of a green screen while a technician projected the perfect Utah scenery and weather for our pleasure. I stretched and said, "What's the plan?"

"This isn't a heist, Samantha. We're going to go inside, ask where the canines are housed. Tell them we are here for the dog and probably sign a paper. Then, if all goes right, we will pick him up and leave."

"What about Summer?"

"She can stay here. I snatched the registration and insurance for the camper when she thought I was sleeping."

"You did?"

"Someone had to."

"We're just going to drive off and leave her?"

"Do you want to drive twenty-three hundred miles across country with her? Who knows what she's got up her sleeve."

Yes. Yes I do. I was not prepared to be alone with Holly. And I liked Summer. Simple as that. In some ways Holly seemed more of a stranger to me. My Holly wore a tie-dyed shirt with cats on it to sleep. Often she'd slip on a pair of jeans and go to class braless, makeup-less, her hair pulled into a pony. I searched Holly's face for my past mischievous friend. Her leaner, more angular self, her pale-yellow button-down shirt. I didn't know this strict person. This humorless woman.

"Holly, we can't just leave her here."

"I think we can, Samantha. What's she doing with us anyway? Doesn't she have some famous friends she can plague? She's unpredictable and could be unstable. All those mists and ointments she's always rubbing into her skin—they're probably hallucinogens."

"You sound like my grandmother. She just seems lost."

Holly smoothed her hair, which was the equivalent of taking earrings off before a country-western bar fight.

"Lost like you, Sam? Does she make you feel better about yourself?"

"Wow, Holly." I shrank back. I tried not to, but I did.

"Say it, Sam. You can't bear to think about being stuck driving with me. You'd rather have that train wreck between us than spend any time with me."

I clutched my hands together to stop them from shaking with frustration. She was right, of course. She could always read me—and there it was, the sadness again.

"Summer may be a train wreck, but at least she's not . . ." Mean? Severe? Unfunny? I hesitated for a moment. My next word might change our relationship forever. If I named Holly, I'd better be careful, because once that label was out there, she would never, ever let me forget it.

In the pause I heard Summer's voice from behind me. "No name-calling. No garbage dumping. No bringing up past grievances. Remember the rules. And Holly, stop trying to trap Samantha, using me as bait. She's not as strong as she seems."

The bright Utah sun brought out the lines in Summer's sober face. Lines that had come from a mix of joy as well as sadness and defeat, just like the rest of us mortals. I was catapulted back to my grade-school playground, feeling again the sting of hearing from girls that my jeans were too short and my cartwheels sucked.

She looked between us. "I came back to get my sunglasses. This sun is brutal." She turned, and as she walked away, she lifted the registration and insurance folder out of her bag and held it straight in the air with one sinewy arm. It was a glorious flipping of the legal bird, and I thought, *Score one for Summer.*

"Dammit. She's sneaky," said Holly. "How much do you think she heard?"

"What difference does it make, Holly? I heard all of it."

CHAPTER FOURTEEN
REJECT BEFORE REJECTED

Holly and I, with our grim postfight faces, stood in the visitor center in the middle of Angel Canyon, possibly the most beneficent spot in the world. As if to highlight our petty energy, a staff member escorted a white short-haired dog missing a front leg through the gift shop. Visitors stopped to pet the scruffy animal like he was a celebrity.

Best Friends was a well-oiled machine. As soon as we explained who we were and what our mission was, we were welcomed, informed, and transported. Peanut, we were told, was in the veterinarian clinic at the top of the canyon. We were ushered into a van for a tour of the premises that would drop us off at the clinic. All I wanted to do was get a look at Peanut. FaceTime Katie. Examine the color of her skin, judge for myself how she was doing.

If we needed a reminder of the trivial nature of our disagreements, here we had it. In the center of the majesty of the Utah hills and valleys, we learned that the founders of the sanctuary had started with a handful of people, cash, and a mission. They had wanted to save animals.

"Michael Vick's scandalous fight-dogs came to find peace and rehabilitation," said the tour guide, and I wondered how I'd never heard of this place before now. The sweeping vistas of canyon and sky were stunning for this Wisconsinite used to flat green farmland and red barns.

I breathed in the dry air and felt the world get bigger with every tire rotation.

I was determined to enjoy the victory of finding Peanut, and, as far as I was concerned, I vowed not to let Holly, who was in full check-her-watch fidget mode, get under my skin at least for the next hour. As we bumped over the unpaved road to the top of the canyon, I decided I was going to practice a technique my grief social worker had taught me to use when dealing with well-meaning parents at Maddie's school who wanted to fix me up. "Try repeating a phrase that doesn't explain, defend, or justify," she'd said. "If someone presses your buttons with judgment or aggression, try saying *thanks*."

"Just plain *thanks*?" I'd said doubtfully.

"Try it—it works." My social worker had short hair with a small swipe of gray in the bangs. She wore wire-rimmed glasses and a knowledgeable expression. Her name was Louise, and she spoke carefully. "There are a few phrases or words that can be helpful in several ways. Here." She handed me a notepad with a dangerously sharp pencil and said, "Write them down, and then we'll test them. Ready? As I said, *thanks* is one. Also try, *We're different; Good to know; Hmmmm, I'll think about that;* and if they say something offensive, just say, *Go Badgers* and don't follow up with anything."

"Go Badgers?"

"Look, an inappropriately aggressive or intentionally wacky question or statement deserves an equally wacky response."

I wrote each phrase on the pad, feeling the scratch of the pencil on the white paper, always a favorite tactile feeling for me.

"Okay, ready?"

I nodded.

"So, Sam. You should try running. It's great for losing weight."

I sat up straight and pulled in my stomach. "Thanks," I said uncertainly. I tried to stop myself, but I continued. "I used to run, but after

141

a few miles my hip hurts. I went to the doctor, and he told me to rest it. I never got back into the habit, and my hip—"

Louise wagged her finger at me, and I stopped speaking.

"You are justifying."

I nodded. "Okay, hit me with another one. I can do this."

Louise dropped into character and said, "You don't go out much, do you? I try to go someplace at least once a week."

I looked at my list. "Well, we're different." I bit the side of my tongue to keep from elaborating.

Louise smiled. "You know, you would look better without bangs."

I touched my forehead and blushed.

Louise gave her head a tiny shake and pointed to the pad of paper.

"Oh! Thanks," I said. I wanted to explain why I had bangs, to cover up a scar from my childhood, but that would be a justification. I sealed my lips.

"You should sleep with more people before you die."

"Go Badgers," I blurted, and Louise leaned forward and high-fived me.

Then she said, "But you should. We all should."

And I, sticking with the program, said, "Hmmmm."

These were my thoughts as we wound our way up the canyon. From now on, when Holly said, *You drive me crazy, Sam.* I'd say, *Well, we're different.* When she said, *Get with the program, Sammie,* I'd counter with *Hmmmm.* When Holly said, *You were a shitty friend,* I'd say, *Whatever I did, I'm so, so sorry. I miss you.* Or, *Go Badgers,* whichever didn't make me feel like crawling into a hole.

When you were a child and you were taught to avoid fighting at all costs, you never got to see the rewards of having the hard conversation. If this continued as you aged, you got the message that the spoils must be so terrible, so ungodly horrible, that nothing was worth an argument. When you were an adult, you could reason yourself out of that, see evidence everywhere that wasn't true, but your child hid and whispered, *But what if the result is worse than the fight?*

One night my mother sent me to bed. I'd heard my father turn on her. His ferocious anger evident in his tone of voice, a bark filled with hatred. "Shut up!"

If she hadn't said, "Okay. You're right," in that small voice, what would have come next?

What if?

If you were me? You listened and kept your piehole closed.

The van stopped at a low, sleek building, and the tour guide hopped out. The thought that we were about to see Peanut and lay our hands on him made my palms sweaty with anticipation. I had to acknowledge that some of my anxiety about this trip came from not believing we would succeed. That Tom would stop us or we wouldn't find Peanut and return him to Katie. That she would only have fragmented Holly and Samantha to comfort her. An unhealed duo, a broken Band-Aid.

Inside the state-of-the-art vet clinic at the very top of the canyon, I realized what this place was. It was a safe house for vulnerable animals. A woman escorted us into the center of the clinic and said, "The veterinarian will be with you shortly. Peanut is in quarantine, so you can't pet him yet. But you can see that he is safe and well cared for." She directed us to an area where a Plexiglas window surrounded a private space, and in the center of that space, on quilted blankets, lay a sleeping Peanut.

Relief and warmth washed over me. My eyes filled with tears, and I placed my open palm on the cool Plexiglas like I'd seen in movies when wives visited their husbands in prison. There was no phone to pick up, so I couldn't tell Peanut we'd made it, we were here, we would bring him home.

"That's him?" Holly said from behind me. "Are you sure? He looks terrible."

I had to admit he didn't look like the luxurious Peanut I remembered. His fur had been clipped, and there were patches all over his body where pink skin showed through. His nose had the mottled heart-shaped birthmark that was Peanut's most distinguishing characteristic visible only to Peanut enthusiasts.

I nodded. "He doesn't look that great. I could kill Tom. What an asshole." I wiped my eyes just as a man strolled into the room.

"So, I hear you're Peanut's family. It's nice to meet you. I'm Griff. I'm one of the veterinarians on staff."

Holly shook his hand first and said, "Not really his family. We are taking him to his owner."

"Oh, you're the transport, then?"

I stepped forward, irritated at Holly and her precise ways, making sure everyone knew everyone's roles in the world. "I'm Samantha." I offered my hand. "The owner is our best friend, but she's too ill to come herself." Griff was, I guessed, my age and had the warmest way about him. He wasn't a heartthrob like Drew, but if Summer were here, she'd accuse my aura of brightening. I couldn't help it. When I meet people who exude warmth, I perk up. I'm like a daisy in need: when the sun shines, I bloom.

"Why is he in this room?" Holly said. "And when can we take him?"

Griff smiled at the sleeping Peanut and said, "Peanut came to us in some distress. We put him in a private room to minimize stimulation and figure out what was happening with his skin. We are very careful and don't socialize dogs until we know they don't have anything communicable."

Alarmed, I said, "Contagious? What was happening with his skin?"

"He came in with mange, but I don't think that was entirely the issue. We're still figuring it out. Animals deal with stress in lots of ways. Hair loss is one of them."

"The Mange? Isn't that like a plague or something?" Holly said, taking a step back from the window.

I gave Holly a look. "It's not the Mange. It's mange. And it's not the plague. It's mites that burrow in a dog's skin." I'd had dogs my whole life until Maddie came along. I wasn't sure if I was equipped to keep myself and a child alive, let alone a dog. I always thought, after Maddie left for college, I'd get another.

"Burrow?" Holly shivered.

"It's not that big a deal when you figure it out. Right?" I looked at the veterinarian like a star student hoping my answer was on target.

"You're right. It takes a skin scraping, and you can treat it with a scabicide."

"Scabicide?" Holly echoed, and Griff smiled.

Peanut's tail moved and out from under it emerged a sleek black ball of a dog. The dog looked like a living, breathing toy.

"Oh, he's not alone!" Holly shouted. Her reaction was so over the top, as if a zombie had reared up and darted at the window.

"For God's sake, Holly, get ahold of yourself."

"I'm not quite the animal lover Samantha is." Holly meant it as a slight. Like my love for animals was a weakness. I couldn't believe that Holly was implying that she didn't love animals at a place whose sole purpose on this earth was to care for animals.

"I bet a few days here will change your mind," said Griff generously.

"Doubtful. We are leaving today."

Clearly Holly didn't need Louise's list of phrases to assert herself. I'd always wondered where all her confidence came from. All that *I don't give a damn what you think; I'm here, I'm crabby, get used to it.*

The veterinarian slid his glance between us. "I'm sorry. There's been some confusion. Peanut can't leave today."

"No! What? We have to go," I said.

"His medical issues haven't been fully sorted out."

"That's fine. I'm sure Katie has her own vet at home. We'll get him there and have all his needs met closer to home," said Holly.

I nodded rapidly, agreeing.

Hearing this, the veterinarian became a stone-cold animal-advocate professional. "He has to stay in quarantine, and we need him on solid ground with his diabetes. Stress is a problem for blood sugar, and he's been maximally stressed lately. It wouldn't be responsible for us to release him."

"He's not in quarantine. He's got that other dog in there." Classic. The only authority was Holly.

"That's Moose. They came in together." Moose was a tiny black dog with a pointy nose and eyes that bugged out like two shiny marbles. He had ears that bent at odd angles and made him look like a bat. "They bonded in the LA facility and don't go anywhere without each other. They both had mange, so there was no cross-contamination. We tried separating them, and Peanut passed out every time." Griff shrugged. "That's the nice thing about working with animals. You don't need a social worker to keep friends and siblings together. You can make your own rules."

I loved it when someone else put Holly in her place. When someone else delivered bad news, even if this news made me nauseous. I checked the time on my phone, a useless move. "We've got to get going."

"When will he be released to us?" Holly paced in a tight circle as if this information had been designed to torture her and not for the good of Katie's dog.

"Peanut has several challenges."

Holly stopped and said, "Okay, let me have it. I'll take notes. What challenges does the dog have, and how long are we talking?" She tapped into a file on her phone.

"He's been treated for mange, and we usually see good results in a few days."

"How few?" Holly said, guarded.

"He's through week one. So maybe three days?" said Griffin.

"Okay, okay," I said, processing this. Three days here, two days on the road. "That's five days before we get back to Katie." This seemed like forever.

"What else?" Holly was a beat cop, a reporter for the *Trib*, a parent giving out curfews. "Give me the highlights."

"We gave him a corticosteroid to reduce his itching. He scratched himself raw in a few areas, and we treated him with antibiotics for infection." Griff glanced at me, and I nodded.

I'd wait until I could pet Peanut before texting Katie, aware that his challenges would become hers. Instead, I texted Drew.

ME: Peanut is not quite fit to travel.

BDREW: I'll wait to tell Katie. I'm with her now. She's sleeping.

He was doing what I asked. Why did that give me pause, make me sad? I shook my head, *Good for Katie,* knowing how silly it was of me to hope.

"He came in with some ulcers on his paws," Griff went on. "Common with uncontrolled diabetes, and we are keeping those clean while still getting him some exercise."

That's when I noticed Peanut had two paws covered with white gauze. Moose actively licked one of them. I pointed to the pair. "Is it okay if Moose licks Peanut's bandages?"

Griffin smiled in a fatherly way at the two dogs. "Yeah, just try to stop him. He's like Peanut's own personal nurse. He keeps the big dog clean and cuddled. It's inspiring."

Holly said, "Look, Doctor—I can see how important these dogs are to you, but this one here is my best friend's, and she has cancer. We're trying to get back home and reunite them. The sooner the better, you know?"

I was shocked to hear a hitch in Holly's voice, and I examined her face. She had that flush she got when her emotions ran high, and

I moved closer but didn't touch her. Her eyes were like a crossing guard moving kids along: keep going, keep moving. But, I'd known Holly once. Her eyes were dry, but she was feeling the stress of this trip.

Griff looked evenly at us. "I understand. As soon as I'm sure he is safe to travel, and you won't have to do anything but deliver him to your friend, I will personally sign the release papers."

Holly nodded. I could see she couldn't speak for fear of losing her steely control.

"I don't know how much you know about diabetes, but insulin levels depend on simple things that nondiabetics never have to think about. Exercise, stress, food, and his insulin needs might change. You two will have to learn how to check his blood sugars and give him the insulin he needs. How are you with needles?" He held out a tiny syringe, and Holly blanched and looked away.

"I'm the one who will take care of Peanut as we drive him home. I've given shots before," I said.

"Good," he said. "Our education sessions won't be long ones, but we want to make sure you know what you're doing. How to read Peanut's symptoms, what to feed him, and what to do if he looks in trouble."

I nodded. "I think I can handle all that."

"Now for Moose. He had mange too."

"Why do we care about Moose? He's not coming with us," said Holly.

Griff looked at me and put his hands in the pockets of his khaki pants. "This is going to be a much longer stay while we separate the two and deal with their grief."

"Grief. You've got to be kidding me." Holly rolled her eyes the way Maddie did when she wanted to broadcast her disgust in a way that there would be no misunderstanding. Hers was the eye roll of eye rolls.

"We're taking Moose," I said. "No discussion." More surprising declarations from Samantha Arias. *WTF, Samantha?* I thought.

Griffin looked closer at me and smiled.

I tried a confident hair flip, but my ring got caught in my hair, and I tried to discreetly free it. My hand hovered near my ear as if to say, *You're just not there yet, honey.*

CHAPTER FIFTEEN

GOT A PROBLEM? GET A DOG.

Holly grabbed my elbow and said, "Excuse us, Doctor, I need to talk to my friend here."

Griff was no idiot. Likely he sized us up in seconds and knew to evacuate. He gave me a quick nod that held a tinge of worry. I hoped he saw the apology in my smile and not my shaky confidence about how to manage Holly.

"We are not taking that sponge of a dog with us."

"Yes, Holly, we are." This was something I could put my foot down about that had no long-term effect on anyone but me. I could see no gray areas for contention.

"No, Sammy, we are not."

I stepped back and looked at Holly. Same perfect appearance despite camper living. A swath of fatigue under her eyes, two frown lines on her forehead, like two exclamation points punctuating her argument.

"Why could you possibly care if I adopt Moose? Furthermore, I'm not sure why you think you're in charge of this."

"Why do you think you can add another animal to this trip?"

"If Moose eases Peanut's transition, then Moose is going with us."

"When I agreed to leave Rosie and travel across country to get this dog—"

"Peanut," I interrupted.

She closed her eyes and shook her head. "I agreed because you needed me, and Katie needed her dog."

I bit my tongue. I did not want to impulsively protest this statement of need. I knew that was how we pitched it to get Holly out of the hospital, where she was irritating everyone from the housekeeping staff to the oncologists. But it rankled. *Needed her,* I internally scoffed. If I'd needed her, it had been when Jeff died or when Maddie was too sick to go to day care or the first time I ran myself ragged caring for Katie.

"Peanut. The dog's name is Peanut."

"Okay. Whatever, Sam."

"Not whatever, Holly," I said, my anger hot and fast. "The dog's name is Peanut. He deserves to be called by his name."

"I don't understand you. Katie doesn't have a child, so her dog can be a substitute. But you have Maddie. Dogs are not people. I should be home with Rosie, and we both should be at Katie's side." Holly leaned into me, her big head on her skinny body, like an authoritarian cake pop without the fun sprinkles.

"We are at Katie's side right now," I insisted. "We are comforting her by getting what she needs and bringing it to her. You don't have to understand why she loves him, although you'd have to be made of stone to not see it."

Holly pulled her head back as if she'd been hit. "I am not made of stone. If any of us are immovable objects, it's you."

"Me?" *Stone! The unfairness!* I wanted to shut up, pull out, stop this fight. I rooted in my memory for Louise's list of safe phrases. Instead, all my loss and pain shoved my denial aside, and I said, "Why do you hate me?" It came out like a middle schooler on a playground who had stepped to an edge and both wanted to be reined back in and wanted to jump.

Holly's blue eyes were the color of lightning when she opened her mouth and raised her pointy, pointy finger. "You act like I'm the hardest person in the world, but I would never do what you did. And here you are being so nice to a dog you don't even know."

For the thousandth time, I desperately racked my brain. "What? Holly, what did I do? You can't possibly be talking about that night and Mike!"

"Ha!" Holly's laugh was like a thunderclap. There was a flicker of old, lovey Holly in that storm behind her eyes. Something like the Sour Patch Kids candy, a sour, sweet flash.

My outrage dissipated. "This isn't about that, is it?" I didn't see her expression because we were interrupted. "Holly," I said at the same time as a fuzzy-headed waif of a woman over Holly's shoulder said:

"Excuse me. Um. Ladies. You need to quiet down. You're inciting the girls." She pointed to a trio of cats, each in their own private metal holding cells. A tabby, a tawny, and a tiger-striped kitty sat alert, their tails twitching. It was like being in a high school hallway, and the crowd was chanting *Fight! Fight! Fight!* It was the pause we needed.

"Girls?" Holly said when she saw the cats. "Oh." But she looked alone, vulnerable. She touched her sternum, and there it was again. That dry-eyed catch in her throat. Holly looked dizzy, and I steadied her, my hand on her forearm.

"Nugget," I said. My old name for her slipped out before I could stop it.

"It's just. If you guys could step outside. That would be great," said the animal urchin.

Holly pulled her arm from my touch. "I don't want to get sucked into your vortex again." Unsteadily at first but gaining momentum, she moved toward a side door, ignoring the *Alarm Will Sound* warning. She slammed through; the alarm sounded.

"She's not supposed to go through that door," the woman said, and I nodded.

"She does what she wants," I said, and I noticed I was winded.

"I can see that." The woman nodded. "You okay?"

"Yeah," I said vaguely. *My vortex?* I was the last woman in America who had a vortex. I had a quagmire. I had a mushy middle. I did not have magnetism of any kind. Unless you considered my attraction to bedding.

The tiny woman and I stared at the glass door as it slid back into place and the alarm hushed. I sighed and the woman pulled a stool over to the room where Peanut and Moose were being held. "You can just watch these two if you want. It's calming."

"Thanks so much. And I'm sorry."

She shrugged. "You'd be surprised at how much that happens here. Couples come to volunteer, and they fall in love with a parrot or a pig, and the next thing you know, we have to call security."

"My friend has never had a pet."

The woman clamped her lips and shook her head. It was like I'd just said, *Holly was born without a head.*

"I think I will sit here for a while, if that's all right." My skin prickling with the electricity of our fight, I rubbed my arms. Who was at fault? Me, Holly, both of us? For years I'd avoided our loss, playing it off in unsatisfying ways: We were kids. I'd read her wrong. Holly was not who I thought she was. We grew apart. These were Band-Aids, and I needed that spray stuff that plugged foundation cracks. One squirt and it expanded to fill all the broken spaces.

I was surprised to see the woman still standing close. "I'm okay," I said.

"Um. Sure."

I turned my attention to the confinement area, where Peanut appeared extravagantly comfortable. I watched him reposition from sleeping on his stomach to lying on his back, his belly exposed, his paws lolling to the side. Moose resettled himself onto Peanut's neck, looking more plush toy than mammal. The diminutive Moose gave me the side-eye, the forever-watchful caretaker assessing my presence.

The stress of confronting Holly had me thick and foggy, but later than usual. I usually shut down in the center of conflict, not respectful moments later.

I rested my temple on the window and watched Peanut's chest rise and fall, rise and fall. It was hypnotic. I knew there was no fighting my sleep disorder, and I didn't think anyone in the clinic would mind if I closed my eyes for a minute or two.

Instead of falling instantly to sleep, I tried to mine my memories. Holly and I had been the best of friends. It hadn't just been youth and circumstance. We would not have these strong feelings if we hadn't started from a place of intensity.

I only had fragments from those years, over a quarter century of them, beginning in that apartment we shared with the hollow doors and thin carpet. My twenty-plus-year-old relics, like still photos, flipped in my mind's eye. Holly, Katie, and I were drinking coffee from travel mugs on the way to class, singing "I Will Always Love You," the Whitney Houston version, Katie's voice ear-splittingly out of tune. Holly's earnest face. Me laughing so hard I couldn't hold a note. Exam week, eating nothing all day and inhaling salty, oily popcorn at night, falling asleep on our notebooks. All that freedom . . . I sighed and felt myself drift off with the cool window soothing my temple.

I don't know how long I slept like that, but pins and needles in my arm woke me. I was used to falling asleep in awkward positions and waking having to shake a limb, stretch my neck, even rub feeling back into fingers. This was the price of a sleep disorder. I laughed at people who needed the perfect Sleep Number mattress or their beloved childhood pillow to get a good rest. As long as I had a place to rest my head and an immovable object, I could catch some restorative z's any day of the week.

"Oh, good. You're awake." Griff, the veterinarian, had returned.

If a sore neck was the price of a sleep disorder, then being discovered sleeping in awkward places by a variety of people was the side salad nobody wanted. I rubbed the numb spot on my head where I'd rested against the glass.

"Sorry," I said, the automatic apology that rested on my tongue along with my neurons, just waiting for whomever would find me.

"No problem. I take naps in here, too, when there aren't a ton of animals making a bunch of noise."

"You do?"

He nodded. With my postsleep, clear-eyed assessment, I imagined him as a boy with a stick on a busy sidewalk moving a woolly bear caterpillar out of the way.

"I usually go to my office, sit in a chair, maybe shut the light off. But I admire a good napper."

"I have a sleep disorder, and when I get stressed, it takes over. I think it's a get-out-of-jail-free card. It keeps me from getting into fights and saying anything I can't take back." I rubbed my eyes and added, "Not today, though. Which is weird."

"A sleep disorder. That's interesting."

I looked at him. "More interesting than watching two friends fight about the value of animals?"

"Kind of. Yes."

"Fair enough. I've had the disorder a long time. I find it very annoying but also sometimes a great escape."

He took the hint and changed the subject.

"It sounds like you've had enough experience with Peanut's medical needs that you won't have any trouble. That's good. Diabetes can be a challenge."

"Does Moose have any other medical needs?" I said, just to prolong a conversation that wasn't difficult.

"Not really. His skin is healing."

Griff the veterinarian was not a looker per se, but he had something very appealing going on. He kept his head shaved in that way men did who knew the fight against balding was lost, but it made him look more masculine, not less. His strong jawline supported good cheekbones and warm eyes behind wire-rim glasses. He didn't have Drew's full lips or striking features, but he exuded maleness. I suspected he was an athlete, but I wasn't sure why.

"I'd like to get on your schedule," said Griff. "We'll have to spend some time talking about how much insulin Peanut will need. How much an increase in activity will change his dosage. How to figure that out with a urine sample."

I laughed. "I don't have a schedule. We just got here. I'm not even sure where we're sleeping now that Holly and I are in the middle of a full-fledged brawl instead of the usual cold war we maintain."

"An odd choice for a traveling companion."

"It's such a long story." I pinched the space between my eyes on the bridge of my nose. "Is there any place I can get a cup of coffee?"

He gestured for me to follow him and led me through the center of the clinic, talking about how important coffee was to the running of the sanctuary. When he stopped and filled me in on details, it seemed as if he was holding eye contact a fraction too long. Not too long in a yucky way. I noticed it because men never did this with me, and by *never* I meant negative-integer never.

I spent my days parenting in the way parenting was for this generation: too much chauffeuring, contributing to fundraisers, traveling to games, discussing AP classes and grade points. Too much of everything. But you couldn't try to leave that treadmill, try to halt the hiring of a British soccer coach for eighth graders, or try dissuading your child from joining another club. You couldn't try to smell the roses, gather enough energy to observe the gaze of a man, or the next thing you knew, your kid would get left behind and you, as the parent, would be more of an outsider than ever.

Who was I kidding? I'd loved being buried in Maddie's life. If you were busy with your kid, you couldn't look too deeply at anything. You couldn't get into anything you couldn't get out of.

Griff stopped and handed me a coffee mug that said, *Got a problem? Get a dog.*

"Listen. Thank you for everything. I'm just so grateful."

He nodded and said, "Drink up. Then let's get you a ride back to the visitors' center with one of our staff. You can take a tour. See what we're about. There are cabins near the entrance. They're not always full. If you're lucky, you can stay there. There's also Kanab. Lots of hotels. Then we'll talk about how to best get you two prepared for the rest of your journey."

I nodded, so grateful again. "So three or four days?"

"Maybe . . ."

"Do not say another word," I said, feeling another tide of anxiety. "Holly is going to kill us."

———

While waiting for the volunteer transport to take me down the canyon, I hit Katie's number and held the phone for a FaceTime call. She answered in seconds, and her friendly face came into view.

"Guess who I'm with!" I said, and I turned so Katie could see me and Peanut through the Plexiglas, in the small rectangle of the phone. "Don't worry. He looks weird because they gave him a major haircut, but here he is! Peanut!"

"Hiiii!" Katie said, her face beaming. "Peanutty, hi, baby. Hi, hon!"

I looked over my shoulder, and Peanut lifted his planet-size head, dropped his tongue, and batted his tail in recognition of the love of his life. While Peanut looked the worse for wear, Katie appeared exhausted. Shades of purplish rings circled her eyes, and she looked somehow thinner than the few days before. I didn't want her to see my concerned face, which I knew showed my pain, so I took myself out of the FaceTime image and let Peanut and Katie make eye contact.

"Who's a good boy?" Noticing Moose, she said, "Are you making friends? Peanut-so-friendly. Did you make a friend?" She crooned and fussed, and I swung the phone back around to me.

"That's Moose. He's Peanut's BFF. Both dogs have had a time of it."

I explained where we were and how we'd gotten to Utah, knowing Drew had in some way filled her in on some of it. I left out distressing details and complicating factors like Summer, the Shaman Shamansky, and the mange diagnosis while adding details about Moose.

"Best Friends Animal Sanctuary. I've heard of that place. I'm sorry, Sam. I didn't think this would be so complicated."

"It's not, honey. The weather has been great, so driving is not a problem. We have Peanut. Should be just a few days more," I said, fudging.

"And Holly?" She rubbed her eyes.

"Oh, you know. She's fine. Bossy. The usual." Pivoting the conversation, I said, "Drew said you went home. That's good news!" Katie wore a sweatshirt that read, *I'm sorry I'm late I didn't want to come* instead of a hospital gown. The gray fabric mimicked her pallor, and I wanted to walk with her to a window. See the sun brighten her skin.

"Yeah. You know how it is. I'm going in tomorrow. They're starting me on a precautionary regimen of hydration and meds."

"Precautionary meds? Because of the blood work?" I asked. She rubbed her face again, and I wished I were there to take her hand. "You look tired." I wanted to sob and tell her I didn't want her to have to go through this again. I visualized cancer as a yoke around her shoulders, one that I could throw off and dead lift into a ditch. Instead, I wrangled my fear and frustration and focused on this phone call, on Katie.

"Is Drew helpful?" I was ashamed that part of that question was for me. What did Katie think of him? What did Katie think of him for me?

"Oh, he's great!" She looked me in the digital eye. "He texts me, had chicken soup delivered from Whole Foods. He says he keeps in touch with you. Said that you were a good friend to have."

Friend, I thought. Friend Zone is what Maddie called it. If you were interested in someone romantically after years of wandering in a love desert, the Friend Zone is not the zone you wanted to be in.

I wanted to hear more about Drew. I wanted to sit cross-legged on her couch with a glass of wine and talk like we did in college about boys. But that's not why I called. Also, what would I say? Drew and I didn't know each other.

"You're eating, then?" I said instead of *Are you and Drew falling for each other?*

Katie nodded, which usually meant she was eating but not enough to merit an audible and firm yes. "I'll be better when you guys get here. Peanut can lie on my bed. You can pluck my eyebrows. It'll all be good."

"So you're going to need the whole thing again?" I couldn't bear to say chemotherapy, treatment, months of hospital visits, but I did feel a bit like I was rolling up my sleeves, planting my feet for a boxing match I'd fought before and won. A bell sounded twice in my brain, *Round two.*

"Gosh no, we don't know that yet." She brightened and sat up straight. "No. I just can't wait to see you and Peanut. I feel better already knowing you are on the way."

Another person might have felt relief, but I knew better. When Katie said, *Gosh no,* it could mean anything. So, I let myself teeter-totter between relief and dread. But what to say? What could I say that conveyed to Katie, *I'm afraid, but I'm here and will always be here,* without fully acknowledging other terrible options?

A woman with a volunteer T-shirt approached me and smiled. She pointed to the door. "Katie, my ride's here. She's bringing me to the admin desk for us to get a room here."

"Okay. Love you!" She waved but didn't sign off.

I met her eyes, and after a beat I said, "Go Badgers."

"Go Badgers," she said with that crooked grin, and it was a good thing she signed off because my eyes filled to the brim with tears.

CHAPTER SIXTEEN
I COULDN'T BE ME WITHOUT THEE

On the short ride from the clinic down the canyon to the visitors' center, I kept my eyes open for Holly. I learned from the driver that Best Friends Animal Sanctuary was not a free-range gaggle, as I'd imagined. No, the animals were counted, housed, and cared for in boroughs named Dog Town, Cat World, Parrot Garden, and others. It was so organized and the mission so clear; I wanted to move in and be a part of such certainty. I wanted to drop my own rollaway next to Peanut and Moose and stay, mange be damned.

After I waved goodbye to the vet technician, who could have gone on for days with facts about Best Friends, I saw Summer strolling away from one of the animal neighborhoods in the lower part of the sanctuary. Summer's T-shirt had been tied around her tight middle, and a light sweat shone on her skin. Red dust collected around the rubber soles of her white sandals. She waved the second she saw me.

"Girl, this place is bananas," she said. "I just got done walking a five-hundred-pound pig named Trixie. It's a job, I tell you. You have to drop food, and they follow you. Defeats the purpose, if you ask me, but who am I to judge a pig's exercise motivations? You do you, Trixie. Whatever works." She brushed her hands on her skirt. "I signed us up to volunteer in the Bunny House and the Parrot Garden tomorrow. Dog

Town was booked, but maybe if we sweet-talk someone, we can get in there. I know you're allergic to cats, so I didn't even look to see if there were openings there."

"How do you know I'm allergic to cats?"

She gave me a look and drew a circle around my face in the air. "Duh, just look at you."

I wasn't going to try to figure out how she sensed I'd had a mild cat allergy ever since my childhood cat died from kidney failure—not enough to keep me away from cats, though. I didn't have it in me to figure out the universe right then.

"Where's Holly?"

"No idea. Grab your bag. I was also able to book us into a cabin. Holly can sleep in the camper and keep her crabby poison to herself. She can shower in our place—that's fine—but that's it."

"Summer, we can't do that to Holly."

"Her negativity is too much. I can't be around it. It's like second-hand smoke. It'll kill you faster than vaping."

"I don't think that's true."

"Why are you two friends anyway? You're such an odd couple."

"Earlier, you called us two peas in a pod. Which is it?"

"Stop changing the subject and answer the question."

"I think we're on the same subject." I was getting used to the flip-flop of conversing with Summer, so I said, "We've been friends forever. Since college. Our friend Katie—Peanut's mom—and Holly and I were roommates. Holly was the funny one, Katie the beautiful, nice one, and I was, I don't know, like their pet. I went along, did a lot of the driving. Made sure everyone got home at the end of the night." I could paint us in any way I wanted with Summer, and I found I wanted to get it right for this stranger, as if she were setting it down in a ledger for historical purposes. I could see Holly at twenty-one, grinning, so sure, and then underneath that satisfied smirk where there was a shiver of *Thank God you're my friend. I couldn't be me without thee.*

"Holly partied?"

"Yeah. God, she was a lot of fun. Maybe she still is; she's just not that fun around me." I had been able to mute the sorrow I'd felt after our friendship had collapsed, but this excursion revitalized everything. It was as if that time in my life had been stored as a flat, dry sponge in my memory banks. These days of togetherness were rehydrating each memory and emotion one drop at a time. Like when we'd found each other after the graduation ceremony, tossing our mortarboards in the air and shouting, "We did it!" And hugged so hard and I cried tears into Holly's graduation-gown shoulder. Or after, at dinner, when we tearfully shared a strawberry shortcake for dessert, and I experienced the salty and sweet mixture of happy and sad. I was right back there at this moment replaying that ache.

Summer watched me as she wound her braids into bundles and clipped them on top of her head. She was the most irritating and enchanting mix of teen girl and wise elder.

"What happened between the two of you?"

What could I say to that? A gnat flew into my hair, and I heard it buzz-struggle to get out. Summer plucked the bug free and let it somersault away. "We." I stopped. "We didn't have a huge falling out." That was true. We didn't. It was more like a *slipping out*. Every time I thought about Holly, I cringed at the memory of my naive self, my immaturity and lack of life experience all those years ago. If I'd realized what was happening at the time, I could have grabbed the tail end of our friendship before it slid through my grasp. I could have yanked it back and set it right. Now, the only way to fix it was time travel. If I could go back, I'd put off my internship for a month. Drive after Holly, call her aunt. Show up at her internship.

But all that action was for movies, not twenty-one-year-old girls who had no idea what years without their best friend might be like— thinking for sure they would reconnect—the youth's ability to believe that they had all the time in the world to fix things.

Frankly, there were other things I might fix if given the chance to zoom backward on the calendar. I thought about Jeff, how I didn't know him. About our marriage, but that wasn't an easy daydream because I wouldn't change even half a second with Maddie. I wiped all those change thoughts from my mind.

"Well, I can see you know more than you're saying. Someday you're going to have to talk about it." Summer narrowed her eyes at me like she did when she was reading some unseeable story over my head. This time there wasn't anything to read.

"I'm not being coy. I don't know, Summer."

"Oh, I think you do, my grasshopper. I think you do."

I shook my head. "Summer."

"You're going to have to push away from the edge of the swimming pool and get into the deep end. If you don't, you'll always be hanging on with your fingertips, afraid." With that, Summer pointed toward a path that presumably led to the cabins. I grabbed my luggage and followed her. Somehow Summer made me feel like a child, like I owed her an explanation for my dirty hands, for my playground disagreements. I hustled to her side. I wanted to show her I could swim in the deep end.

"If you had told me then that after graduation Holly and I wouldn't be friends, I would have laughed at you. Laughed and told Holly, and we would have pooh-poohed it together. As if we'd ever let anything get between. It was not possible."

"And yet," Summer said over her shoulder.

"Katie was the warmest of us all. And brilliant. Anything she read she remembered. If it weren't for her, I wouldn't have passed my astronomy elective. Holly and I studied, but Katie, she could sit in lectures and ace the exam."

"I never went to college."

"No?"

"Nah, my mom got me into commercials right away. There's a lot of money in commercials. Especially if they run a long time. I was the girl sniffing coffee in the Folger's commercial."

"You were in a Folger's commercial?"

"And Juicy Fruit gum, Johnson Wax, and Taco Bell. I had to eat so many tacos, I won't go near them now."

We took a few more steps. It was a relief to talk about her history instead of mine. I felt like I was getting close to something, but I couldn't reach it, like a popcorn hull caught in a tooth crevice, and I was fishing around and making everything else sore.

"The show, though. That must have been fantastic."

"Yeah," she said without enthusiasm. "Fantastic."

I waited, thinking she would elaborate. The ruddy dust on the road kicked up a cloud as we stepped into the sagebrush. I was just about to fill the lull when she said, "You don't have friends when you're in show business. Just connections. People who can connect and people who can't. Once you become someone who lacks connections, all your so-called friends disappear."

"What about your cohost? Matt what's his name? Isn't he in those comic book movies now?" She trudged ahead of me on the path, switched her bag from one shoulder to the other. "You guys seemed like the best of friends."

Summer stopped walking. "I was in love with him." The sun was behind her, so I couldn't read her expression, but I didn't have to. Her voice dropped, not in volume, but as if the next words were a burden. "Best friends are hard. You, of all people, know that."

———

Summer's vulnerability, the ease with which she dropped this painful piece of history, made me admire her openness while feeling so very sad for her. The night held us in this moment, and I heard her sigh.

We approached the cottage, which was four cement walls and a tile roof, where we would spend the night. The camper sat, slightly off kilter, on the rock driveway.

"She found us," Summer said out of the side of her mouth. "The jig is up." And boom, Summer the jokester was back.

"The jig?"

"There's no way we can exclude Holly from sleeping with us. It was a good idea, Sam, but not well executed."

"It wasn't my idea. I didn't even know about these cottages."

"Now you're being ridiculous."

Holly lounged, phone to her ear, in the only chair outside cottage number four. A scattering of moths bombed the light over her head, but Holly didn't seem to notice. Nor did she see us. I stopped, unsure of what to do with my awkward apprehension. Summer, a few steps in front of me, swung her arm back and drew me along.

Holly said, "I love you, Rosie. I'll be home soon. Yes." She nodded, hung up, and wiped her eyes.

Something akin to love washed over me at hearing Holly's gentle voice, a voice I used to know so well. I resisted Summer just enough to postpone what would inevitably be another difficult moment with Holly, a moment that would squash this warmth I was feeling.

We grabbed the rest of our stuff from the bus, and Summer stepped onto the narrow porch and put her hand on Holly's shoulder. "Let's get you out of the heat. The people at the welcome center said the door is unlocked."

I tried to make eye contact, but Holly averted her eyes from mine, and once again my fatigue whispered, *Why bother?*

In the cottage, Holly dropped onto one of the double beds and lay flat on her back like a starfish. Summer began unpacking on the other bed. I sank into an upholstered chair and rested my head against the painted concrete wall.

"Okay," said Holly, staring pointedly at the ceiling. "We'll push the vet to give us an itemized rehabilitation plan for Peanut. Then we'll insist we leave sooner. I'll check the statutes. I don't think they can keep him." Holly frowned, and one deep wrinkle between her eyes appeared. Her complexion was otherwise so smooth that a wrinkle stood out in high relief.

For a hot second, I thought about suggesting that Summer and I could do this without Holly. That she could fly home to Rosie. This would reduce conflict on all fronts, with the sanctuary and between Holly and me, and get her home for Rosie and Katie.

I rejected that thought almost before it was fully formed. It was clear Holly thought I had ruined our friendship. That I somehow hadn't been a sufficient friend, hadn't defended her from Mike, hadn't made amends. There was no way she would believe my motivations were pure, because in fact they weren't entirely. This was what I did where conflict was concerned: pacify, pander, and comply. Holly and I had to get to the finish line together.

"Also, I'm not like you guys. I have to eat. I'm going to find some dinner," said Holly.

With that, I closed my eyes and drifted off to sleep.

———

When I woke, my back stiff from the unforgiving chair, it was twilight, the room was empty, and I had the strongest urge to see Peanut. And, I suppose by proxy, Katie. There were texts on my phone from Maddie.

MADDIE: Mom, I can't decide if the kids like or hate me

Where are you? I need help with a scholarship letter

Another text minutes later read,

You're probably napping but I love Boulder. Can I go to college here?

And then the last one that said,

Can I take a gap year?

Each text was like notes in a frantic song moving toward a crescendo. I could feel Maddie's insecurity about the kids, her desire for the *right* future, and uncertainty about what decisions would get her there. I thought about what to text back, but there were no short, meaningful sentences that would calm her or direct her future. If I even tried, she'd be either annoyed or have already moved on to another perceived issue. It all caused me the usual parent anxiety but also made me happy. I was not totally out of sight, out of mind.

Plus, I was no expert on how to make a life work. What would I say? What would Katie's lesson be? Put your heart and soul into something and get cancer anyway?

A buzzing text from BDREW read: Do you have dog news?

There it was, that stab of *feel good* when a text from Drew appeared. I was rapidly becoming a test case for phone addiction and endorphin release.

ME: Yes. The Great Pyrenees has landed!

BDREW: Excellent! So, what's your ETA?

Was he asking because he wanted to see me or because he was so invested in Katie that he wanted to ease her wait? Or both? Or just the latter? Most likely the latter. *Ugh.*

ME: He's sick. Her ex did not take care of him. I told Katie we'd be home in a few more days.

BDREW: She's pretty down. She got discharged but her WBCs spiked. She's being readmitted. PS. This is not privileged information. She texted me this.

A frisson of fear shot through me. High white blood cell counts are the bane of all those admitted to the hospital. WBCs could mean so many things, from a dangerous infection or illness to stress. With Katie, though, it could be the worst news possible.

ME: Do you know something else?

BDREW: No. But we both wish you were here.

ME: I wish I were there too.

I waited to see if there was more. I thought about how wise it was to involve a stranger in all this. But I *wanted* to involve this particular stranger more deeply. And that made me feel guilty and opportunistic. My feelings were a water board of torture.

BDREW: You're a comforting person.

ME: I am? *I'm not.*

BDREW: Yes. Katie says you are her most loyal friend.

I felt the heat of confusion thinking about those two talking about me. I picked at something crusty on my leggings.

ME: She means so much to me.

I wished I'd taken a picture of Drew, creepy as that would have been. I would like to see his face. Be reminded that he was the right person to ask for help. That I had done it for the high-road reasons and not because I thought he was attractive. I wished I could see his expression while he texted me. Was it soft? Amused? Friendly?

BDREW: Send a photo of you and Peanut, okay?

ME: To Katie?

BDREW: No, to me.

And literally, it was like the crowd watching a home run on a baseball field went wild in my head. And that wildness felt like a mixed-up bag of possibility—but of what? Joy? Loss? Fear? Love? "Good God," I said as I walked out the door. "Sammie, you are a wreck."

CHAPTER SEVENTEEN
I DO, BUT I DIDN'T

Outside the cabin in the dry evening air, I released the pressure in my back with a tall stretch. Just ahead and down a short drive, I saw the white horse corral and fence equipped with electrical wires. A handful of horses grazed inside a grassy field. I heard the click of a door opening to my left. A woman in the cabin escorted a sleek fawn-colored pit bull out to pee. She waved gaily and disappeared back inside, shutting her door with another click. Neither Summer nor Holly were anywhere in sight. I pocketed my cell phone and stepped closer to the fencing.

I didn't have the keys to the camper. I was hungry, and I wasn't sure how I'd get to the top of the canyon to see Peanut and Moose. The two dogs were a couple in my mind now, a couple of one—fused. Like Holly and Rosie. Like Katie and me. Together, forever-after.

The possibility of forever-after being terribly close for Katie. The thought of going up against cancer again made me feel exactly how I felt trying to do a pull-up for the President's Fitness Challenge in middle school. Shaky, hanging in limbo, and unfit.

Losing Katie would feel like touching the electric fence, a nasty current that would stay with me forever. I took in the wide green of the grass, the mountain range, and the flawless darkening blue sky. My feelings of powerlessness made larger with the wide sky, tears pricked my eyes, and my cheekbones were wet.

A nut-brown horse in the field, his coat blurry with softness, ears tall and tight against his head, stopped chewing and stared at me. His stare was such a horsey look of curiosity. It was as if he were saying, *What exactly is happening over there?*

I tried to define it for that horse and myself. It wasn't sadness I felt. It was, if I had to put a name on it, *verklempt*—choked with such a chopped salad of unnamable emotions that the fiber of it all felt stuck in my throat.

With grand, deliberate purpose, the brown beauty stepped toward me as if in a procession. One hoof forward, knee high, evenly paced and stately, he kicked up dirt on his way.

I froze. I always wanted to be the kind of person loved by animals. Like that dog in Japan who, after his owner died, hung out at his train stop for years after. But as much as I acted like a Try Hard where being a best friend was concerned, I was also a Try Hard with animals. Dogs put up with my efforts to connect with them out of sheer doggie pity, but cats would have nothing to do with me. Their disdain when I called out to them was unmistakable.

When the powerful animal arrived in front of me, he turned his head and stretched it through the fence. His big globe of an eye, like a satellite, turned to meet mine. I remembered hearing that you shouldn't pet a horse on their face. They preferred to be touched on their neck, but I had the feeling that this horse wanted me to touch his nose.

Slowly, I let him smell my hand.

"I don't want to startle you," came a male voice to my right.

I pulled my hand from the soft black muzzle. Griff the veterinarian stood next to me. "I'm sorry. I don't know what the rules are. He seemed so intent. It felt rude to not touch him." The horse stayed in place, waiting.

"You're fine. Don't feed him, though."

I was aware that my face was wet with tears, and I was sure I had that bedraggled look I get when I cry . . . a red pinched nose, rheumy eyes, and patchy pink skin under my chin. I wiped my face with my shirtsleeve. "I don't know why I'm crying." Why did crying in public feel shameful?

"This place knocks the tears loose from everyone," he said with a sympathetic head tilt. "There's something about horses. This one's name is Tony. He's a fan favorite."

"I've never been a horse girl." I reoffered my hand to Tony, and he nuzzled my fist. "Not like my neighbor Jessica, who spouted horse facts nonstop on the way to soccer games when we were kids. Let's see if I remember any." I opened my hand and the horse let me cup his cheek. "You can tell if a horse is cold by feeling his ears. And a baby horse can run right after they're born."

"Excellent! Any others?" Griff's open face, so happy to find a horse enthusiast.

"Not that I can recall. It's been a while."

"Here's one for you. Horses can read your intent. Tony didn't come to comfort you. He came to your side because your energy wasn't preda-tory, and so he got curious. He came to say, *Who dis?*" Griff seemed to be trying to comfort me.

"Well, Tony, I'm Sam, and I mean you no harm." His soft, warm cheek fit into the curve of my hand. "I kind of wish he came to comfort me. Or he came because he knew I was a good person."

"Oh, he knows. Horses are very careful."

"I'm not a big crier. I'm a worried mess about my sick friend." I put my hand on the bridge of the horse's nose; there was nothing soft about the bony ridge between Tony's eyes. "The scale of this space is overwhelming. How could this sanctuary be here, and I'm only now discovering it? I wish my friend could see this place." I promised myself I would bring Katie here, and my heart seemed to skip a sad beat.

"This is the kind of place you either know about or you don't. Once you see it, you can't unsee it. That's what it was like for me." Griff had changed from his professional veterinarian clothes to jeans, Australian boots, and a stretched-out navy T-shirt with *Yankees* on it. His expression was relaxed interest with a wash of familiarity. He spoke as if we were already friends. "My name is Griffin. First and last name, by the way."

"You mean it's always been Griffin?"

"No, my name is Griffin Griffin. My parents thought it was adorable, and also maybe they hated me."

"Dr. Griffin Griffin?" I forced myself not to laugh.

"Dr. Griffin Griffin. Thank you for not laughing right away."

"Can I laugh later in my cabin when you're not around?"

"Absolutely, I expect most people do." He shrugged. "I don't know what my parents were thinking. By the time people started making fun of me when I was a kid, I'd lost my parents. I never got any answers."

"I'm so sorry to hear that." This was another moment in my life where a cliché was the only thing I could think to say and was inadequate.

"It wasn't awesome, but there was no more laughing at the orphan boy with the odd name." Griff swiped at a fly near his chin. "It was so long ago."

There was a comfortable moment when neither of us spoke, then Griff said, "I was visiting a sick pig and saw you here. I came over to see if you'd like to visit Peanut, maybe get something to eat."

"I would. Both. I'm starving." I peered at his face and wondered if this was what his life was like. Working all day, talking with volunteers, possibly finding people who would donate money and help sustain the sanctuary.

"I can take you into Kanab, or we can see Peanut and eat leftovers from lunch. We have a vegan chef on-site and whatever is uneaten from the cafeteria gets delivered to the clinic. You know, in case we have an all-night emergency and need something to eat."

"Let's go to the clinic. I might not have enough energy to go find food, eat it, and then visit Peanut. Maybe if I spend more time with him, he'll get better faster. You know, like when they hug babies in the hospital."

"Dogs heal so fast. He'll be ready." He took a red bandana from the back pocket of his Levi's and like a stoic cowboy in a movie, gestured for me to wipe the tears from my face. It was startling to have this kindness from a stranger.

I followed Griff to the staff room within the clinic, and he opened the refrigerator. "It looks like we have cold sesame and peanut noodles." He moved a container to the right. His broad shoulders obstructed my view. "We also have fruit and gazpacho on the one hand, and two beers on the other."

"Wow, I was expecting far less appetizing or healthy. I lose my appetite when I'm super stressed and I keep forgetting to eat. This is such a nice thing for the volunteers who don't have any place to go."

He looked puzzled but kind. "The cook is amazing. I've never eaten so well as after moving here."

"Is that right?"

"I'm a single guy. I ate a lot of frozen pizza. What can I say?"

I smiled and distractedly thought about Maddie and our dinners. Happy affairs where she'd chat about simply everything. Once, her class had watched a documentary about how Chinese labor helped build the transcontinental railway, and she got up and acted some of the parts out. The memory of Maddie's sunny face, her happy chatter, her call out to me, "Mom, mom, mom!" if I wasn't fully focused. I might have been living for my daughter, but you'd never convince me that it wasn't all worth it. My heart swelled and deflated in equal measure, the bellows that lived in my chest, the love that fueled my heart.

"I guess pizza is in my future too," I said as much to him as to myself, and I felt a stab of loneliness for my future without Maddie at home. Possibly without Katie—and as quickly as it had appeared, I shoved that thought out of my brain. I would not bring that to fruition by considering it. I would not. "My kid is lactose intolerant and won't eat anything but chicken. But she's graduating and leaving soon."

"Oh, you're married." I saw his eyes dart to my empty ring finger, and he gave me another unreadable expression.

"Widowed. When my daughter was an infant. I was a single mom."

Griff nodded, handed me an open beer, and I took a long swallow. I felt the cool liquid slide all the way down my throat. I pulled out a folding chair at a table with a few empty coffee mugs that held the orange Best Friends logo. I took pride in clarifying my singledom by saying I was widowed. Despite my quiet single life, I had not been divorced, had not been given up on. I had not been at fault.

"I'm sorry. That must have been very hard."

"At this point it's my history and my reality." I speared a clump of noodles with the plastic fork he'd given me. The cold noodles tasted like the best thing I'd ever eaten. I also felt the effects of the alcohol, which seemed impossibly fast and unfair.

"I'm a widower too."

"You are? I don't know many other widows. It's rare. I'm so sorry."

"Well, you know. It's an unusual place to be in the world. People don't know what to do with us, do they? They can't blame us for being single, they definitely pity us, and then there's this romantic notion surrounding it. A kind of Heathcliff-on-the-moors thing when he was lovelorn, before he got filled with rage."

"Exactly!" I said with such vigor that a piece of noodle flew out of my mouth and landed on the table between us. I wiped my mouth and the table quickly, embarrassed.

Griffin Griffin laughed. He'd nicked himself shaving, and there was a small scab he touched with his fingertips when he talked. "If you're keeping score, I'm an orphan and a widower."

"Oh Lord. Yes, you are," I said, enjoying this banter even with the tick-tick-ticking of lost minutes and our delayed arrival back home. I tried to focus on the moment instead of my time-urgent worry.

"If I become an amputee, I could be my own joke. An orphan, a widower, and an amputee stagger into a bar."

"Or an action movie: *Orphan, Widow, Cripple, Spy.*"

"Cripple? You're calling me a cripple?" Griff said good-naturedly.

"No," I said laughing, "I'm not. You aren't an amputee. Did you forget?"

"Oh yeah. Well, it's something to look forward to."

I covered my mouth. "I'm sorry. You just told me you lost your wife, and I made a joke."

"You were provoked. If you can't joke with someone else who's widowed, who can you joke with?" His eyes were wide and bright, and he had a swipe of oil on his lower lip.

In a mom moment, I brushed a bit of green onion off the side of his mouth.

"Thanks." Without breaking eye contact, he licked his lips and his thumb. And that's when I figured out what was happening. Slow as a sloth, my mind crawled out of its ditch at the side of the road and clawed into the oncoming traffic of emotion. This man, this Griffin Griffin, was flirting with me. And my brain crept from surprise to astonishment to a five-alarm fire bell.

In a movie the two widowed people would fall into each other and apologize in the morning. But I wasn't drunk; nor had I shaved my legs or anything else for that matter for too many years, which might have been a funny thing to consider at that moment, but old habits die hard. I could be under anesthesia and know the status of my body hair.

The larger barrier, besides my very low attractiveness and self-esteem, and my slowness to interpret mating signals, was, I realized spectacularly, Drew. For the first time in ages and ages, I was thinking of a man in a romantic way and was hoping he was thinking of me.

And there was something else. I'd often suspected if anyone—
anyone—ever showed interest in me again, I'd be so desperate for
attention I'd fall on my back like a submissive Labrador. But no.
Look at me! I was considering two attractive men and choosing one
over the other. I mean, fake choosing because I did not have confir-
mation that anyone was truly interested in me. But if I was reading
the room, and I think I was, I had options. Thrilled was the only way
to describe what I was feeling in that moment.

Back to reality. I could only imagine what I looked like. I had
wriggled into a pair of black leggings and running shoes in the back of
the camper. Thank God I'd swiped some deodorant on. I took another
swig of beer, smoothed my V-neck T-shirt, and straightened the small
gold chain I always wore around my neck. Maddie wore the same one,
with a tiny gold bumblebee charm on it. My phone buzzed with an
incoming text.

"What are you thinking about? Your expression is all over the
place."

"It is?" I said.

"You would make a terrible con artist."

"That's fine, because I don't often get pulled into the long con.
The grifter life." I tried a sideways peace sign to show how hip I was,
and he shook his head. I pulled my phone out of my pocket and read
Drew's text.

BDREW: Yoo-hoo!

ME: Is Katie okay?

To Griff, I said, "This is my friend who is watching over Katie,
Peanut's mom. He promised to keep us all informed because our Katie
will only say she is fine."

"Carry on." Griff gestured amicably to my phone.

BDREW: I'm with her. She's sleeping now. Maybe call her in the
morning.

ME: Has something changed since earlier?

I held my breath, my heart rate elevating.

BDREW: She's feeling terrible about sending you guys to get Peanut.

Drew was with Katie right now. Sitting next to her bed. She was telling him her feelings about our friendship. I felt flush with satisfaction that I'd asked him for help, but I wanted to be the one with Katie. At the same time, I wanted to have Drew's concern focused on my face, because apparently I was a greedy jerk.

ME: Drew. What else? Can I call you?

"Is everything okay? You don't look happy," Griff said quietly.

"I'm not sure. I think my friend isn't doing that well, but I'm not getting enough information to know for sure." I waited for the bouncing dots to turn into information, and I felt my vision telescope.

"Go ahead and call if you need to. I'll give you some privacy," said Griffin.

BDREW: I just left her. I have to meet a resident. But I can text.

I stood abruptly, wanting something to do. Something concrete. "Can I see Peanut? Get a photo. Maybe with me in it too?"

"Sure." He stood, and his folding chair screeched against the floor. I followed him to Peanut's room. "Today was his last day in isolation, so you can even pet him."

"Thank God. We can leave soon."

ME: I'm going to send a photo of me and Peanut.

BDREW: Good idea.

Griff unlocked the door to Peanut and Moose's room, and the two dogs opened their eyes. Peanut angled his front paws in a comical parody of a human stretch. Griff crouched, and Moose stood and bumped his head against Griff's knee.

"Hey, boy," he said as he scratched the dog's ears. "How's your pal doing?"

Peanut stood slowly and moved in for some love. The dog hit Griff's face with his long, pink, taffy-like tongue without effort. Griff wiped his mouth. "Peanut always hits me right between the lips. His aim is grossly good."

I knelt down, and Peanut seemed to recognize me. He knocked me into the door with full doggie weight and enthusiasm. I let the dog lick my hands and bump his head against my shoulder. The noodles and beer in my stomach flip-flopped, and I wished I hadn't eaten.

"Careful, Peanut." Griff stood and pulled Peanut by his collar just enough to contain him. "You're going to get slimed. He has a lot of saliva."

I was about to stand, but Moose rolled onto my lap. I took him in my arms. Peanut, out of respect for his friend, sat on his haunches and retracted his tongue. He looked like a very intelligent anthropology student observing another culture. Their two bodies pressed against mine made a warm body blanket that ramped up my desire to get this luxury home to Katie.

"Hey, Moose. You want to come home with us? Meet my friend Katie?" I touched his sleek fur, like that of a baby seal. "I'd bet cash money that any saliva dropped onto this guy's fur beads up and rolls right off." I handed Griff my phone and said, "Take a picture, and I'll send it to my friends." I scooted over to Peanut, and all three of us smiled at the camera, my attempt at joy the shakiest of all. "Wait!" I grabbed a blanket and wrapped it around us to hide the worst areas of Peanut's shaved fur and pink skin.

"You look like a small manger scene," Griff said and aimed the phone. He examined the picture and said, "Look how cute you all are!"

I peered at our faces on the screen. Peanut had the radiant white-toothed smile of the Great Pyrenees. Moose looked anxious but happy.

"Wow, I should wear dogs and a blanket more often." Something about that picture lit a fire in me.

I sent it to Drew, and to Katie so she'd see it when she woke.

BDREW: Wow. Nice. When will you get here?

ME: We leave tomorrow or the next day with Peanut. I'm talking to the vet right now.

"Griff. You've got to get us out of here. We've got to go." It was Holly.

Clenching my teeth, I pulled up her number and texted: You're right. We've got to go.

BDREW: Atta girl.

CHAPTER EIGHTEEN

SHUT UP. SHUT UP. SHUT UP.

Griffin saw the determined look on my face. "We'll finish the paperwork tomorrow. Give Peanut one more bag of IV fluid. Both dogs ate
dinner tonight, which is big. They hadn't been eating well." He had his
hands in his front pockets and looked like he was in professional mode.

"Good." I rubbed my hands on my thighs. "Can you drive me
down to the cabin? I have to talk to the others."

He nodded, and as we walked into the dry evening air, he said,
"You'll need dog food. I'll give you a kit with insulin, et cetera. I'll make
a list and get their meds and supplies together."

We made our way down the canyon, the tires bumping in the ruts.
"Thank you so much. I know we haven't been the most gracious group."

The van banked as he pulled into the gravel drive, the headlights
hitting the sagebrush. "You're wrong there."

I never knew what to do with a compliment, and my shyness inten-
sified; I didn't know how to react to Griffin's attention. "I wish we had
more time here, but I also wish we could leave tonight."

"Me too," he said, and I stole a glance at him. It was nice to be
liked for something other than being a responsible parent at bake sales.
I wondered how much I was creating in my head.

I slid out of the van, and the dark night covered me like a cloak as the lights of Griff's van swung away and receded. I walked toward the front door of our cabin, the grinding gravel and occasional chirp and rustle of wildlife the only sounds in the air. I smelled cigarette smoke, and as my eyes acclimated, I saw the outline of Summer, seated at the café table on the front porch.

"You smoke? Summer, I am seriously shocked."

"Don't judge. You think it's easy to look emaciated for the paparazzi every day? You have to smoke to make it work."

Holly would have pointed out that there were no publicity hounds at Best Friends trying to catch Summer the celebrity being *just like us. They hug puppies!* But I was nicer than Holly. Clearly.

Summer offered me a cigarette, and I said, "No, thanks. Is Holly in there?" I gestured to the cabin door.

"Yup." Summer texted and held it up for me to read.

Holly get your ass out here.

"You're brave, Summer."

I saw her lift her chin and exhale out of the side of her mouth. "So, the vet, huh? Solid choice."

"I'm rolling my eyes at you."

"Why? Why not have some fun? You're away from home. Stuck here. No responsibilities. Single. You could do worse than the vet. My guy at the pig house grew a beard. I barely recognized him." She took another puff on her cigarette. "Did you know that all potbellied pigs grow up to be full-blown porkers? That's why they end up here. The potbelly grows up to be a full-on pig, and people give up their beloved, smart, hungry pet." The night breeze shifted, the cigarette smoke returned, and Summer waved it away. "But we were talking about you and the vet."

"Should I let him have his way with me on one of the exam tables?" Drew, not Griffin, popped into my mind, and I didn't chase him out.

"That might be chilly, but sure. Why not?"

"I was kidding! Oh my God." I was glad she wasn't looking at me; my face felt warm.

"I never kid about sex. Sex is wizardry that keeps the old lady parts fresh. If you can get a young man, their jism is magic. It's the fountain of youth."

"Rein it in, Summer. I am not going to sit out here and talk about sperm and how I should be using it in my skin care regimen."

"Not on your skin, girlie. Sex with a young guy is like a shot of stem-cell sorcery right in your hot pocket."

"The mother in me can only think of a safe sex reply about condoms." But that wasn't true; I thought about Drew's hands on my phone.

Two cabins down, an outside light came on, and a man emerged with a dog on a leash. He walked in a circle with the large buff-colored dog and then went back inside, leaving the light on.

Summer said, "You can adopt an animal for a night if you want as a trial run before you bring it home. It's like animal Tinder if you ask me, but who am I to judge? Have you ever tried e-dating?"

"I don't date." I knew I sounded as if I'd rejected something more outrageous than swiping on a phone screen and having a cup of coffee with a man. I realized this was not an inappropriate question, and I softened my response. "Men don't ask me out. I rarely speak to single men. If a single man, say, delivers a package from Amazon, he sure doesn't look at me for anything other than a signature. I deal in married men, parents, and teenage girls." After my speech I said sheepishly, "Although I do think Griffin likes me."

"And the blind can finally see." Summer lifted her hands like a preacher. "Things have changed, no?" She stubbed out her cigarette and slipped it into her ever-present bag. I didn't object. Things were changing.

Holly pushed her way out of the cabin and said, "What do you want, Summer?" To my amazement she saw me and moved toward us, not away. She wore a pair of clean jeans and didn't look tired or annoyed. I dropped my shoulders, relieved. A truce?

"It's time for weed, my friends," announced Summer. "And don't give me the shocked *country girl* response, Sam. You're gonna take a puff of this pen and relax. If you say no"—she lowered her voice to a stage whisper—"I'm leaving you alone with Holly for the rest of the trip."

"I heard that." And damn it if Holly didn't say it with a wry smile.

When Summer handed me the slim, almost-weightless pen, I shrugged and gave her this victory. It was easier than sex with the vet on his exam table. I inhaled and coughed like the amateur I was. I didn't even care. I wasn't here to be anyone I wasn't, and I sure wasn't a cool pot-smoking quick-sex-haver.

"Your turn, Holly," she said, and I watched Holly inhale.

Jeff and I had smoked the traditional doobie with a roach clip in college. That was before weed quality control. Weed is a spa experience these days, and I immediately felt relaxed and calmly dizzy.

I kicked out the metal chair for Holly, and she sat, looking looser than she had the whole trip. She sat equidistant from Summer, and I felt a new, hopeful quiet in her presence.

Summer squinted at me. "What do you do for fun, Sam? You know, when you're not taking care of somebody."

I made a face. "I'm not always a mom." Knowing that wasn't even close to true. "I belonged to the Friends of the Library Book Club that should have been called Gossip and Netflix with the Girls. Our book discussions lasted maybe a minute—the group wasn't a literary sort." I gestured for another hit.

"Hells yeah, Sam!" Summer handed the pen over.

I inhaled. "The group mostly wanted to talk about the book covers or if they wanted to be friends with the protagonist. Marjorie, the youngest of the group, listened to all the books on her speakerphone and lamented authors who used too many cusswords. She said that her kindergartner, Peter, who had terrible adenoids and sounded stuffy year-round, had started saying, 'Mom, I want some more ducking rice.' And 'Where is ducking Buzz Lightyear?'"

Summer laughed and took a hit. "That's the question for the ages. Where is mother-ducking Buzz Lightyear?"

"Mostly the group talked about what show we were binge-watching and how hot Idris Elba is."

"Right? Smoking hot!" said Summer.

"No argument there. He is gorgeous," said Holly.

I let myself enjoy that second of agreement from Holly before saying, "After several glasses of wine, one night the conversation turned to vibrators."

"As it so often does with book clubs," said Summer.

"You guys, I don't own a vibrator."

"Not even a little one?" Holly asked.

"Nope. I shut that part of my life down with Jeff."

Summer sat up, serious now. "You have not had an orgasm since your husband died two thousand years ago?"

"Well, no. I mean. Sometimes I have one accidentally when I'm sleeping. I have this great recurring dream with Dwayne 'The Rock' Johnson."

"Accidentally?" Summer was doing the interviewing but Holly was listening.

"Spontaneously, I should say." I knew I was high now, or I'd never have said this out loud.

"God, your body is trying so hard to live, and you are shutting it down on a daily basis. But why?"

I didn't hesitate, which is why I don't do pot on a regular basis. It's like truth serum. "Twenty years ago I said *I do*, but I didn't, and then he died."

"And?" Holly exhaled smoke into the night.

"I don't know."

"Yes, you do," Summer said, not bothering to look at me. Her wise and childlike face lifted to the stars.

"Okay. I've thought about this a lot." I closed my eyes, and without thinking it through, I said, "It was a reprieve, but maybe it was also the punishment. I don't know if I have what it takes to start or finish a new relationship. I don't have the skills. Either way I looked at it, I made myself miserable, and I'm being careful not to make myself miserable again."

"Oh yeah, you do seem happy living between wanting everything and running away," said Holly, but not with her usual rancor. She said it like old, funny sarcastic Holly. The one who liked me.

"Hey," I said and swatted her arm. And we both stared at each other. Holly and me.

Then Summer slapped me, and I let out a whoop and dodged her. A dog let out a bark, and someone from one of the cabins shouted, "Go to bed."

Summer widened her eyes, and we laughed at the admonishment. The dog lover who wanted other animals to go to sleep and stop messing around.

"Not to be a buzzkill, but it's time to get out of here," I said.

"Agreed," Holly said and rested her head on the nearby stucco wall of the cabin. "Let's make a list of things we need from Griffin."

"Done."

We were all quiet for a few moments, and Holly pointed to me and said, "Time to get this ho on the oad," and we laughed until we got yelled at again.

———

The next morning I woke after a restless night sleeping with Summer in a double bed. My thoughts went instantly to Katie and getting Peanut to her. Holly lay under the covers, and I rolled to my side and watched Summer, already dressed, smearing lotion on her arms.

"Good. You're awake. I've signed you guys up for volunteering. We have to attend a quick orientation, and then we can go to our posts."

"Nope," Holly said, as if she'd been up for a while. "I'm not doing that."

"Yup, you are. I've signed you up. This place runs on volunteers. If you don't show up, they won't have enough help."

I had to hand it to Summer. She read the tidy, groomed, hyper-responsible Holly and saw who she was at her core. Holly would never, ever back out of a commitment, even if she hadn't committed herself. I was starting to think Summer was from a higher power to screw with us.

"I put you in the cat house for obvious personality similarities, Holly. Sam, I'm sorry to say that there were no spots in Dog Town or the Bunny House, so you're in with the parrots. You'll love it. They are crazy cool."

Holly said, "Where are you volunteering, then?"

"The pigs, of course."

"Why 'of course'?" I said.

"They're obsessed with food. I'm obsessed with food. Plus, my guy is over there. He gets me pig privileges."

"I don't want to know what pig privileges are," I said.

"I wouldn't tell you. You wouldn't understand."

———

We went to a quick orientation with a roomful of other volunteers . . . a trio of women in matching shirts, a married couple who held hands through the film on animal safety, and a man with a white ponytail who was eager to interact. "Your first time? I've volunteered sixty-five times. I like the bunnies best, but lots of times I go to the cat house."

I was about to make a joke about cat houses and hookers, but Summer elbowed me. I glanced at Holly, who was texting but smiling, and I had the feeling she was smiling at the people in the room, the oddball collection that we were a part of. Even after all these years, I knew what Holly was thinking. We thought the same things were funny, and although Holly was not aware of my connecting us in the moment, I felt closer to her.

After we finished, the volunteer van dropped us at the top of the canyon, and we separated. I watched Holly stroll to Cat World with her hands in her back pockets, which I knew meant she was feeling shy. My heart pinched for her, the usually bold Holly out of her familiar role of being in charge of everyone. Seeing her from the outside like this was like peering at your hometown after being away. All the sights generated mixed feelings of curiosity, melancholy—and in the city that was Holly—the grief and confusion of our loss.

"Have fun with the kitties, Holly," I said, but not loud enough for her to hear me.

I walked to the Parrot Garden with a married couple who had met one another volunteering and came back every year on their anniversary. Cheryl and Joel were from Phoenix and drove an RV that had all the comforts of home. They were volunteer pros, if there was such a thing.

"Samantha, is it?" Cheryl said. "Remember—you can't put the parrot dishes in with the cockatoo dishes. You can't cross-contaminate any of the dishes. Remember, no cross-contamination."

I nodded. As we got closer to the birds, their shrieking became louder, and I looked at my companions for any sign of alarm. Joel opened the door, and an earsplitting squawk came from somewhere in the building.

"Yikes. If we were out in the world and a person was yelling this loud, we would call 911," I said, laughing.

Cheryl and Joel exchanged looks, and through pursed lips Cheryl said, "They're just talking to each other."

"No, I know. I was just joking."

I felt a tug at my elbow and heard Griff say, "Cheryl, I'm borrowing Samantha."

Married Cheryl turned her frown upside down when she saw Griff. "Anything you say, Doc." She beamed.

A bird shouted, "Shut up. Shut up. Shut up!" and Joel said, "Okay, Romeo, that's enough."

When we were out of earshot, I said, "Cheryl likes you."

"She is an exacting volunteer," Griff said, dodging my observation. "I saw you were signed up to help in here. I think you need a Best Friends experience that has more romance than the Parrot Garden."

Romance? How to feel? How to handle? Must make a joke. "But Romeo," I said.

"I promise I'll get you some one-on-one time with Romeo," he said.

"Please tell Romeo my true love is ice cream." I tried a hearty laugh, but it came out cartoonishly loud while my mind was turning over the thought *maybe?*

CHAPTER NINETEEN
NICE LADY

Griff and I hiked across the parking lot and over the dusty terrain to the now-familiar veterinarian clinic. "Visitors often think volunteering here is all about playing with puppies and petting kitties, but we need the most help with cleaning cages and general upkeep. The volunteers keep this place going. I don't know what we would do without them."

Okay, I thought reasonably. He's charming to all the volunteers to soften the blow of giving them dull jobs. A golf cart driven by a young woman with a gray stocking cap and a springer spaniel riding next to her bumped by. The dog's ears flew behind him, and his mouth was wide open in a smile. The cart hit a divot, and the woman's arm shot out and made sure the dog was secure.

When we entered the clinic, I was the only volunteer with Griffin. And I considered Griffin again. Why did I care what he thought of me? What anyone thought of me?

A staff member, a small man with glasses, stopped Griffin to ask about supplies for the clinic. I watched them speak, tried to puzzle out what was going on with me. If Maddie had been here, I could have focused on a teachable animal moment, or made sure she knew where to get lunch. But she wasn't, and I had the time to think about me.

Another staff member pushed out of the clinic and saved me from the reverie. "Hi, Marcy," Griffin said. The woman stopped, fished a note out of an apron pocket, and held up a laminated card I couldn't read. She wore canvas shoes with *Vegan* written on the top of each one. Griff read the message on the card. "Clinic, then Dog Town," he said.

The woman turned to me and held up a different card for me to read. It said, *I won't speak until the animals can.*

"Oh," I said.

She had a defiant look on her face, then she turned an invisible key at her lips and stalked off.

"She doesn't talk?"

Griff took a deep breath and said, "This is a great place for people with strong convictions."

My phone buzzed as we moved into the clinic, announcing that we were in the real world, despite feeling on the edge of it.

I peeked at the texts. Maddie, right on cue.

MADDIE: What should I do with my day off?

The twin zing of worry and delight buzzed through me. I had no idea how to answer my daughter. Had I taught her to ask for suggestions rather than to dial into her own wants? What I wanted to do was focus on what was happening right this minute. Was Griff interested in me? Was I interested in him? Awake. I felt awake.

"I haven't been here long, and already the outside world is moving way too fast. Asking for too much."

"That's what happens. I thought I'd be here just to heal, but I can't imagine jumping back into the regular world."

MADDIE: Yoo hoo

ME: I can't right now.

MADDIE: Rude, mom

And I didn't reply.

When Holly blasted into the clinic, I was busy folding laundry, trying to be zen about this day delay. I had just decided to FaceTime Katie—I needed to see her smile, assess her color, and reassure myself. I found a place to prop my phone, but, as if in slow motion, I felt the door whoosh open, saw Holly's panicked face, and heard her high-pitched shout. "Help!"

Holly had less of a mad-at-Sam look and more of a this-is-a-real-emergency expression. It was shocking to see the always sardonic and composed Holly rattled, but I was relieved that I hadn't caused this particular crisis.

The clinic door slid shut behind her, and she shouted louder this time, "Hey!" while cradling a blanket in her arms. Griff moved with unruffled certainty, and a vet tech put her arm around Holly's shoulders and said, "This way."

Holly said, "Help it."

Griff took whatever Holly held with practiced gentleness and placed the bundle onto the stainless steel exam table. A warm overhead light clicked on. Gently, Griff plucked the soft fabric aside.

Holly stood, wringing her hands, her face white as a paper cup. "I don't know what happened. He was fine literally one minute ago."

Griff said, "Fill me in."

"I was in Cat World like I was supposed to be. There were pans to clean. I had been petting Fluffer Nutter in the Community Cat room earlier. I've never had a cat. I don't know how to pet them. Is there a way to pet them?"

I peered at the bundle and said, "Fluffer Nutter?"

"I touched his back; he flopped over. Then something came out of it. A huge moving blob of poop came out of it."

"A moving blob?"

"Of poop," she said with increasing volume. Holly grabbed my arms and with wide, frightened eyes said, "It was horrible. He made this horrible mewing sound like someone had his tail in a door or something. I grabbed the first towel I saw, wrapped him and the poop up. I didn't look. I just brought him here. I couldn't find my staff person. I couldn't find her!"

I rubbed Holly's forearm, something I hadn't done since she was a drunken, emotional college student who threw up chili in the dorm sink after drinking too much red wine.

"I'm sure you did the right thing."

"The noise he made."

"He's quiet now, though. You did the right thing."

"Is he dead?"

I put my arms around her shoulder, and it felt so good. I said, "I'm sure he's not dead. Nobody dies from pooping."

I knew what Maddie would say watching this interaction. She'd say, "Mom, why are you so nice to Holly when she's so mean to you?"

The answer was so simple. I wanted her to love me again. I knew it was piteous. Maybe it was part of that weird thing we humans do. We only want to be a member of the club that won't have us. Maybe it was my almost-desperate need to be liked, and here this person was, wildly, aggressively not liking me. But when Holly was vulnerable and needed somebody, I just wanted to comfort her, and I wanted her friendship because despite everything, I still loved her.

"Let's go over and see Peanut."

"Peanut?"

"Katie's dog? The reason we're here?" I tried to guide her toward the room where I knew Peanut and Moose lay quietly together, but she resisted. A young woman in blue scrubs said, "She's having her babies. Fluffer Nutter is a mama."

"Well, that explains it, Hol. She was pregnant."

"He's pregnant?"

"She is. Fluffer Nutter is a she."

Holly gaped at the table, at Griff and the kitten. "I moved her. Midlabor, I picked her up."

"You picked up the baby too. They're doing fine though, right?" I said.

The woman smiled and nodded.

Holly looked at her hands and shuddered. "It looked so gross. And it was a baby? Babies aren't gross."

Griff laughed. "If you're not used to seeing this kind of thing, it's definitely gross."

"I almost passed out," Holly interrupted him.

"Okay. Let's get you a chair." I steered Holly to a tall stool.

"You were so good with Maddie when you delivered her."

Surprise washed through me. I was so eager for any positive morsel tossed my way from Holly, but it stunned me when it happened.

Katie had been by my bedside and called Holly to come and bring her a change of clothes in case she had to stay the night. Holly came in at the worst possible moment. Right at the second when Maddie slithered out of the birth canal and into the doctor's arms, followed by every other drenching membrane that came with birth.

But then she left.

"You were so dignified. It was so wet. All of it. So oceanic."

"That's one way to describe it."

Holly shook her head. "So much of everything. Wetness, pain, stretching. I couldn't take it. Katie stayed right by your side. Held your hand, remember? I had to go."

I'd thought for so many years she had walked away in indifference. Now, seeing that Holly had been overwhelmed, not detached, I wanted to soothe her, to tell her it was okay. It would overwhelm anyone. "I remember you brought me two roast beef sandwiches for after."

"I was going to drop them and leave, but I froze. I wanted to stay, but I was worthless. You don't know this, but in the hall I got super dizzy and had to lie on a gurney. Somebody had to get me off it. It was for someone going to surgery. I threw up in my coffee."

"I had no idea?" I knew I sounded incredulous, but I remembered nothing. During the delivery I'd had drugs and couldn't process what was happening around me. Afterward I didn't have time to think of Holly. I was too busy bonding with Maddie. Now here we were, Samantha and Holly, talking like old friends.

"I can't handle all this." She waved her arms around the clinic. Pointed to Griff, the cat, the exam tables with their large overhead lights. "This. Hospitals. All of it."

It occurred to me then that what I was seeing was Holly's future labor-and-delivery stage fright. She was worried for Rosie. Scared she would identify the baby as moving poop and freak out.

My tender feelings for Holly had me responding, "You and Rosie will be great. You rise to every occasion. You two seem to be able to do anything you want."

Holly snapped her head up, eyes lit from within, furious. "What's that supposed to mean?"

I stepped back, bumped into one of the cold examination tables. "You're good at everything."

"That's not what you mean, though. Rosie and I are just as able and qualified to be parents as you and Jeff."

"I know that." And I did. Of course I knew that.

"Do you? I don't think you do. I think you're pissed at us. Me. I think you don't believe a child should have two moms."

"What are you talking about, Holly?" I said so loudly that I shocked myself. "I was a single mom. Two moms would be much better than one mom." I flashed a look at Griff, who didn't seem at all alarmed by the drama on the table or from the two women getting into it in front of him.

"But you did have a man at one time."

"What are you getting at?"

"Your thinly veiled homophobia."

"My what?" I laughed bitterly at the ridiculousness from a woman who should have known better.

"Yeah, except it's not so thinly veiled, is it?"

I backed away from Holly, but she stepped into the argument. I planted my feet and said, "Is this about graduation night? You can't still be angry about Mike."

"You don't like us, do you? Rosie and I. Us as a concept. Us as a couple."

"You know that's not true." I wasn't even angry at the notion. I didn't feel defensive, but I did feel misunderstood. "This is why you hate me? This made-up thing you have in your head about my being homophobic?" I should have been angry about the label, but instead I felt deeply hurt, saddened. I wanted to understand her thoughts, what had I said or done that was so obviously insensitive.

"Hate? How could you even say that to me?"

I felt wobbly, and my edge of sharp understanding began to dull with fatigue. I tried to clear my head and said, "I have never understood what happened to our friendship. I never thought you were disgusting. Mike was a jerk. Is this what we have to get over to be friends again?" I hadn't heard my voice this shrill in years. I knew I was stepping into it. And I didn't care. I wanted it over. All the tiptoeing, all the shame of feeling responsible for this great wrong in my life and having no way to right it.

The barking started low and almost conversationally. I heard it but had more to say before the lights of my focus succumbed to darkness. I lightly slapped both cheeks. I would not take a pass on this. I would stay awake.

"I'm sorry you're not prepared for the grit of childbirth, but you can't take out your fear on me." A series of louder whines followed the lower rumble.

"You will never be ready to talk about anything, Samantha. Everyone who knows you knows that." A sharp series of dog complaints filled the air, and Holly added over the din, "And don't think for one minute I'm not ready to be a parent."

"Stop it, Holly. When did you get so ruthless?" I wished it had come out stronger. But I was feeling a wash of sleep-disordered fatigue that was all-consuming. I imagined it was the same for an epileptic who felt a seizure coming on and was not able to stop it. If I could get a glass of cold water. Maybe that would help.

"I swear to God, Samantha, if you're going to pretend to fall asleep right now—"

That did it. "Stop it! You're a bully, Holly."

I needed to sit somewhere. Put my head down, clear my thoughts. The dog barking, Holly, it was all too much. I felt an arm around my shoulders and another at my waist and heard Griff's voice. "Holly. Go calm Peanut down. Samantha, you come with me."

I looked over my shoulder and glimpsed Peanut standing on his hind legs, howling. Moose stood on all fours, emitting a series of high-pitched, staccato yips. I felt more supported by those two dogs in that moment than almost anyone in my life. It was clear Holly had no idea how to calm down the chorus of animals, but for once she did what she was told. I saw her move to the kennel, her hands out in front of her, saying something I couldn't hear.

"She's so . . ." I struggled to label her in the way she had labeled me. "She's so mean," I said like a kid on the playground to the teacher who had come to rescue her.

———

Griff guided me to his office, set a tall glass of water in front of me, and left me alone. I'd have given anything for one of my pills. If I took one just before I fell asleep, I'd wake in twenty minutes feeling like a superhero. Normal humans called this a coffee nap, but mine would more appropriately be called a speed nap. I drank the water, rested my head, and fell sound asleep.

When I woke, it was as if my thoughts were a child, waiting for me to reengage. *Homophobic? Am I homophobic? Is there a Google quiz on this? I mean, I'm sure I have prejudices I don't even know I have, but homophobia? No,* I thought. *I'm not.* But maybe that was exactly what homophobic people thought. There had to be types of homophobia exhibited by well-intentioned people who didn't understand their own biases. Was that me?

I shifted my position, closed my eyes, waited for the relief of my thoughts. I blinked. When did she come to this conclusion? When did Holly decide that I was against what she was at her core?

I dialed Katie, and she picked up on the first ring. "Hey, Nugget," I heard myself say with delight at resurrecting our bond with one word.

"What's wrong?" Katie examined my face for the distress I thought I'd ironed out before I'd rung her.

"Nothing! One more day here. The vet says we can leave, and boom. On the road."

She wagged her head disappointedly. She knew me inside and out. I could hide nothing.

"Holly said I'm homophobic."

"You're not homophobic." Boom. No preamble. Just real talk, real support, in real time.

"I don't think I am. Maybe I said something once that was insensitive? I'm sure I did. Who doesn't?" I thought about it. "You, I guess. She talks to you, so she doesn't think you're homophobic."

In college Holly's sexual orientation wasn't a question. She dated guys, and later never came out as far as I know. "One minute she was in New York alone, and the next she was in New York with Rosie, and then when she called and it was, *my wife and I*," said Katie. I heard the frustration I felt in her voice.

"Okay, Katie, it's all so pointless." I felt like I did when my dad was yelling at me, making me feel like I couldn't get away from the reprimands, and if I tried to defend myself, his anger would intensify.

"Are you going to make her talk about it?"

"Make her? Have you tried to make Holly do anything?"

"You'll have the time in the car. Maybe you two can talk. You're going to need each other." Katie sounded worn out.

I held my breath. "What's going on?"

"I'm not in remission anymore." Her voice took on the false pluck of a girl who just didn't care that she didn't make the cheerleading squad. She was going to continue to do cartwheels just the same.

I clutched the phone. "Oh, Katie." I pulled the sleeves of my sweatshirt over my icy hands. I had known this was coming, the petechiae, the red marks on her legs. "Like the last time, right? Did they say this is like the last time?" Already I was planning: We'd get the cold cap for her hair. We wouldn't forget to ask for the nausea drugs early this time. Dum-Dum lollipops, only the red and purple ones. I'd stock up on rice cakes to settle her stomach. My thoughts raced, my body itching to run to her side, to start the process of saving Katie.

I heard a woman's voice. Katie said, "Sam, I've gotta go. The nurse is here. I have to get in the shower, then some tests."

"Wait. I need more information." I heard the anguish in my voice. This was not the voice of a confident person. It was the voice of a person who knew this time was different, worse.

"There isn't anything yet. I'll call you as soon as I know more."

"I am coming home," I said, standing, shoving my chair back into the wall. "I'll be there as soon as I can. I'm just going to get Peanut and drive."

"Don't speed," she said. "I gotta go."

The phone went silent.

There was a short rap on the door, and Griff poked his head in. "How are you feeling?"

Wild eyed, I said, "I'm so sorry we brought all this to your sanctuary. Can I pack whatever Peanut needs so we can go first thing tomorrow?"

In a calm voice Griffin said, "Everything is ready. He's going to get his final dose of meds and his last bag of fluids tonight. I'll have him bathed with Moose and ready when you wake in the morning. There's three of you. You can drive all night."

"What can I do?" I heard my voice crack, but I said it again. "What can I do?"

Griffin took a beat, then said with care, "Let's get you back to your cabin."

CHAPTER TWENTY

DON'T BE MAD

I launched myself out of the van and stumbled across the pea gravel to the front steps of the cabin. The door stuck, and I had to kick the bottom of it so when it opened into the cabin, I tumbled inside. Summer was washing a cup at the sink, and Holly was in the midst of folding a white T-shirt. "I just talked to Katie." My voice sounded loud and frantic. "Holly." I said her name as a touch point, to get control of my emotion. "She's out of remission."

Holly's quiet reaction, a rapid blinking, told me she already knew about Katie. That was fine. I saw that I didn't care. In fact, if she knew, we'd be on the same page to get out of here with as little fuss and fighting as possible.

My bag lay on the floor, and I stuffed in my sweatshirt and a pair of jeans I'd worn the previous day. My toiletries were in the bathroom. I'd need those tomorrow. What else could I pack? "Do we have to strip the beds tomorrow? I'll check out and pay right away. Should one of us go to Kanab and get water, food for the rest of the trip?"

Summer put the cup down and said, "I can do that. Get us coffees. Something to eat. You guys settle up and get the dogs."

"Good. Yes, Summer. Thanks. That would be great. Holly? What did Katie say to you?"

"She didn't tell me anything useful. I don't think she knows very much."

I remembered how important it had been for me to know who Katie had called first when this all started. What pettiness. Such a waste of time. In the past when there was a crisis—Maddie's broken arm, Jeff cleaning out our accounts—there was always something to do. Get to the emergency room, go back to work. I could do, do, do instead of feel. Today there was nothing to keep me busy. Katie was gravely ill, Holly and our gulf were unresolved, and we were miles and miles away from getting Peanut to the hospital.

"How's Rosie?" I said, and Holly's face pinked.

"She's feeling good."

I nodded. "I need something to do."

"I know you do. There's nothing we can do right now. We will get on the road tomorrow and drive."

"Griffin is helping us. Peanut is out of the clinic. He's no longer in quarantine. Griffin knows what we need to get on the road."

"Good work, Sam." Holly's all-business face had less rigidness, more consideration.

My puppy heart, so eager for approval from its owner, skipped a beat and sped up, hoping, begging, for another pat on the head.

———

We spent the evening quietly. Even Summer was subdued. She offered us more weed but half-heartedly. We ordered a pizza. Ate it silently. Holly examined Google Maps, looking to save us minutes off our drive. I didn't want to talk to anyone other than the women in the cabin. I had no desire to contact Drew, tell Maddie and manage her anxiety, or commune with the horses. I wanted the morning to come.

When we shut off the lights, I heard every rustle and sigh while we took turns sleeping, waking, using the bathroom in the night. When the morning sun streamed into the cabin, I rolled to my side and saw Holly was already gone. I looked at the time on my phone. I felt less nervous, more resolved. Today was a *do* day. I knew how to *do*.

I stood, gathered my things for the shower, found my tennis shoes. Summer peered at me from under the covers. My eyelids felt gritty, but I felt more rested than I'd expected to.

"You Midwestern girls get to it, don't you? Holly out for her run at dawn, and she's already at Cat World volunteering. You off to get this show on the road." Summer sat up in bed; her right breast, as perfect as a teenager's, popped into sight, and she covered herself with the sheet.

"Are you naked? Are you naked every night?"

"That's kind of a personal question."

"You know Holly thinks I'm homophobic." I found this less important this morning. More silly and pointless than damning.

"I heard."

"Did she talk to you about it?"

"God, no. You two are the talk of the entire sanctuary."

"Are you serious?"

"Yup. You and Holly and you and the vet. Nobody needs Netflix with you two around."

"There is no me and Griff. Nobody thinks there is a me and Griff." The thought that others were watching this drama play out startled and embarrassed me. I'd striven to live so quietly. Here, my life was a show for others' enjoyment, when I didn't know what I was doing.

Summer stood, pulling the sheet off the bed with her, but not bothering to cover her backside. "It's like one big buzzing soap opera around here. 'Did the crabby one talk to the nice one? Did the nice one kiss Griff yet? Is the pretty one'—that's me—'going to stay at Best Friends after the crabby one leaves? Is Griff going to help them when Tom shows up?'"

Summer clapped her hand over her mouth and turned to look over her shoulder.

I froze. "Tom? Katie's ex-husband? He's coming here?"

"Don't get mad."

"What did you do?"

"I didn't have permission to take the camper."

"What? I saw Misty give you that folder. She waved to you as we drove away."

"Right! Misty said I could use it to pick up Peanut, but she texted me and said Tom was mad. It's his camper after all, not hers." Her eyes widened, and she said, "I fully expected to drive it back to her. But then you guys said we had to go to Utah and finish this caper."

I turned on her. "It's not a caper, Summer. None of this is a caper. This isn't fun for us. This is about survival! Don't you see that?" I grabbed her by the narrow shoulders, as if she were a child who needed focus. "What have you done?"

Summer looked stricken.

I dropped my hands, considered the implications, my mind sluggish without coffee. "You're saying we stole the bus?"

Summer tried to lighten the news with a nervous smile. "Turns out we did a bit. But I texted her that we were at Best Friends because Peanut got moved out of the California place."

I pointed my angry finger at her. "That's why Tom is on the way. He saw the camper was gone, and he knows where it is. Dammit, Summer. This isn't fun and games."

Summer gave me a panicked look. "Obviously when I texted Misty, I didn't think it all the way through." In a high voice she said, "I was trying to help. Make Misty understand why we didn't return the bus immediately."

"Is he coming with the police? Will Tom take the camper? How are we going to get out of here?"

Summer frowned. "Oh, that never occurred to me. The police." She dropped her sheet and pulled a T-shirt over her bra-less torso. "Misty didn't say anything about the police."

"Please stop making me ask questions and tell me what is going on."

As she quickly pulled on her shorts and slipped her feet into her flip-flops, Summer's eyes drifted to the window behind me. "Get down, Sam." She yanked my arm hard, and we dropped to our knees. "He's here."

I peered out the window. Tom climbed out of one of the sanctuary golf carts and waved a thank-you to the driver as the volunteer moved off. He walked in a wide arc around the camper. He looked tan and as fit as I remembered. I was sure the female California Invisalign crowd loved perfecting their blinding smiles with the Culver City dentist.

"It turns out Misty dumped Peanut while Tom was taking a big dental acupuncture course in Florida. She said she was sick of that dog moping around for his ex-wife, and one day she drove to the humane society and dropped him off. Then she felt bad and called Katie."

"Misty dropped off Peanut?"

"I told you that," said Summer, which of course she hadn't.

"I could strangle you, Summer." Furious, I added, "How could you not have told me all this?"

"Lots of times I don't know what to say, and I'm afraid everyone is going to be mad at me." She said this like a little girl, and my rage dimmed, but my resolve was not to be messed with.

Tom opened the sliding door of the bus and looked as surprised to see its internal transformation as we had been. I considered what to do. Should I race out, confront the man? I knew Tom, and if you went at him, he would fight you to the finish. He held all the cards in this situation. I needed Holly. She would know what to do.

"What else do you know, Summer?"

"Misty isn't all bad. She texted me that he was on his way. She hoped that I'd still have room for her on my new talk show despite this snafu."

"What talk show?"

"What?"

"What talk show did you promise Misty?"

Summer looked at me. "I don't have a talk show anymore, Sam. You know that."

I let out a groan of frustration just as Tom closed the side door of the bus. I couldn't see him anymore, but the gravel crunched under his feet as he moved to the driver's side of the vehicle. The door screeched open, and the bus listed with his weight as he crawled in the driver's seat.

"He's going to take the bus without even talking to us?"

"That's what quid pro quo is, Sam."

"Summer," I hissed, not wanting to alert Tom but wanting Summer to understand how serious this was. "He's taking our only wheels. How are we going to get home?"

"I thought I was helping! Misty thought Tom would be as happy as she was to see the last vestiges of that marriage. But she got it wrong." She was speaking quickly, trying to deflect blame. "Tom is still super pissed at Katie—you know, for whatever reason men are pissed at the women they divorce after they've been caught in an affair."

I watched Tom, my anxiety ratcheting up as our ride pulled out of the driveway.

"I'll stop him!" said Summer like an energized Tinker Bell, but I grabbed her by the arm and yanked her back. As if her bones were hollow, she ricocheted away from the door and crumpled next to me.

"We can't overpower him. We have to have a strategy. He's going up to get Peanut." I wrenched my phone out of my fanny pack and dialed the vet clinic number. I waited, and when the line connected it was the answering machine: "This is the Best Friends Animal Sanctuary Veterinarian Clinic. We are working with the animals right now. Please leave your name, number, and message, and we'll call you back."

At the tone I said, "Griff, this is Sam." I thought about what to say—there was no time: "Don't give Peanut to the man." I hung up.

Summer said, "Nice, Sam." And she gave me a closed-fist solidarity hand signal like we were part of a teamsters' picket line.

I slapped her hand down and said "Summer!" like I'd said "Maddie" a thousand times before. "We have to get up there. We've got to stop Tom." I pulled up Holly's number and texted her: Tom's here. Has Van. Peanut!! I hit send, and immediately I heard a buzzing sound. Holly's phone sat on the bedside table. "What? She always has her phone!"

"I texted my pig guy," Summer said, looking at her phone. "He said we can use a golf cart to get up there. But Sam. He's going to take Peanut. We can't stop him."

"That is not happening," I said. "Not happening!"

CHAPTER TWENTY-ONE

SUMMER SANDY

"Doesn't this thing go any faster?" We rolled up the canyon at a speed that felt so much slower than the blood rocketing through my veins.

Summer, to try to make up for her crap, leaned forward like a champ, willing the vehicle up the winding unpaved path. There were two roads on opposite sides of the sanctuary that led to the veterinarian clinic at the top of Angel Canyon. Tom surely had used the paved road, where the VW couldn't topple over into a canyon. We were on the shorter, rougher route.

What would we do when we got to the clinic? Confront Tom? Kidnap Peanut? Disable the camper? When we got up there, I'd go get Holly from Cat World. We'd need her firepower if we were going to go head-to-head with Tom.

"I'm going to fix this for you guys."

"Just go to the clinic. Try not to make things worse." She mewled like she'd taken a hit. "Summer, I know you were trying to help, but we can't lose Peanut. I'm not mad."

We pulled the golf cart into a side stall, and Summer bolted. She crouched and in a zigzagging pattern, like she was dodging sniper fire, ran to the clinic. If I hadn't been so pissed, I would have laughed.

I looked over my shoulder at the clinic and jogged to the cat house. I took the front steps two at a time, pushed the door open, and called out, "Holly?"

Cats draped on every surface, climbing tree, countertop, and armchair sat up with startled expressions as if to say, *Must you?*

"Holly Dunfee?" I turned a corner and ran into a volunteer cuddling the fattest feline I'd ever set eyes on. "I'm looking for a tall woman. Holly?"

The woman did not match my intensity and scratched the chin of the languorous cat. "Bossy? Kind of grouchy?"

"Hey," I said, suddenly defensive. "She came to help. She has her own ideas, sure . . . but"—I shook my head—*Keep going, Sam.* "Yes. Where is she?"

The woman said, "Maybe the cafeteria?"

"She eats only at mealtimes. It's not breakfast or lunchtime. She's not looking for snacks." I said the last sentence like I was Norma Rae protesting a textile mill. *She's not looking for snacks!*

"Whatever you say." I could almost hear her describing this encounter with the other cat ladies: *Dude, it was intense.*

I jogged a quick circle through rooms that resembled a grandmother's cottage: overstuffed chairs, chintz cushions, and a smell that might have been urine but could also have been soup. Holly was nowhere. I pivoted and charged out of the cat house. Summer left too long unsupervised was problematic.

At the clinic I eased open the side door. I heard Tom: "I realize you have procedures, but I'm sure you understand my position. My dog was erroneously donated. I've come to retrieve him."

From where I stood at the side entrance, I could see Tom facing off with Griff. Neither man saw me as I stood protected by the corners and equipment. Tom had his arms crossed, sleeves rolled up, and chin lifted. Griff was relaxed in his authority, unintimidated.

"I do understand, but we have a process for adoption."

"I'm not adopting this dog," Tom interrupted without rancor. "I'm reclaiming him." He looked around. "Where are the women who drove the camper?"

"He came to us quite ill," Griff said, ignoring the question.

"Oh, I get it." Tom smiled, part of the bro network. His wallet in his hand, he extracted a credit card. "You need your money. I get it. How much?"

This was what he'd been like with Katie: reasonable, logical, emotionless, and in the end, demoting all Katie's concerns to a matter of money. I remembered when he did that early in her health issues. He wanted to go fishing in Canada, and Katie had just had a suspicious pelvic exam. She'd asked him to stay until she was certain her mysterious bloating was nothing. Instead of staying and holding her hand, waiting with his wife for the results, he'd offered to send Katie and me to a spa for a long weekend while *we* awaited the results.

"Go wherever you think will help you feel better. Take Sam. Hell, take Sam and Maddie. She never goes anywhere without that kid anyway." He'd said this like I was needy and weak to want to be with my daughter.

I'd overheard all of it. I'd been in Katie's kitchen. We were filling baggies with Chex Mix for one of Maddie's bake sales. I'd had the impulse to rush into their conversation. Call Tom out on his selfishness. Instead, I continued putting the salty cereal mix into individual snack bags and pricing them. My conflict avoidance forever in attendance.

This time I wasn't going to stand around and do nothing. Katie needed Peanut, and even though we didn't have a leg to stand on, at least we could put up a fight. This time my *I* was a *we*, and if Holly, Summer, and I weren't exactly an army, we were definitely a noisy quorum.

I straightened, took one step toward Tom and Griff, and thought, *Shut up and join the fight, Sam.*

———

Before either man saw me, a barking frenzy broke out. Two staffers held the clinic doors wide while Summer strode through them, restraining four enormous Great Pyrenees dogs. She looked like the goddess Diana holding back remarkably friendly hounds of hell. Each animal had the full white-toothed grin of the Pyrenees breed, and each dwarfed Summer's diminutive but regal posture.

I stepped behind a post, looking on in horror when I realized that Peanut was among the others. He was smiling but looked notably less luxurious than the other dogs. His fur hadn't grown back around his face and ears, and more than one spot on his torso had a raw patch of spotted pink skin showing.

Two veterinarian volunteers took hold of the leashes alongside Summer, who wore the blue lab coat of a veterinarian assistant. I was about to join the great white parade, try to reason with Tom, but Summer warned me off with an *I've got this* expression that froze me to the spot.

My heart broke for the innocent Peanut, who had the same beaming smile as the other grand canines. He had no idea he was about to become a bargaining chip. Katie's flushed face came to mind, the feel of her warm, soft temple when I kissed her goodbye.

Summer spoke not in her familiar breathless California girl voice but like the other professional staff at the sanctuary. "Hello, Dr. Griffin. I understand you wanted us to deliver the Pyrenees that came in from California. I wasn't sure if there was a particular dog you wanted, so we brought them all. We're cleaning the kennels. It's our time for controlled exercise."

Griff did an excellent job containing his surprise. The dogs' heavy panting and occasional yips gave everyone a minute to catch up. Summer smiled a radiant smile, and with that smile, Tom reacted presumably like many men had before him in Summer's life. He touched his full head of black hair and put out his hand.

"I'm Tom."

"Sandy," said Summer, brilliantly thinking to change her name. She handed Peanut's leash to Griff. It was like watching a clever vet-magic trick. The handoff, the intensity between Tom and Summer-Sandy. The baffled but game Griff and the guileless Peanut. How could I ever have doubted her?

Summer offered her hand to Tom, held his gaze, dropped her head, and batted her lashes. In the fist that still held a leash was Peanut's doppelgänger, give or take a tan hind leg and an inch in height. She was offering a different dog to Tom and banking on the guess that he wouldn't notice.

Breaking gazes with Summer only briefly, Tom said, "There's my good boy; there's my Peanut." He took the new dog's face in his hands and said, "I've been looking everywhere for you, buddy." Tom glanced at the dog before returning to Summer, who smiled charmingly.

The silent volunteer who had sworn off speech had just caught on to this case of mistaken identity. Her eyes darted between Griff and Summer, Tom and Peanut, and if she hadn't been holding the leashes of two other enormous, wiggling dogs, she would have flapped her hands in a version of sign language or grabbed a Sharpie, scratched out a message on her tennis shoes, and ruined the whole con.

"It's so fantastic that you want to take Peanut and nurse him back to health in your lovely home. Two women just left who were initially interested in him but didn't take him because of his bowel challenges," said Summer-Sandy.

While Tom loved being the hero and praised by a beautiful woman, the phrase gave him pause. "Bowel. Challenges," he repeated, and I could see him picturing what this kind of challenge might entail.

"Giardiasis," said Griffin. "It's a parasite. He's shedding it. He's on day two of getting metronidazole." I could see he was having fun, and that took some of my panic away.

"Doctor?" Summer said, glancing his way. "The mucus is less, don't you agree? But his stool is . . ."

"Copious."

"Abundant, I'd say; wouldn't you, Doctor?"

"Plenteous." Griffin nodded. "A marvelous green, though."

I cringed at the image but wanted to shout, *Plenteous!*

Summer nodded gravely. "It's a funky parasite, but we got it on the run." She punched the air with her arm. "Peanut isn't that bothered when he lets it go. We'll send a plastic tub with you so you can bathe him. We have buckets of a special shampoo that handles the odor well."

"Odor." Tom grimaced as if that was the biggest issue in this conversation.

"Most people want us to finish up his meds and have him shipped . . . ," Griffin said.

"Is that an option?" All of a sudden Tom was wildly interested in the best care possible for Peanut. "I don't want to rush him." The counterfeit dog moved toward Tom, and he stepped back.

"Sum . . . Sandy, can you help me?" Griffin said. "We'll get Peanut's records for Tom. Don't forget the rubber gloves and absorbent pads."

This was an impressive display of theater, and I felt deep admiration for the cast involved.

Alarmed, Tom said, "Pads. For the camper?"

The real Peanut lifted his nose and spied me hidden out of sight, behind the file cabinets. He barked two sharp barks and pulled on the leash to get to me. I put my finger to my lips to shush him and shook my head no.

Summer pulled a folder from under her arm. "I've got some of his records right here," she said, beaming.

I knew without a shadow of a doubt that was the folder that held the camper's registration, which she'd been carrying around in her bag this past week.

She held out the tattered folder and said, "The rest of the paperwork can be completed at the visitor center while we finish up with Peanut."

"Um. You know. I'm not in a rush." Tom pretended to consider an extremely difficult decision. "Maybe I should do what you suggest." He arranged his features to display compassion with sympathetic eyebrows and a careful frown. "Leave him here? Have him shipped."

I saw the audacity of the plan and watched with rapt attention.

Summer retracted the folder slowly, as if not to scare a skittish squirrel. "If you think that's best."

Summer and Griffin looked at each other, and Griffin added, "We have big bathtubs here for when things get nasty. You can finish the paperwork online, and we can have him delivered. We have transit vans that go back and forth to LA fairly regularly."

"Do you drive these vans?"

"I certainly could," said Summer pleasantly, seductively.

You could see Griffin was enjoying the fun parts of this escapade, but his ethics were being challenged. I adored every minx-like characteristic of Summer in that hot second and knew I would forgive her everything going forward.

"Tom," Summer purred, "it's going to be dark soon; you'll want to get on the road."

"I have to return my rental. I'm driving a different vehicle home." If he wondered why no one asked him about having two cars at the sanctuary, he didn't show it.

"Silly, we'll take care of all that. No problem. We do everything for our animals and their forever parents. You can rest easy." She rubbed his arm. "I'll walk you out. Get the rental car keys and paperwork, and you can hit the road." Summer slid her hand down the back of Tom's arm and chattered all the way out the door.

"Look at her go," I said, impressed.

CHAPTER
TWENTY-TWO

WILLY NILLY

The side door of the clinic clicked shut.

Griff and the silent volunteer turned their heads in unison to look at me. "What just happened?"

"Tom just got Summer Silva'd. That's what happened," I said, suddenly no longer the slightest bit angry at her.

Griff said to the mute volunteer, "I'm assuming no one is cleaning the kennels."

The volunteer shook her head no.

"Would you please return these dogs to their units? We'll keep Peanut. The real Peanut."

The mute volunteer shook her head with great disapproval, turned the dogs around, and walked out the front doors.

"I'm afraid to make a move," I said. "Do you think he'll figure it out?"

Griff crept across the shiny linoleum floor to peer out the smoked windows at Tom and Summer. I followed behind, touching the real Peanut's back, running my fingers through his long fan of a tail. "I guess Peanut doesn't look like himself," I said. "The other dog, what's his name?"

"Rambo."

"Rambo does look a lot like Peanut before he lost all his fur." I knew from approaching the windows for the last couple of days that it was easier to see out than peer through the smoked glass into the clinic. This afforded us some cover for viewing the goings-on.

Tom and Summer chatted, and she used every flirty-girl tool in the flirty-girl arsenal. She ran her fingers through her hair, touched her lips, brushed an invisible something off his shoulder.

"Look at her go," Griff said.

"Yeah."

Griff and I were so entranced by watching Summer hypnotize Tom that I didn't hear Holly enter the clinic until Peanut started to whine, and she said in a voice that was decidedly not part of a stealth operation, "What's going on?"

Griff jumped and let out a girlie scream. Holly had a tiny cat on her shoulder, the same cinnamon color as her own hair. When she saw who we were looking at, she said, "Is that Tom?" She took a step to the door, and I grabbed the cuff of her jeans and hung on.

"That's our bus!" Holly yanked against my hand. "Does he have Peanut?"

"No. Hol. Peanut is right here."

She glanced at Peanut, who sat with perfect posture next to Griff like he was getting ready for a photographer. "Is he taking our bus? Is Summer leaving with him?"

"Get down." I tugged at her leg, and she pulled back.

"Let go of me. That dick. I've got a few things to say to him."

She pulled so hard I slid toward her and felt Griff grab my waistband to anchor me. "Holly. Wait. Stop!"

I said it with such authority that Griff let go of my pants. Holly stopped pulling and peered at me. We must have been a sight. Two adults crouched beneath a window, spying at two *other* adults standing outside, an almost-bald dog panting at our sides.

"He came for Peanut. We told him Peanut had a parasite and was pooping everywhere. Summer and Griff convinced him to let Peanut get better, and after that she would deliver the dog to Tom. Summer showed him a different dog just in case he didn't go for it. Summer is getting him out of here." I saw Holly heard me, but the information didn't seem to cool her anger or change her plans.

"He thinks he can just come here and undo everything we've done. He thinks he's the only person with rights."

I held my breath. We were minutes from getting away with something, but it was clear I wasn't going to be able to dissuade Holly from confronting Tom. She had her hand on the door. In one second either Tom would turn his head and see her, or Holly was going to stride out like the High Plains Drifter and take him down.

"Holly," I said desperately, "if you're going out there, please give me that kitten on your shoulder first."

I felt the tension go out of her. She touched the kitten, and in that moment of softness, I added, "If he gets out of here, we can leave today."

The kitten on Holly's shoulder nuzzled her neck, and I saw Holly put the pieces together. "Peanut's not sick. Summer showed him the wrong dog."

"Keep your eye on the prize," said Griff. For some reason that struck me as funny, and I let out a hysterical giggle.

"He's going to leave him here," she said.

"Probably forget about him." I wanted Holly to see how crucial this moment was, but I couldn't get control of my laughter. I clapped my hand over my mouth, and my eyes teared up.

Griff nodded, and his shoulders started to pulse with suppressed glee. "This is all kinds of wrong," he said.

"Is this okay?" Holly looked at Griff, and he shook his head.

"We deny people pet adoption for all kinds of reasons. We aren't denying Tom anything, but he'll never have him delivered. No way. I can spot commitment issues a mile away." He said this like a balloon with a pinhole leaking air as he laughed into his sleeve.

I peeked over the windowsill. Tom opened the driver's-side door while Summer looked on. He turned toward the clinic, and Holly dropped like a stone next to us. She landed on my leg and clutched my arm. I grabbed her bicep, like I used to.

Neither Griff nor I could breathe, we were laughing so hard.

Holly smiled, and it looked like she might laugh too. If I could have, I would have held my breath. Then she let out a muted cackle, a fraction of the unbridled laugh from her college days. The kind that when she let it loose, people in the bar stopped drinking and looked on with their own private memories of happy times.

I stopped short of hugging her, but my aura reached out and circled her as if it were valentine red and filled with cotton candy.

Holly peered out the window. "He's in the cab. He just shut the door. The brake lights are on."

Griff and I pulled it together and scrambled so we could see out the window. Summer stood at the driver's-side door, Tom said something to her out the window. She smiled. He patted the door twice, and the camper rolled forward.

"Okay, but how are we going to get out of here if he takes the bus?"

"Summer has it figured out. We're going to drop off his rental in Kanab, and we can get one for us."

Summer gave us a surreptitious thumbs-up, but then the camper's brake lights flashed, the white reverse lights came on, and the camper crept back into position.

"Crap," said Holly.

"Hide Peanut!" I said.

Griff sprang into action. He took Peanut's leash and led him back into his old quarantine room.

Holly crouched next to me, and we watched Summer jump lightly onto the running board. It was easy to see her as her younger self, before life and time pushed the girl into a woman. A surge of affection for Summer bumped my anxiety up another notch.

Summer stepped off the running board and jogged toward us. She slammed into the clinic and shouted, "Shampoo! He wants the shampoo for home!"

Holly turned to me, and as if the word *shampoo* were the baton in a relay race, shouted at me, "Shampoo!"

I turned and was about to shout to Griff, but he rounded the corner at a sprint hugging a heavy plastic jug with a pump top.

Summer tossed Holly the rental car keys and paperwork.

Tom opened the camper door. "No! He's getting out of the bus," I said, thinking he really wanted to impress Summer. Make like he was a good guy.

Griff handed off the jug to Summer. It had to be heavy, but she bore it like Wonder Woman.

Summer waddled to the door, pushed her back against it, and moved into the sun in time to intercept Tom. He smiled and loaded the shampoo into the trunk.

"Get into the bus," I said.

"Get into the bus," Holly repeated, and I felt myself smile, and it was like no time or anger had ever lived between us.

Summer said something, and Tom handed his phone to her. I'd seen this in movies, so I knew what was happening before Holly said it.

"She's putting her number into his phone," I said.

"She is truly taking one for the team," Griff said.

We watched in wordless reverence as a Tinker Bell look-alike, master manipulator, got up on her toes and gave Tom the kind of hug no man would forget. She wrapped her long, slender arms around his neck like a high school girl at a nineties prom dancing to the theme from

Titanic. When she pulled away, Tom coughed, smoothed his shirt over his torso, and reluctantly stepped into the cab.

"Go home, Tom," Holly whispered.

Summer pointed down the canyon. We all held our breath and watched the camper's taillights until they were out of view. Summer turned, wiped her hands on her pants like she'd touched something foul, and walked into the clinic.

Holly started a slow clap, and we all joined in. One by one, in deep appreciation of Summer Silva, the girl weaned on the teat of the fake Hollywood screen kiss, we applauded. Unlike any love interest that ever existed, she brushed her hands together and without a smile said, "Do you think he bought it?"

I rushed Summer and hugged her.

She gave me a pat as if to say, *Okay, sweetie, we were never in danger.* "Oh, for sure." Summer held three fingers in the air and counted down. "And, three, two, one." The bird whistle that was Summer's text notification chirped. With a flourish, she pulled her phone from her back pocket and read. "And so it begins." She typed something.

Griff came up next to me and whispered, "What's happening?"

"We are watching what every reality show is based on. Who is the better player?"

"I am a mother trucker," Summer said and winked at us. "I just sent him a heart emoji. That is going to make him crazy."

"It will?" Griff asked. Summer looked at him with such unabashed pity even Holly sighed.

"I'll drive the rental car to Kanab, get us another vehicle," Holly said.

"Nope, I will," said Summer. "I got us into this. I'm getting us out. You and Sam have to adopt some dogs."

Holly had a shimmer that I hadn't seen this whole trip. These hijinks were what College Holly fed off. Even if she wasn't shining at me directly, I felt like I had helped bring her some of that joy.

Summer giggled with glee but got serious. "As soon as we get a few miles between us, I'll block his number, but I'll be able to track him. I turned on his location share on his phone." We waited and watched in wonder at the celebrity slash CIA operative in front of us. While I'd been learning that *lol* meant *laugh out loud* not *lots of love*, Summer had probably been planting cameras in her bushes and filming a reality TV series.

"If we adopt Peanut, does that trump any future ownership for Tom?" I asked Griff.

"Yeah. If you officially adopt him right now, he's yours."

Holly and I shared a glance that said, *Let's go!* And we bolted from the clinic.

———

Holly and I race-walked to the office of adoptions. The dry sand beneath our feet hushed our steps, and I felt the sun heat the back of my neck.

"Let's get the papers signed for Peanut and Moose and then see where we're at." I cringed at my accidental mentioning of Moose. I was sure to get pushback from Holly, and I didn't want to hear it. It was none of her business if I was bringing Moose home. I gave her the side-eye, and she looked determined and not mad; relief shot through me.

"Please tell me Summer isn't going to do something crazy," said Holly.

I wiped the sweat from my upper lip with the sleeve of my T-shirt. "I don't think she will," I said breathlessly, trying to keep up with Holly's long strides. "She knows she almost screwed this up for us."

No admonishment from Holly, no blaming me for bringing Summer along. We were going to get Peanut out of here and to Katie. We were working together without a fight. My heart whispered like an excited sorority girl, *OMG!*

Inside the adoption office, Holly pushed past me and spread her hands on the counter. "We need to adopt some animals," she said with the intensity of a parched cowboy approaching a barkeep and demanding a shot of whisky. "ASAP," she added.

The staffer said, "Yes! Griff called. I have the papers right here for Peanut and Moose."

"And Utah," said Holly. "I'm taking Utah with me."

The kitten that had slowed Holly down from confronting Tom was on her shoulder, the threadlike fluff of a tail curled lightly under her chin.

I wanted to examine Holly's face. This was not a development I had predicted. Instead, I said to the adoption staffer, "Okay. And apparently Utah." I drummed my fingers on the counter, wanting the laid-back woman to speed up and catch our turbo-charged energy.

Holly looked at my fingers. "What, Sammie. What? Only you can make a snap decision and adopt an animal willy-nilly?"

The staffer blinked, and I said, "Please allow my friend to adopt Utah willy-nilly." Holly lashed out when she felt vulnerable, and I let our shoulders touch to demonstrate, however subtly, unity.

The woman pulled out a form, and I watched her write *Willy Nilly* for the adoptive pet name. I considered correcting her for one-half a second, but decided instead to not say a thing.

I touched the map app on my phone. "Kanab, Utah, to Madison, Wisconsin, is twenty-four hours of driving. Three of us driving all night, we will be home by noon tomorrow."

"Three of us? Summer's not coming."

I stepped back, examined Holly's face. She looked like a little kid testing a parent, like she knew she was expected to protest, but there wasn't any conviction there.

"I think she'd like to come, and I hope that's okay with you."

"First Moose, then Summer? Are you that afraid to be alone with me?"

Instead of firing off a defensive comeback, I examined her face. Pragmatic but vulnerable Holly looked back at me.

"I'm not afraid to be alone with you, Holly." I did not look away.

Holly's expression didn't change, but she cleared her throat. "Three people is better. Also, we can shave off some time if we speed."

"Oh, we're going to speed, all right." I knew that for all our differences, we had the same goal in that moment. To get home.

———

It took an hour for Summer to get back, but she'd done the job. With our adoption papers in hand, we met her in the parking lot of the clinic. She had our luggage stuffed every which way in the trunk of what Holly and I simultaneously saw was a sky-blue Prius.

"Oh boy," I said. Three grown women, two dogs, and a cat would be stuffed into that sustainable vehicle all the way to Wisconsin. A clown car if clowns had dogs. I didn't dare complain; Summer looked proud, with a few strands of blonde hair stuck to her damp forehead and her cheeks flushed from exertion.

At the car, Summer whispered, "I think Griff likes you" and bumped me playfully with her hip.

I peered around for him, nervous, and saw him moving toward us. "It's nice to be liked. Get in."

Holly, with her long legs, moved out of the clinic, and we all stood back as Griff coaxed Peanut into the back seat of the Prius.

I skidded to a stop, knowing how readily Peanut passed out when faced with a tiny space. Griff, with steady hands, ushered Peanut toward the car. He said something we couldn't hear, and the dog stepped into the back seat and settled like a Victorian traveler waiting expectantly for the train whistle to blow.

"What the heck?" Holly said. "How did you get him in there?"

Summer dumped a bag of dog food into the trunk.

"We noticed he had trouble with small vehicles when he came, but we move animals around in golf carts. We had to get him comfortable. This thing he's wearing isn't a harness; it's a ThunderShirt, and that helps a lot."

"A ThunderShirt?" Holly asked, holding Utah close to her chest.

With surprising energy Summer heaved the last piece of luggage into the diminutive trunk, along with an empty ice-cream bucket and a milk jug of water. "It's that thing that came from Temple Grandin's research on reducing animal stress. You wrap them in a kind of Spanx, and they feel secure."

"She's right. Not Spanx exactly, but it's the same girdling principle," Griff said. "Plus, I put this pheromone ointment on his nose. Moose is with him. Peanut is ready for travel."

This was happening! I was more than ready to say goodbye to the sanctuary with a new roommate in the loyal and adorable Moose.

Griff hustled to my side, holding what looked like a man's travel shaving kit. He unzipped the case filled with syringes and insulin, and I steadied it. Our hands brushed, and we made eye contact. He wanted to say something to me, but while I felt his attraction, I didn't want to encourage it. I saw that I could enjoy someone, even feel attraction to them, but hold myself apart. That if someone showed interest in me, I didn't have to or wouldn't just slide into a relationship without making an active choice. Most of all, choice didn't have to entail a conflict, but it did require knowing what I wanted.

"What are you going to do if Tom completes the paperwork?"

"He won't. He doesn't want Peanut. We protect animals here. We do not hand them over to people who don't take care of them. Remember what condition Peanut came here in? Summer saved me from having a confrontation."

"Good. I'm glad. We wouldn't be happy if we'd compromised the ethics of you or this beautiful place."

"You have his feeding schedule and food. Try not to deviate from it. Under no circumstances should you give him one of those whip-cream cups from Starbucks."

With her kitten on her shoulder, Holly said, "We don't have cat food." She pivoted on her heel and jogged into the vet clinic.

"Not to be mean, but whenever she moves fast, she looks exactly like a daddy longlegs," said Summer.

"Have you tried NoDoz? For the sleeping thing?" Griff asked me. He pulled a plastic container out of his lab coat pocket, lifted the top with a pop, and extracted one oval capsule. "It might help."

"You *are* a full-service veterinarian, aren't you?" I asked, wanting to say something lighthearted but also as a segue to something deeper.

Summer's phone whistled, and she yelled, "Shotgun!" And dove into the passenger seat.

"I can't thank you enough for all you've done," I said to Griff. I considered offering my hand to shake and rejected that idea.

"I'd like to see you again," he said, his brown eyes warm and direct. "You should come back."

Summer stuck her head out the passenger door. "Get in, Sam. We gotta get on the road."

Griffin looked at the spot on my forehead that I'd heard other mothers call the elevens. The two vertical lines that developed after years of world-class brow furrowing from worry and trying to understand Common Core Math. With a calloused thumb, he brushed softly at the bridge of my nose. I closed my eyes, and he swept his fingers over my brow. It felt nice, but I felt no zing, no magic. Not like I did with the few moments I had spent with Drew, and we hadn't even touched. I wanted that for myself. Even if it wasn't with Drew. I wanted the rush and tumble of chemistry plus possibility.

Holly came scuttling out of the clinic, one hand on her shoulder anchoring Willy Nilly and the other clutching a bag of cat food and a cup. I smiled at the physical comedy of the legs, the kitten, and the determined look on her face.

He opened the door, and I dumped myself into the front seat. I lifted my eyes, my hand with the keys automatically finding their place in the ignition. Griff pushed the door shut and secured it with his hip. I tried to find the window control, only succeeding in locking and unlocking the doors in frantic succession.

The car swayed as Holly heaved the cat food into the trunk.

I finally got the window to roll down, and I said, "Thank you, Griffin. You're really something. But I don't think it's good for either of us to consider something so far away, on such a small time together. But I won't forget what you did for me here. Or what you do for these animals."

Griffin didn't look disappointed or hurt. Instead he seemed to understand and appreciate my candor. For my part, I realized that putting your thoughts and emotions into simple sentences was easier than building a life where those sentences would never have to be uttered.

At the front passenger-side door, Holly rapped hard on the window.

"Out, Summer. That's my seat."

I saw Summer silently mouth *shotgun*. Out loud she said, "We have got to go!"

Summer hit the door unlock, and Holly, without her usual outrage, slid into the back seat next to Peanut and Moose.

"I am not sitting with these two for long. It's like a hot, hairy, humid Roman bath for dogs back here."

"Griffin! Thank you for everything."

"Yes!" Holly said and stuck her hand out the window.

I hit the gas, and we were off.

"Turn right onto US-89 N." The GPS spoke, and Summer pinched the screen and said, "It looks like we're on 89 for an hour, but then it's I-70 for almost five hundred miles."

I calculated seven hours of driving during my leg of the trip. I wasn't sure I had the staying power for that many miles despite my resolve to pull my weight behind the wheel. I felt my arms sag, and Summer said, "I'm working on a driving schedule. You won't have to do this for too long."

I heard a telltale gagging from Peanut, a sound all dog owners are familiar with. A repeated hiccup-swallow sound that usually ended up in a pile of grass and undigested food.

"Peanut just threw up on my shoe."

"Are you okay? Should I stop the car?"

Summer hit the sunroof, sucking some of the odor from the car.

"No. Keep going," Holly said, but it came out, "No"—gulp, cough—"keep going."

"If you give Moose a minute, I'm sure he'll just eat it anyway," said Summer.

"Gross," I said and glanced at Holly. She looked pale but not too sick, considering.

"Way to hold it together!" Summer said. "Just fifteen hundred miles and twenty-two hours to go!"

CHAPTER
TWENTY-THREE
FIRE DRILL

I had a good long look at the map on my phone. We were leaving Utah soon on I-70 and would have to travel through Colorado, Nebraska, Iowa, and into south central Wisconsin. There were precious few turns, lots of similar climate and landscape—almost nothing stimulating.

"Let's call Katie." I pulled my phone forward. "Summer, hold it up so we're all in the screen." Summer rested her hand on the dashboard, and I hit Katie's number so we could FaceTime.

I heard Holly repositioning in the back seat. "Peanut, look alive. Moose. Not you. You're fine."

The phone rang and connected, and to my surprise Drew said, "Hi, Samantha," enthusiastically but also confusingly because he was lying down in a hospital bed. Had I dialed Drew? But, no. I hadn't. Drew had Katie's phone. The view shifted to Katie dragging an IV pole on wheels out of the bathroom. The thrill of our victory at Best Friends had my emotions sailing high, but the sight of Drew, so familiar and fun with Katie, slapped me back to reality.

"Katie's here." Drew's voice.

The ceiling came into view, and Drew groaned. "I was trying to fix the position of Katie's bed. We can't get the head of the bed at the right angle."

We.

Drew and Katie. I guessed that would be right. My valiant heart bucked up and said, *That's fine.* And I knew it would be.

"Hi, Katie!" Holly said. "Look who we have." Summer focused the camera so that Peanut's face obliterated everything else on the screen. I didn't know what expression was on my face, but I did feel a tinge of disappointment.

"Peanut," Katie squealed. "Hi, boy. Hi, lovie, it's me. Mama. What a good doggo, baby. Who's a good boy? He looks good, you guys. I mean, weird too. I've never seen so much of his face before."

Hearing Katie's joy made me feel so proud of all of us. Then she switched to the voice she used for Peanut that had a lisp. "Of courth you look handthome, Peanutty. You're my Peanut. You are the motht hanthome dog in the land."

Drew laughed, and Katie said over her shoulder, "What? You don't have a special language for your loved ones?" Drew repositioned again, and Katie slung her arm around his neck. "Thanks for sending Drew. He's terrible at Words with Friends and doesn't smell that good, but he knows where all the ice cream is at the hospital."

"I smell fine," he scoffed, then said, "Where's Samantha?"

"I'm driving, guys!" That felt nice, but I wanted to poke my head into the picture and see Katie's face.

"Is that wise?" Drew said. "I'm joking, Sam!"

"You look great!" said Holly, and I looked closely at my best friend. She did look pretty great. If a little greenish beneath her Revlon foundation.

"Drew's off tonight. He's bringing curry." Then abruptly the signal died, and we lost both of them.

"Get them back," Holly said, and Summer hit the screen several times in an attempt to reconnect.

"We must be in a dead zone," Holly said. "I'll text her. Tell her we'll call her when we're closer to a town."

I heard Peanut drop back onto the seat. Summer was uncharacteristically quiet. I felt Holly's hand on my shoulder, and I heard myself say, "Katie hates curry."

Summer propped herself against the passenger-side door to take both Holly and me in and said, "Okay. I know what you're thinking. Let's look at the evidence."

Holly's phone rang. Thank the Lord. I did not want to look at any evidence; I knew what everyone was thinking because I was thinking that too. Katie was not better.

Holly answered saying, "Marlene. Hi. Is something wrong? How's Rosie?"

Marlene was Rosie's mother, and Holly looked scared.

"Okay. Okay." She nodded like she was in the room with the woman on the other end of the phone. Holly flexed her jaw. "And her blood pressure now?"

I swung a glance at Summer, and we locked eyes. Summer touched my arm. "She'll be fine," she murmured.

"When can I talk to her? No, I understand. Tell her I know. I'm not at all worried. Please keep me posted and have her call as soon as she's able." Holly hung up and said, "Pull over. I'm driving."

Peanut sat up, and his globe of a head filled the rearview mirror.

"What's happening?" I said, trying to see Holly's expression. Worried.

"Samantha. Pull over now." Moose let out a yip. Peanut dropped his tongue like an anchor off the side of a boat and panted. I slowed the car, moved to the gravel at the shoulder of the road.

"You can't pull over here. There's no shoulder." Summer grabbed the steering wheel and shoved the car back onto the highway.

"Hey! Don't!" I pushed her tiny hands away from the steering wheel.

"There's a rest stop just ahead." A car whizzed by, the driver pressing the horn as it passed. Peanut let out three sharp barks, and Moose mimicked in a higher range.

"Hit the brakes. Sam, come back here. I'll drive," said Holly.

I braked again, guarding the steering wheel. Holly was the authority as always, but she had real anguish in her face that I wanted to soothe.

The car slowed to a stop, and I slipped the transmission into park. The driver's door was yanked out of my hand, and I climbed out of the car. All in now, Summer yelled, "Let's move, team! Get home."

Summer ran around the car and deposited herself right back where she'd been seated the whole trip, in the passenger seat.

I pushed Peanut over and flopped into the back seat. I felt the car move forward a few inches and screech to a stop. Both Moose and Peanut slid off the seat in a lump. I heard Peanut's teeth clink together as he hit his chin on the front seat.

"Where's Utah?" Holly looked as if she were on the verge of having a stroke.

I squinted at Holly from the back seat, and Summer had a confused look on her face.

"Utah! Utah!"

Summer pointed behind us, and I realized that Holly meant the cat she'd adopted.

"I'm sure she's back here," I said, searching for the cat.

Holly launched herself out of the car. "No, she never leaves my shoulder."

She yanked the side door open, threw her body across mine, and tried to look under Peanut's butt. Peanut grumped, and Moose wedged himself between Peanut and the seat. I touched his sleek fur and searched the floor.

"She's not back here."

Holly straightened and like a skinny quarterback, arm extended to oncoming traffic, of which there was none, high-stepped it across the road. "There she is!" she screamed in a girly voice and disappeared into the brush.

Summer rushed out of the passenger seat and clipped the leashes on the dogs.

"I'll quick get everyone to pee if you can help Holly. You guys. Let's take a pee."

The top of my head felt light with anxiety for Rosie, Holly, and Utah. Just as I was about to charge out of the car and start searching, I felt a soft brush against my ankle. There, emerging from under the driver's seat, was Utah. "Summer. Here's the cat!"

"Hit the horn."

I leaned into the front seat. Hit the horn. One long and three short, then dropped like a sack back into my seat.

Holly's head appeared like a prairie dog over the small mound of grass and trees.

"We have her!" I screamed and frantically waved her back into the car.

Limbs lanky and unorganized, Holly paused, looked both ways down the highway, and galloped back. Her face was wet with tears, and when she got to the car, she took Utah into her arms. She nuzzled the kitten. Oh, to have Holly look with such fondness on you.

"Oh my God. Oh, Utah."

Summer looked at me and said, "Sam found her under the seat."

"Thank you, Samantha." She looked at me while she nuzzled Utah. "Thank you so much, Samantha."

Serious Holly again said, "Rosie's blood pressure is off the charts. I have to get home."

"Absolutely. We are going to get you there."

"By hook or by crook," Summer added.

———

I shifted positions slightly, not wanting to disturb Peanut. His body had conformed to mine, and Moose lay like a jockey across the larger dog's back. Someone farted, and I stopped breathing through my nose.

Holly driving fed her need for control, and Summer navigated and chatted about being in an episode of *Friends* and how she and Lisa Kudrow were practically sisters. Holly was tense but quiet. I liked how Summer kept the mood in the car light, talking about a show Holly had rarely watched, and a sistership that had a 97.9 percent chance of being false.

I opened the window for some fresh air, and the noise alerted Summer.

"Hey, girl. How you doin'?" This in her best Joey impersonation.

I touched the short, soft, shaven fur on Peanut's haunch and said, "How's Rosie?"

"Okay for now," Holly said.

Summer read the last text on Holly's phone. "She's been medicated and is being discharged."

Peanut yawned and moved his leg closer so I could pet him more effectively.

"We're not going to stop except to feed the animals, pee, get gas, and grab food," Holly said.

"No stopping for anything that isn't absolutely necessary from here on out," added Summer, like she had to make it clear to the kids fooling around in the back seat to pace themselves with their water bottles. In a quieter, almost meek voice, she said, "Thanks for letting me tag along, you guys."

Summer looked out the windshield, and Holly reached over and squeezed her leg. I waited for a flippant reply, a bit of humor to ease any discomfort there might be with such a blatant emotional display, but instead I saw Summer try to swallow.

"I don't have a lot of friends."

Holly offered an understanding smile to Summer, and my mood sank. I repositioned, and Moose lifted his bat-like head and with his part-buggy-Chihuahua eyes and part-pug frown appraised me. We made eye contact.

"How'd you and Rosie meet?"

I saw Holly assess me, gauge my sincerity.

"She worked for a competing law firm. I met her in a bar after work."

Holly hesitated. I wanted her to know I was a safe haven. That I wanted to know what love at first sight looked like. "What did you guys talk about?"

"Not the law. It was like we didn't have that in common. I asked her about the dress she was wearing."

"What did it look like?"

"I don't remember. It wasn't about the dress."

Even though she was driving, she was gazing into her past, seeing Rosie for the first time again.

"I was a goner."

Summer rested her head against the window. "What was that like?"

"Like they say in the movies. Like being struck with a sparkler on the Fourth of July. But it didn't burn; it felt exciting."

"Did she feel the same?"

"Rosie said I was wearing a red dress with a wide belt, but I don't remember. She said she asked me to borrow my lip color because she wanted something that my lips had touched."

"I've never felt that," Summer said. "I've felt excited, but it petered out into nothing."

I didn't bother to tell these two women who knew me that I hadn't felt it either. I was so happy Holly had felt this. It's what I wanted for Maddie in the future too. Love that felt like love.

This stream of information whetted my thirst for more, and I remembered something about Holly in that moment. College Holly had managed her anxiety by talking, and I'd helped her by listening, and I put my head back and listened as if we were back staring at the water stain in the shape of Italy on the ceiling of our old apartment.

After thirty minutes Holly said, "Close your eyes, Samantha. I'm feeling better," and I did, and I felt better too.

CHAPTER
TWENTY-FOUR
SO MUCH MORE GOING ON

I woke to the roar of a semitruck thundering by, pelting us with small rocks and spray. I inched away from the door.

"That truck felt close."

It had rained while I dozed, and we were kicking up water, and the air felt muggy. I looked at my watch. Colorado?

"I think he's playing a game with us. We've been passing each other for the last hundred miles. He gets past me, lets me catch up; he blinks his lights. He has a sticker on the back of his truck that says, 'Truckers are the hero of the highway.' I suppose that's true. They bring us everything, don't they? Produce. Fencing. You name it."

Holly sounded cheerful—even, I dared say, peppy. I did not expect this. I expected tired, distracted by Rosie, maybe impatient.

I glanced at Summer. She wore noise-canceling headphones and an eye mask. Her head rested on a blow-up bathtub spa pillow in the shape of a seashell.

I stretched my legs under Peanut's weight and discovered a sticky, wet drool spot on the top of my thigh. Utah had wedged herself between the headrest and Holly's shoulders.

"How long have you been driving?"

Holly shrugged. "Summer gave me some Adderall. I don't think it's affecting me, but this trip hasn't been that bad. I'm pretty sure I can drive the rest of the way tonight."

"Summer has Adderall? All this time I haven't had any of my sleep medication, and Summer has had a stash?"

"I don't think this is the stuff you take. Like I said, I don't think it's affecting me. I'm just naturally energetic."

I recognized the Adderall virgin. I had been one myself before I went for a sleep study and found out what I already knew, that I fell asleep too quickly during inappropriate times and slept too much for a healthy woman my age. Adderall felt like euphoria to a good girl who lived on one cup of coffee a day and for whom getting drunk was having one frozen margarita on Fridays—which was me more than Holly back in the day.

After the drug kicked in, you felt like your attention had been scrubbed clean and you could multitask—hell, multithink—and finish the things you'd had on your to-do list since the sixth grade. Your appetite went unnoticed while your mouth was like a swamp. It was a small price for the searing precision of your thoughts.

"Do you have a water bottle? I'm super thirsty," Holly said.

I handed her a warm bottle of water. "That's a side effect. Have you heard from Rosie or Katie?"

"No. No news is good news. See, we're coming up on the truck."

I checked my phone. There was a message from Drew.

BDREW: Catch me up.

I got much less of a bump of delight now that I'd seen Katie and Drew together.

In my periphery, I noticed the eighteen-wheeler slow as we approached. Holly hit her turn signal and pulled into the left lane. We crept up the long length of the vehicle, passing the rear lamps, the axle, and the exhaust system just behind the cab. As we moved parallel, the trucker turned on his overhead light and held up a sign.

"What does that say?" said Holly, squinting around Summer's hair.

Through the rain-streaked window, across the road between us, I ducked my head and read the sign.

BLOWJOB? All block letters with an enormous question mark after the last *B*, which struck me as funny. The guy used punctuation to make sure whoever he showed it to knew it was a proposition, not a nickname.

"Blow job, Holly. It says blow job. Gun it and get out of here. That guy wants a blow job." I jostled the dogs and leaned forward.

Our car swerved away from the trucker at the same time Holly hit the accelerator, and the engine surged and passed him. She overcorrected, yanking the wheel back. The tire hit the pavement edge and balanced there. I leaned into the dogs. The wheel spun off the asphalt edge, and the Prius came so close to the front wheel of the semitruck that I threw my body across Peanut and Moose, closed my eyes, and braced for impact. I felt the car veer again and heard the front wheel hit the gravel, but miraculously the tire lifted out of the shoulder, instead of being yanked into it and shoved into the ditch. The car lurched back and forth, working to find solid ground.

"Jesus." Summer pushed the headphones off, along with her sleep mask. "What the hell, you guys?"

Everyone in the car sat at attention, panting. I whipped around, and out the back window I saw the trucker recede, his headlights blinking, the massive face of the truck appearing to laugh at us.

Holly lifted a shaky hand from the steering wheel and repositioned Utah more squarely against her neck. Her shoulders heaved as she caught her breath.

"We should change drivers," I said.

"No! I'm not pulling over and risking that trucker grinding up next to us at this time of night."

"You've had a shock. We all have," I said.

Summer protested. "I haven't had a shock. This crap happens every day. In fact, it's a weird day when someone doesn't whip their dick out in Hollywood and ask for a blow job. It should be getting better since Weinstein and all, but they're getting sneakier. You don't see as many wrinkly dicks, but you have to pay attention and not say *yes* to anything without making sure when they offer you a sweet potato it is in fact a potato and not their pet name for their weirdly shaped penis."

I couldn't help myself: I laughed, saying, "Sweet Potato," but I was giggling so hard it came out "Sweet. Sweet Pot. Sweeeet."

Summer said in all seriousness, "Well, once someone offered me a Summer squash, and I thought it was a kind of dirty joke. Like 'Summer, do you want to squash?' *Squash* meaning like, you know, screw. But then I learned a summer squash is a vegetable. I mean, I've heard of zucchini, so, I guess."

Holly gave one of her low, throaty giggles that changed into a guffaw. The laugh rolled to her shoulders, and she threw her head back. Listening to her made me laugh harder, and I felt tears streaming down my face.

"I have to pee. Oh my God, I have to pee," I said.

For once Summer looked pissed to be the butt of a joke, to not be in charge, but after a second of outrage, she started laughing too. In between our laughter, I could hear my phone buzzing.

BDREW: Hey, nice lady. Catch me up.

ME: I will if you will.

BDREW: Katie is doing pretty well. Lots of stories about you and Holly.

Me: Holly is driving. We just got propositioned by a guy in a big rig. Summer is our BFF now. I am dating Peanut.

BDREW: Don't get too attached to Peanut.

ME: Story of my life. Moose is now my plus one.

CHAPTER TWENTY-FIVE

BY HOOK OR BY CROOK

We were hours in, many miles down the road with maybe five hours left to go, depending on pit stops. We'd played I Spy, the Alphabet Game, and Cows on My Side, which was a silly game that no one was into but Summer, who yelled "Cow!" at every billboard just to be funny. After an hour Summer lost interest, fell asleep, and I must have too.

When I woke and shifted in my seat to release my tingling left butt cheek, I realized the car wasn't moving. We were parked under the yellow lights in the parking lot of a decrepit gas station, the keys were in the ignition, and the car was idling almost noiselessly. Holly must have run inside to relieve herself. Summer was asleep in the passenger seat with her neck bent in what looked like a very unpleasant position.

Peanut sat alert, panting and staring out the windshield. His thick pink tongue dripped stringy goop onto the center console. Peanut's heavy breathing transitioned into a high-pitched whine, and I reached back to give the dog a scratch under his chin. He pushed my hand away with his nose.

"What's up, Peanut?" He licked his lips, flicked his gaze at me, and returned to staring out the windshield. I reached forward and opened the glove compartment for a paper napkin to wipe the dog's chin, and that's when I saw it. The shiny red cab of an eighteen-wheeler parked near the diesel fuel pump. I recognized the decal, Tiger Paw Trucking.

"Holly? Summer! Is that the blow job truck?"

Summer popped up from the back seat, seemingly fully alert. "Maybe? It could be. Yeah, I think it is."

"I'm going to look for Holly. Lock the doors after I leave. Watch the dogs. If we come out running, unlock the doors and let us in. Okay?"

Summer nodded, eyes wide.

I launched myself out the door of the Prius. The ground was wet, and heavy drops of water fell from the one streetlamp above our car. My tennis shoe skidded as I slammed the car door. Head down, I jogged the short distance to the convenience store that was attached to a one-door garage. The place appeared empty. No one stood behind the counter. I couldn't see Holly. I eased the door open a crack, smelled something deep fried, and slipped inside, my body tingling with adrenaline.

The brightly lit interior was crammed with shelves filled with cases of beer and rows of chips, beef jerky, and candy. Against the back corner, near a carousel of sunglasses, stood Holly. She cowered, her back against a dingy wall, and said, in a voice I'd never heard from her before, "Please give me my cat. She's just a baby."

I crept to the side, tried to see who she was speaking to. Beyond the rotating hot dogs and dry jumbo pretzels dispenser stood a man. He was a full head taller than Holly and wore a ratty mesh ball cap on his head.

"I think she wants to go home with me."

"Give her to me." Holly looked like she had in college minutes before throwing up, either from drinking or the flu. There was no joy in seeing the imperious, regal Holly taken down a notch.

"I'm just trying to be friendly. Smile, sweetie." He lifted Utah, and the kitten's tiny body dangled unsupported.

All I wanted to do was get in there and empower Holly, see her rise up and take him down. I swept through the candy aisle, knocking a Twinkie packet off the shelf on the way. The good, careful girl in me almost stopped to pick it up, but I thought, *No, Spider-Man does not pick up sponge cake. He does not tidy.*

When I got to Holly, I threw my arms around her, and surprising both of us, I said, "Hey, lover. What's taking so long?" Then I kissed her on the lips. Almost. I caught Holly on the corner of her left nostril, missing her lips altogether. I knew enough about emergency situations not to try to stick the landing. I pivoted and threw my arm over Holly's shoulders. She grabbed me around the waist and said in a surprised voice, "He has Utah."

I turned to face the trucker. "Oh, you found our cat," and I plucked the kitten right off the man's hand.

"Sweetie," I said, tucking Utah under Holly's neck. "You've got to do better keeping an eye on this girl." Holly secured Utah on her shoulder and murmured something. I could feel my friend, *my friend,* pull herself up straighter, fill her lungs with air.

The man had a colossal beer gut and mustard-stained fingertips from years of smoking from packs just like the one that pushed against his breast pocket. There were two burn holes on the right jacket sleeve of his brown Carhartt coat. He needed a good toothbrush.

My brave-ish display of support for my friend did not intimidate the man. "Your friend lost her way. I caught her coming out of the men's room." He slid his eyes over Holly. Sure enough, we stood in front of the closed door of a men's room and within a foot from a hall that led to what would surely be the moldy shower stalls of a truck stop.

"The women's bathroom is clogged." Holly cleared her throat, sounded stronger. Held me around the waist with a firmer hand.

"I told her we could share." The man leered at both of us. It occurred to me that the attendant of the gas station was out of sight on purpose. This situation had a surreal quality to it, as if it was happening to someone else, say on a movie screen.

Maybe that's what finally did it, the dreamlike feel of the moment. That, and my general fed-up-ness of feeling powerless for no real reason. I was so sick of men who thought they could rule with intimidation, like my father. Or felt entitled to a sick woman's dog during a divorce just because he had money.

I stepped between the man and Holly. Sweeping my arm like an usher, I said, "We don't want to keep you from showering. Off you go. Grab a toothbrush on us." And I winked. For the first time in my life, I coordinated my eyes in a one-two punch.

He dragged his eyes over my body from the top of my head all the way down to my sneakers. "You're a bitchy thing."

"You're a trope," I said. "A cliché," I clarified for his tiny brain. "A troll! A troll who picks on women and kittens and probably babies too." My rusty insult skills were cringingly on display.

He took a step forward. I had no plan. The wall behind us too close. I could smell diesel fuel, and I spotted a piece of taco chip in his beard. Which was not a useful detail.

Holly grabbed my arm with cold, viselike fingers, tugged me so we were standing side by side, and Tough Holly Ballbuster reborn said, "Get out of our way, you troll."

It must have sounded so much better in her head. The trucker took another menacing step toward us and raised his fist. I shrank back and closed my eyes for impact at the same time that Holly shoved him in the center of his sternum.

We heard Summer before we saw her.

"Hey, dirtbag," her Disney voice rang out.

The three of us turned, like an ungroomed synchronized swimming team. Summer held a red-and-white plastic baseball bat, with the cardboard packaging on it, over her head. I would have laughed if I hadn't been so astonished.

Summer took a wide, uncoordinated swing and knocked a bag of Lay's potato chips onto the floor. I watched as she regrouped, raised the bat again, and although she didn't say it, we knew she wasn't finished.

"Get away from them," Summer said through clenched teeth. A brown head of hair and black-rimmed glasses emerged from behind the cash register and Plexiglas barrier.

"You!" I called. "Hiding like a coward. Call the police!"

"Call the police!" Summer repeated with her eyes locked on the truck driver. She took another swing; this time she was oddly precise in her aim. A bag of chocolate-covered pretzels flew from a hook near the beef jerky packages and took flight. We all watched as it slowed at the peak of its arc by a sprinkler head, then dropped somewhere out of sight.

"What the . . . ?" the trucker said.

"Hey!" the man behind the counter shouted. "Leave the merchandise alone."

Summer lifted the bat over her head and brought it down on the top of a display of Funyuns. And, oh my God, at that moment I finally got it. Fun Onions! Uninhibited and into this vigilante justice, she swung the bat and toppled the revolving sunglasses display. Plastic frames skittered across the floor followed by a loud crash of the flimsy tower. "That's for not calling the police."

"What is wrong with you bitches?" the trucker said with real wonder, backing away from Holly and me.

"Bitches?" Summer yelled. "Bitches?" She looked between the manager and the trucker, who was now making a break for the door while grabbing the keys that hung from a chain at his pocket.

"We *bitches* are getting our friend and her kitty and by hook or by crook getting out of here."

"By hook or by crook?" I said. Don't get me wrong. I was in full admiration mode. Summer was rocking a baseball bat in the middle of Nebraska, scaring the bejesus out of a big, imposing man, but the phrase *by hook or by crook* was a buzzkill. Honestly, it was worse than *trope*.

The manager hit the button on his intercom-microphone. There was a loud static-feedback screech followed by a nasally voice: "Ma'am, please put the bat down, and come up and pay for your snacks."

Summer slammed the baseball bat on top of the ice-cream novelty case and shouted, "We will not pay for the snacks."

And I thought, *Oh, what the hell.* "We will not pay for the snacks!"

"Blow job," Holly shouted.

"Blow job!" I shouted.

Holly and I joined hands and grabbed Summer and ran out of the gas station breathing hard like three ecstatic high school girls who'd just stolen condoms.

CHAPTER TWENTY-SIX
FRIEND-DEMENTIA

The moment we three stepped into the cool night air, I heard the dead bolt click into place behind us. The gas station attendant flicked off the hanging neon **OPEN** light, and the sidewalk went dark. But the shaky effects of my adrenaline rush couldn't be switched off so easily. I heard the slap of our tennis shoes echo on the pavement.

I'd stood up to somebody. Not just anybody: a giant, sexual-favor-requesting, hostile man. Or, I should say, *we* did. Sure, the tiny Summer had to rescue Holly and me, but when push came to shove, I didn't slip into unconsciousness. *Au contraire.* I aggressed! I always wondered if, in a survival situation, would I be the person who peed and cried, or would I grab a floaty and jump?

It was clear. I was a jumper. We were jumpers!

"You guys! Holy crap!" We were still holding hands.

Summer let out a "Whoop!"

I peered at Holly; she was oddly silent. Was she pissed at me for kissing her? Was she insulted? She let go of our hands first, and I took a deep breath in and held it.

"GAAH!" she shouted into the night air. She dropped her head back, put a hand over her face, and shouted again. She shivered all over like Peanut or Moose would if they'd just come out of the rain.

I waited, unsure how to feel. I knew Fun Holly from college and grown-up Fierce Holly, but Paralyzed Holly and now Screaming Holly? I was at a loss. I needed a prompt.

"Let it out," Summer said, and she herself let out a loud, prolonged scream.

This time the dogs got involved, letting out short yips from the car as if to say, *Absolutely! Yes! Also, what's happening?*

I said, "Go, Team Katie!" But that didn't do it for me. I tried again. "GO, TEAM KATIE!"

We made eye contact before all three of us shouted, "GO, TEAM KATIE!"

A loud squawk punctuated our voices, and a speaker from the top of the gas pump crackled, and a man's voice said, "You don't have to go home, but you can't stay here."

The three of us laughed so fully and completely that at that moment we felt like one person.

While we'd been inside the gas station, Peanut had moved to the driver's seat, and Moose to the passenger side. Both dogs sat with humanlike anticipation. When Holly opened the driver's-side door, one hand steadying Utah, Peanut pivoted and threw his bulk into Holly's arms. One paw went up to her shoulder and the other navigated the kitten respectfully and landed on her chest.

"Whoa," she said, just before Peanut washed the length of her face with his tongue. "Peanut!"

I sprinted around the car and slid my fingers under his collar. "Okay, dude. This is not okay."

"No. Leave him." Holly, averting her face from Peanut's slobbering, let him lick her neck while she shielded Utah. "I've got him."

"I think he's glad you're okay. He was worried. That's why I went looking for you."

"Is that right? Peanut, were you concerned?"

There was no way I was going to ruin this moment by pointing out that she usually called him "the dog."

"He was. Concerned. We all were." I gave Summer a quick glance.

Holly scratched the big dog's ears and then helped him out of the car while wiping her face with the back of her hand.

The dog bumped his head against her thigh as we walked to the back of the Prius. Holly put Utah into the makeshift cat box. Her expression darkened as she watched the little bundle. I could see the victorious Holly humbling again as we all calmed down.

"How am I ever going to be a parent?" she said, her eyes still on Utah. "That man walked right up to me and took Utah. I couldn't stop him." She glanced at me, the expression on her face filled with angst. "Rosie is going to have that baby, and they are going to send her home to us." Her voice went up an octave when she said, "It's harder to adopt a dog than to take a baby home. We are going to walk out of the hospital with a human and try not to kill her or lose her for eighteen years. There are men like that out there. Just taking whatever they want, and we are having a girl. *You* had a girl. How did you do it, Samantha?"

"Oh, Holly." Everything about Holly's hardness about Peanut, Moose, and even Summer, her difficulty with empathy outside of her tight circle, this was all fear. Fear that she wouldn't come through for love.

"How did you keep her safe? I can't protect Utah. I couldn't protect myself."

"You could have. You would have. I know you would have."

"No, Sam. No. I wouldn't have. I didn't."

Summer appeared at Holly's shoulder and said, "Safety and the idea that you can keep anyone safe is an illusion. But, loving someone is the ultimate safekeeping."

Holly and I looked at Summer, the woman who continued to amaze us with her insights. "She's right. No matter what happens to us in life, we can always come home to the people who care for us. They are our safe harbor. We are. Holly. We are here for you," I said. Finally getting to finish a sentence that was started all those years ago when Holly walked out the door.

Curing yourself from avoiding conflict wasn't just about stepping up to fight. It was also about learning to lean into discomfort. Maybe the process was like washing windows on a sunny day: the big dirt was easy, but the final smear on a filthy windowpane could be the hardest to rub out. With the last bit of bravery juice slowly leaking out of my nervous system, I said, "Do you want to talk about what happened in the gas station? I feel like something else was going on in there?"

Holly lifted Utah and handed the kitty off to me. I took her soft, warm body into my cupped hands and cuddled her to my sternum. "Remember the house party, graduation night?"

"Of course," I said softly, slowly. "I wanted to kiss Jim Calhoun, so I hung around the pool table the whole night."

"Upstairs. Yeah."

"So long ago. But I can smell the stale beer."

"Ugh. Me too." She stopped speaking and waited so long I wondered if she was going to keep going. She started up again. "I ran out of wine, so I went down to the keg room. Tucker was down there."

"Tucker. Yeah. I vaguely remember him. Tall with that scruff on his face. The goalie."

"That was him. We took all those classes together. Anyway, someone threw a beer can at him. Split open his eyebrow. There was blood everywhere. Tucker pulled me into a room where the light was better, asked me to look at the cut on his head. Wanted to know if he needed stitches."

"Obviously he didn't know you."

"That was before blood made me woozy. I'm pretty sure that's why I don't like looking at stuff like that," Holly said quietly.

I didn't try to lighten or evade this conversation. Instead, I put myself at the party; I felt the thrumming music and saw the Christmas lights hung everywhere even though it was May. The ruddy painted concrete floor in the basement—sticky, downright wet, even. I hated the basement of that house and rarely went down there.

"I was stupid. Had no experience with boys." She paused, and I willed myself not to say anything. To just listen. "He'd stopped bleeding, but his wound looked terrible. I thought I could see a bit of bone. Then he shoved me, hard, and I fell onto a bare mattress on the floor. That's how I got covered in beer. My cup flew out of my hand and spilled all over both of us. It must have surprised him because I had just enough time to raise my knee. I accidentally caught him right in the nuts. His full weight came down, and he rolled off of me. Called me a . . . dyke. You know, there were rumors even then. He spit on me." The muscles of her jaw flexed.

I heard myself gasp in shock. "Holly. My God, why didn't you tell me this?" I racked my brain, tried to remember that night more clearly. My disappointment turned to grief.

"I was drunk. So embarrassed to be so stupid. Also, back then, it was just what happened at parties. Date rape and assault, they weren't things. I thought I shouldn't be such a baby. Nothing happened."

She'd come up the stairs looking wild eyed, soaked in beer. She threw up in the corner of the party house. Behind the front door. I tried to remember what she looked like, how I could have missed that she'd almost been raped. Wondered if this is what made her so angry at me. Did she blame me for leaving her alone?

"We got home, and you threw up a bunch more."

"The hate in his face. Real hate. He pushed me so hard, I had a bruise on my collarbone forever. My head grazed the cement wall. There was nothing playful or sexual about it—it was violent. It changed me."

An icy feeling in the part in my hair moved down my neck and into my shoulders as I ran through my own memories. "I thought you were emotional about graduation and leaving." I began to see that I'd missed so much of that night. It was no wonder I hadn't been able to understand what had happened to us.

"There was that too. I thought he was my friend. I realized you can't trust people."

"Then we had that thing about Mike and that disgusting thing he said. You must have felt surrounded by"—I searched for the right word—"traitors?" It felt satisfying to name it, to attach careful words to it. I'd watched an archeologists' dig on television once, was amazed at the painstaking precision it took to unearth a fragment of the past. This felt like that.

"Who's Mike? What disgusting thing?" Summer asked, reminding us that we were not alone talking about this very private thing.

I hesitated, giving Holly a chance to answer or protest. When she didn't, I said, "Mike was a guy Katie was seeing. He made this gross gesture insinuating that Holly and I were having sex in the living room."

"Were you?"

"No," I said. "We were very close. We spent all our time together."

"We did spend all our time together." She quieted. I could see her remembering.

"I don't have any memories of college without Holly and Katie in them."

Holly sighed. "I never drank like that again. I never get drunk."

"Is that what happened to you two?" You had to hand it to Summer. For a woman with the girth of a Popsicle stick, she never shied away from the fray.

"No!" Holly said. "No," she said again.

Ugh, I thought. *Ugh*, there's more. I felt sick to my stomach. There was more to consider. More to our story.

The ringtone for Rosie jingled from Holly's phone on the dash. A wash of disappointment flooded through me. I was ready to hear the rest, however terrible it might be. Holly answered the phone and motioned for all of us to get in the car. "Hi, sweetie. Why are you up?" She gestured for me to get in and drive. I heard Summer maneuver around the dogs and slam her door. I pulled out of the gas station parking lot while listening to Holly.

"How close? Is the baby moving?" Holly listened and said, "Remember what they said about 411. Four minutes apart, lasting *one* minute, for at least *one* hour. Then hospital."

I could hear the tinny voice of Rosie on the line, but not what she was saying. I caught Summer's eye and mouthed the word *labor*.

"I'm not driving. Sam is. Why? Just tell me." She paused and said, "What's going on?"

I plugged one ear, leaned toward her, tried to hear what Rosie was saying.

"You have to go to the hospital!"

My worry ratcheted up with the volume of Holly's voice. I touched her forearm. Summer had a hand on Holly's shoulder.

"When your water breaks, there's a greater chance of infection." Holly's voice became high pitched and I accelerated in response.

"No. Not an Uber, honey. Call Luther next door. He knows what to do. It's not a bother. No, remember. We gave him all that zucchini bread for just this occasion." In a more forceful voice, she said, "Do not take an Uber—do you hear me?" She sighed. "I'm sorry. Sweetie, I'm sorry for that tone. I just. Okay. We are about four hours away. We'll be there in three. I love you. I love you more. I love you most of all."

She hung up the phone and looked at us. "Can I drive?" A typical Holly demand that came out instead as a respectful ask.

"We're going to get you there, Holly. Tell her, Summer. Read the universe. We'll get there, right?"

"I mean, there was never any doubt, you guys. Never," Summer said, leaning forward.

"How many babies get delivered a year, do you think?" Holly asked.

"Like in the world or Wisconsin?" I said, hoping to distract Holly.

"I'll google it," Summer said.

"Let's just do the US."

"Three point eight million."

"If you divide that by three hundred sixty-five days in a year, it comes to like"—Holly paused for a breath and said—"ten and a half thousand babies delivered in a day."

I'd forgotten how good Holly was at math too. All those years of learning about her in college and then all those years forgetting, because she was no longer around to remind me. We had friend-dementia. Moose wheezed his signature sigh as if to say, *What a waste.*

"How many of those deliveries go badly?" Holly asked but abruptly changed her mind. "Wait, I don't want to know."

"Rosie is healthy, and I'm sure has taken great care of herself. She isn't high risk," I said.

"How much did it hurt? It looked like it was agony." For the briefest of seconds, Holly and I made eye contact. I knew what she was asking. She didn't want facts; she wanted reassurance.

"You don't have to worry about that. They have epidurals. I didn't get one because they missed the window with my progress." Holly was listening. I could see she wanted details. "After my water broke, it still took hours for Maddie to come, but I don't remember those hours. I remember some pain, a lot of pushing, and the most fabulous release. Then Maddie, on my chest already looking to nurse."

"I saw you delivering Maddie without Jeff. I had to get out of there. It made me too sad," Holly said softly.

I let that sit in my brain. She left not because she hated me or didn't care. It was because she did care, and suddenly I had another layer to add to the memory of Maddie's birthday. A balm for a rough patch that had always existed in my memory.

"Katie was there. I was in such a fog of pain, but it was so good to get a glimpse of you." Realizing I'd said *pain* and reminded her about Rosie, I added, "You really do forget everything once the baby is in your arms."

"I don't want her hurting without me."

"Rosie knows you're trying your best to get there. She is so lucky to have you."

"I shouldn't have left Rosie so close to the end."

"She's early, though, right?"

Out of the corner of my eye, I saw Moose sit up. He let out a yip like he was feeling the speed and was as uncomfortable as I was.

Holly glanced at me. "I'm no good in emergencies. Rosie says I'm missing an empathy gene."

"I think that makes you good at emergencies." Moose let out two sharp barks and a growl. I turned, and the usually almost coma-quiet Moose stood on his hind legs, his front paws leaning on the back of the front seat. His buggy eyes reflected the lights on the dash.

In slow motion, my brain went from *This is unlike Moose* to *Why is he doing this?* to *What does Peanut think of this?* to *Peanut sure is quiet* to *Oh no.*

I pitched forward so abruptly, the seat belt, afraid for my life, clutched me tightly.

Summer started. "What's happening now?"

"Peanut!" I reached back, felt his warm fur. "Peanut!" The dog didn't move. Moose barked again. I looked at the time. He hadn't eaten for a while. "Peanut's blood sugar might be low."

"Summer. What's going on with Peanut?"

"His eyes are open, but he looks super tired. Peanut, sit up. Come on, boy." I could hear her moving around in the back. "He's acting like he's asleep, but he's looking at me."

"Get Peanut's insulin kit out of the glove compartment, Holly."

She hit the button, and tucked neatly into the tight space was the small case Griffin had given us. Inside, I knew, were insulin, syringes, blood-testing materials, and a container with a sugar solution in case of low-blood-sugar emergencies.

"Holly, you have to test Peanut's blood sugar."

"Here. You do it." Holly shoved the black nylon case toward Summer, who put up her arms.

"Holly. I'll hold Utah and Moose. I will assist you. But, you know as well as I do that you have to do this."

"I can't do it! Pull over, Samantha. I'll drive. You do it."

I leveled my gaze at Holly. "Summer's right. Rosie needs us ASAP. There's no exit. It's quicker if I talk you through it."

At that, Holly unzipped the bag filled with lifesaving supplies. "Yuck. It's sticky. There's goop all over the equipment." I hit the switch for the overhead light. The glucose solution must have broken open.

"Let's get his blood tested," I said calmly. "See where we are at. That thing there." I pointed to the pen that held the blade. "It's loaded. Hold it on his paw. Hit the button. It will stab him for you."

Holly unclipped and got on her knees. Summer pulled Utah from Holly's shoulder.

"You have to have the test strip ready to drop the blood onto it," I said. "It's not hard. Can you see?"

"You stab him, Holly, and I'll collect the blood. I've done this with my grandma, and honestly she was almost as hairy as Peanut." I saw Summer reach for the strips, heard the top pop as she opened the canister.

"You guys." Holly coughed. "I feel dizzy. I can't."

"You're fine. I'll keep the car steady."

Holly hung her upper body between the seats. "Hold up his paw."

"Get the needle in place," I said.

"Seriously. Don't say needle," said Holly.

"Open your eyes, Holly," said Summer.

I heard the click, and Holly shouted, "Did I do it? Did I get it? Summer, is it working?"

"Yes. There's blood. I'm getting it," Summer said excitedly. Happily.

"I do feel dizzy."

"Don't think about it," I said immediately, soothingly. "Think about statutes and torts. Or contracts. Contracts make you feel steady, right? Stick the thing into the slot on the reader."

Almost to herself she said, "Contracts don't bleed." There was a silence, and then: "Do you think Rosie is going through this right now? They're probably taking her blood."

The car hit a divot and wobbled. "Holly, concentrate on what we're doing. Can you read the display?"

Holly, heroically holding it together, held the monitor up to the dome light and read, "It says, 2.98 mmol slash L."

"His blood sugar is low. We need to give him something sweet."

"There are cookies in my purse. I have cookies," said Summer.

"He can't eat a cookie," I said. "He's not totally awake. He might choke. We have to give him some syrup. Something to smear on his gums."

"The squirt bottle in this kit is empty," Holly said, sounding frantic.

"I have maple syrup!" Summer shouted suddenly. "It's under your seat, Holly."

Holly flipped around, and I heard her rummaging. "Got it! Thank God you're a slob, Summer."

"I am frugal," she said primly.

Back on her knees, Holly peeled back the foil on the tub of faux pancake syrup. "Summer, can you open his mouth?"

"Yeah. Okay."

It was quiet while Holly, I presumed, aimed cheap maple syrup into Peanut's mouth.

"It's getting in!" Summer said.

"Now massage his throat to help him swallow," I instructed.

"His lips are floppy," said Summer.

"Does it matter how much I give him? It's kind of everywhere back here," said Holly.

"That's what diabetes is. They have to have some sugar but not too much," I said.

"Peanutty, how you doing, big guy?" Holly crooned.

"Awww, Moose is licking him," said Summer.

The cooing in the car was like a symphony of caring. Holly's and Summer's voices were high, calling encouragement of all kinds:

"Come on, buddy."

"Katie loves you, big guy."

"Moose, here, you missed a spot."

"Come on, dude."

Then Holly cried, "His eyes are open. He's licking his lips!" She rotated on her knees and looked at me with triumph.

Summer put her hands up, and Holly slapped her ten. "Disaster averted!" Summer said.

"I'm going to let Peanut lick my fingers." Holly's voice trembled, but my heart swelled at her words. "But if you guys don't mind, I might barf out the window again."

"No, you won't, Holly," I said, my throat thick, my eyes wet. "You did it! You saved Peanut."

"We saved Peanut," she said. "We did it."

She grabbed Summer's and my hands with her sticky fingers, and my inner deer spirit animal whispered, *Good job, ladies. Nicely done.*

After Holly let go of my hand, I must have touched my eye because my left lid felt gummy and slow to respond when I blinked. Holly grabbed the water bottle from the cup holder and squirted it into the McDonald's paper bag. She wiped her hands and gestured for mine.

I felt cool water in my palm and Holly's warm hand cupping mine.

"Nice job back there. Med school isn't far behind."

"I haven't had a flu shot without a Valium in years."

"I was squeamish too. But, your college barfing, later working in the hospital, and being a mom takes the squeee out of the mish. If you know what I mean."

"I'm never a fan of the mish, as you know." She gestured for my other hand, and I reached across the steering wheel. "Maybe I'll be more help to Rosie now."

With Holly holding my hand, I had the courage to say, "When you love someone, you can handle all their wetness. Blood, poop, barf, all of it. It's not enjoyable, but it's an honor. This is why it was so easy for me to take care of you in college." I flicked my gaze into the rearview mirror and saw Summer winking and gesturing to her headphones. Slipping them on, she covered her ears, gave me one of her magical thumbs-up, providing Holly and me the privacy to talk. "I need to know what happened to us, Holly. Can you finish what we started? Please tell me."

Holly stopped rubbing and held my hand. I saw she was just as ready to put the past in order as I was. "You never read my letter, did you?"

My heart beat steadily, and my hands were calm on the steering wheel. "What letter?" I said.

"I realized it on this trip. You didn't see it. Didn't read it. That's why I never heard from you."

"Back up. What letter?"

"Before I left that morning. After graduation. I put a letter in that junky backpack we razzed you about. Your favorite thing in the world."

"You wrote me a letter?"

Holly nodded.

I wanted to stop time, find that letter. "A pen exploded, everything was covered in blue ink. I dumped the backpack, didn't even go through it. I threw it away."

"There was a letter in the side pocket." I heard Holly's voice catch. "Oh, Samantha. I should have known that. I should have figured that out."

The road sounds retreated; my head felt light. "This is what happened to us. Isn't it?"

Holly's face, filled with pain and loss. She shook her head as if wishing this all away.

"What did it say?" Strung between us was a heavy tension wire, a current of history and sadness passing back and forth and through the years. I saw the apartment again, two floors, like a town house, dated green Formica countertops in the kitchen around the corner from the main bedroom.

"It was a love letter."

The breath went out of me. "Oh." I touched my sternum. "A love letter. I see now. I get it. Holly. I didn't understand."

I thought about that night. I'd braided her short hair to keep it out of her face. Rubbed her back. Holly's pajamas white with tiny horses. Helping her wash her face, throwing her jeans in the laundry. I reframed this memory with this new information. Lovers? Friends? What was the difference?

She brushed her hair away from her face, and I saw how hard this was for her. "I wrote it all in a letter. My phone and address where you could reach me. I was trying to figure it all out."

I let myself feel the crushing loss of us, the abject misery of unrequited love, but it was visualizing Young Holly waiting for me to respond that made me groan with pain.

She stopped, sighed, started again. "I was terrified of my feelings for you. Of rejection. Of losing our friendship. Part of me didn't want to talk about it, but even then I knew I couldn't let it go. So when I didn't hear from you, I was relieved and furious. I pretended it was all your fault. For years." She washed her hand over her face and groaned. "What a stupid, stupid waste."

My arms were so heavy on the steering wheel, my throat so dry. I glanced in the mirror, saw Summer's sympathetic eyebrows, her wet eyes. I realized she was listening in, providing support from the back seat. "I'm . . ." I searched for the perfect words, wanting to get it right after so many empty years without Holly. "I am so sorry." I looked at Holly, reached to cup her face with my hand. "I'm so filled with sorrow for you and me. And I'm . . . angry. But not at you. I'm angry at young me. And young you." I took my foot off the gas, steered the car to the shoulder, heard the car crunch onto the gravel. I put the car in park. I took my seat belt off and turned with my arms out. Holly unbuckled her belt and leaned into me. I hadn't hugged this woman in years and years, and yet she smelled like college and cake, like vanilla and best friend. Her long arms wrapped around me. My muscles remembered, and my heart beat like the wagging of a dog's tail. *I know this woman,* it said. *She's home!*

"Don't apologize. That's not right," she said into my hair, her breath warming my temple.

"I'm not saying I'm sorry to you. I'm saying I feel deeply sorrowful."

"Yeah. I owe you the apology." She pulled back, looked me in the eye. She wanted to clear the air, but I saw something else. She wanted forgiveness and to be my friend.

"Homophobic," I said, finally understanding.

"I wanted to stay righteous," Holly said. "My anger was really rejection, and this was more important than our friendship. Rosie tried to tell me. She tried to make me see that maybe I didn't understand everything. I wouldn't listen." She removed my hand from her cheek but didn't let it go. "Coming out doesn't mean you have everything figured out. The phrase says it all. Coming out is a process. It's an opening door. There should be a term for post–coming out. Maybe *arrived*? Like after you have your sexuality figured out in the context of this binary world. But nobody needs that phrase. Nobody has arrived. We're all just moving through doorways with every person we meet. It's a specific thing. Not a general thing."

I thought of one of the many conversations Katie and I'd had over the years. We didn't care that Holly was gay. We cared that she hadn't told us. "Maybe it's enough for her to come out—like is she required to send out announcements?" Katie said when we learned that Rosie and she were moving home together. Like together together. "For example, I knew I liked men, but I didn't announce it. Why do we require people to announce the category of where their love sits if it's not a man and woman?" Katie smiled. "I love assholes. Should I send a card to my Christmas list? Happy Holidays, everyone! I found a new jerk to date!" We'd laughed. Then I'd thought, *I'm not on Holly's Christmas list,* which I knew was too whiny to say out loud.

"Katie and I speculated about what happened a lot. Neither of us had the answer because none of us had all the information."

She let go of my hands and covered her face. "I'm so ashamed, Samantha."

"Oh, Holly." I felt her distress. "Don't be. We were so young. I don't think we should blame our younger selves for not being our older, more experienced selves."

"I didn't understand this back then, but I do now. Loving me like that wasn't even in the realm of possibility for you. It never occurred to you. While with me, it was who I was. How could I have expected you to understand when I had my own troubles coming to terms with being gay. On top of that, I thought you'd read the letter and didn't bother to respond."

My throat closed, and I tried to clear it. I ached for the newly graduated Holly who'd left her best friend a love letter and that friend never responded. For all our lost years.

"I didn't trust you."

"I should have tried harder to find you. I should have fought for us. Maybe my dad was right. You get what you fight for, so you'd better learn to fight." I rubbed her shoulder and said, "And, boy, do we know how to fight now."

With her headphones around her neck Summer sat forward and joined our loose embrace. It was awkward, the three of us, the back of the front seat between us. We were all tearful and looking for something to say, to put this all behind us.

Summer, with a little twinkle, said, "I knew it was something like that, you guys; I just knew it."

I dropped my head back with a laugh at the same time as Holly's phone trilled and lit up with a FaceTime call from Rosie. Holly hit the green *accept* circle, and the phone screen illuminated her love, anxiety, and devotion meant only for Rosie.

CHAPTER TWENTY-SEVEN
THE CHIEF RESIDENT

"Rosie! Baby. Hi, honey. Hi, lovey."

I smiled. Listening to Holly talk to Rosie was like hearing old Motown tunes without the music. So much sugar, so much honey, so much love.

Rosie spoke softly into her phone. "I don't want you to worry. They admitted me. I have preeclampsia."

Holly's eyes shot over to me.

"Her blood pressure is up," I said gently. "That's what *preeclampsia* means."

"Your blood pressure?" Holly said to the screen. "Isn't that an old-man problem? You're not an old man."

"It's a pregnancy thing, too, honey." I heard Rosie's calm, creamy voice through the phone. I thought about her child listening to *Goodnight Moon* read with that voice. What a lucky baby.

"Okay. Okay. Now what?" In one graceful movement, Holly lifted Utah off her shoulder and deposited the kitten into Summer's waiting arms. A pushing-up-her-sleeves moment, a foreshadowing that the future hours would not be for kittens.

"Holly, back up from the phone, I can only see your nostrils," Rosie instructed. Holly extended her arm, and now both of us could see Rosie's perfect skin and kind eyes.

"That's better," she said. "Now don't go crazy. I think they're going to give me something to speed up my labor."

"No! I want to be there for you. I want to hold your hand."

"It might be the safest thing," I said, touching her wrist.

"It might be the safest thing," Holly repeated in the quickest turnaround ever.

Rosie's face softened with relief and then pulled tight again. "Hang on. I feel a contraction coming on."

"Breathe, sweetie. Put the phone down."

Rosie disappeared, and the orderly hospital room jostled into view. I watched Holly's face turn from loving to terrified. "She's in the right place with experts," I said quickly. Summer put a comforting hand on Holly's shoulder while Holly's eyes remained glued to the phone.

"Take a deep breath, baby. Okay, let it out," said Holly. Except for Rosie's breathing, a low moan, there was no other sound, and we held our own breaths and waited. Rosie repositioned the phone.

"How bad is it?" Holly's brow knitted as if she herself was in pain. "Give me some of the pain. Pour it into the phone."

"Oh God!" she shouted. Another moan, a pause, and then Rosie gasped. The contraction dissipating. "I'm not afraid, Hol. This baby is meant to be."

"We are meant to be." Holly looked as if she wanted to crawl through the phone screen to be by Rosie's side.

"Oh, hey," Rosie spoke to someone off-screen. "Okay, sure." To Holly she said, "They're going to check my progress."

And that was when things went bananas.

Rosie said, "You're kidding. God, Holly. The baby."

"What's happening?"

In the calmest voice in the car, Summer said, "Holly, the baby is coming now."

"Start driving, Sam. Let's get us there, right, Holly? We'll get there soon, and you can hold the baby." Holly nodded rapidly, and I saw she was holding her breath.

"Keep breathing, Holly. You can remind Rosie too," said Summer.

"Right. Remember, Rosie. Breathe through."

Peanut sat at attention. I couldn't see Moose, but I assumed he was mimicking his best friend's posture. I heard Peanut panting, and I knew he was feeling the charge in the air. The anticipation of new life.

There were metal clanking sounds and a chorus of mixed voices. Someone said, "I'll take the phone." There was a wild, swinging view of the previously empty room now populated with bodies. An unknown woman's face appeared and said, "You're Rosie's wife?"

"Yes!" Holly said, her voice frantic and high pitched.

"We've done this hundreds of times. We're good at this." The phone flipped, and Rosie's face appeared in the screen. The woman's voice filled the speaker. "She's doing great. She's our focus. Just be encouraging." Summer's fingers clutched both of our shoulders.

Holly dropped her hand to the gearshift, where mine rested, and gripped it tightly. I moved so I could hold her hand properly.

Rosie shouted, "Can I push?"

Holly cut her eyes to me. "She's ready to push?"

"It happens fast sometimes. Superfast. But that's not a bad thing," I said.

Holly nodded, trusting, childlike.

The guttural wail that followed gave me chills. Holly tightened her stranglehold on my hand. Summer placed her cool hand on top of ours. I'd given birth. I knew what it felt like. There was a reason women told and retold their labor-and-delivery stories. The experience was like Vegas—wholly over the top and with an entire foot over the line of decency. Labor was the original slot machine, with higher stakes, greater fear and anticipation, with the promise of an epic prize in the end. The gift that kept on giving. A family.

Summer whispered, "This is wonderful" as she angled her phone over Holly's shoulder and captured the entire delivery on her phone.

Unnamed voices spoke encouragingly; someone said, "Okay, now the shoulder"; Rosie sucked in a breath and bore down, let out a slow groan that seemed to fold inside itself.

Holly, Summer, and I froze. There was quiet in the hospital room, as if the entire world had taken a slow-motion jump on a trampoline and we were all suspended in the air, waiting to touch back down to Earth.

And then we heard the baby make a noise between a mewl and a cry, and Rosie's tearful laughter. "She's here, Holly. Sweetheart, our little girl is here."

From my perspective as a bystander, it was revelatory. Despite the medical degrees in the room, all the book learning and classes, in that instant the doctors and nurses became nothing but door holders, ticket collectors, spectators. It was as if Rosie's body was a rock star on a stage shouting, *Stand back, brainiacs—a mother is in the house!*

———

Clamors of celebrations, tinny and joyous, leaked through the speaker.

The person holding the phone shifted, and there, in the iPhone rectangle, was a black-headed, soaking-wet baby.

"Oh, Holly," I whispered. I wanted to pull over. To stop rotating my gaze between the highway and the baby, but I knew this moment was about taking care of Holly, not creating a better moment for Samantha.

"Hi," Holly said, and the baby gave a cough and whimpered. Holly made a delighted sound, wiped her cheek of a heavy, fat tear.

Summer sighed and said, "So little!"

A woman in blue scrubs lifted the slippery-looking infant and placed her on Rosie's chest. "Hello, darling girl," and she flashed a quick look at Holly. Holly's face, shown in the light of the screen, radiating warmth. Rosie's face was dry and sure, but soft and buttery with love. And I knew this moment was a gift from the universe. That after all these years, I could be present for Holly and be a witness for all this. I wanted to say, *Wait, wait. Slow down. Look!* to everyone in the room cleaning up around Rosie as if nothing out of the ordinary was happening.

Whoever was holding the phone must have gotten distracted, because the phone dropped, and a thick, bluish-white, shiny rope filled the screen.

Holly gasped. "What's that? What's that thing on the baby?" She gagged and coughed, looked away.

"It's the umbilical cord," I said.

"What? That huge thing?" She gagged again, which made me laugh.

"We can't see the baby," Summer shouted.

The phone shifted, and Rosie said, "Don't watch, Hol. We're going to cut the cord."

Holly squeezed her eyes shut, then changed her mind and opened them again. "No, I can take it. It's okay." But she gagged twice despite herself, adding, "Are they doing that right? Is that the chief resident because I don't want a med student giving our baby a weird belly button."

And just like that, Holly was back to being Holly.

———

The next fifty miles were filled with the soundtrack of Rosie and Holly's love and their new baby attempting to latch on to Rosie's breast. Unable to tear her eyes from the screen, Holly told me and Summer, "We chose Eleanor as her name as soon as we knew it was going to be a girl."

It was hard to keep my eyes on the road, but I was determined to get my friend home to her family. I tried to give them their privacy. This was such a personal time for a couple. I knew because I hadn't had it with Jeff. Katie had accompanied me to all the childbirth classes. She knew to lock eyes with me during the transition stage of labor, supported my shaking legs in the final pushes.

Listening to Holly and Rosie, I returned to the well-worn path of what I'd missed over the years by sliding into marriage instead of actively choosing a partner. Staying instead of leaving because I couldn't speak up and get out. In the past, the intensity of that loss was made worse by knowing I hadn't done the work, hadn't learned how to ask for what I wanted because of my fear of conflict.

I'd learned so much on this trip. I tried to hide the first tears that leaked out and slid to my jaw. Those tears were followed by more tears. I heard Peanut reposition, and his head appeared at my shoulder. He licked my jaw, catching the salty liquid. I laughed, but it came out half giggle / half blubber—the release so rich and whole, so satisfying, it was as if I'd swallowed something delicious.

Summer peeked around Peanut and said, "Awww, Sammie," kindly, and I decided this nickname had a new feeling to it.

"Eleanor, I'd like you to meet my friends," said Holly in the singsong tone that every mother adopts the second a baby shows up.

CHAPTER TWENTY-EIGHT

LIFE PARTNER

Ten miles from Saint Mary's, the hospital that housed both Katie and Rosie, Holly unhooked her seat belt and shouldered her bag. The safety alarm sounded.

"We have ten more minutes," I said.

"I know."

"Holly."

She reclipped her seat belt but looked ready to vault.

"I don't think you can bring Utah in there. At least not until we clear it with the hospital."

"I'll put her in my purse."

"You're going to hold the baby. Kiss Rosie. Utah is an animal that has been with a bunch of other animals. You can't expose Rosie or the baby to any kitty critters. Leave Utah. Wash up. Go see Rosie."

Holly blinked.

"I'll take care of her," Summer volunteered and moved to cradle the purring kitten against her chest.

Holly fidgeted and wrapped her cold, bony fingers around my wrist. "I'm nervous. I can't believe I'm going to meet my daughter."

She released her seat belt, and the alarm sounded again, like a game show ding-ding-ding right answer. Holly threw Summer a kiss. "Take care of each other."

All together we said, "We will!" and chuckled at our unified enthusiasm.

I steered the car into the circular hospital entrance and stopped. Holly ejected herself from the car and loped across the pavement, and it was as if I was back one hundred years ago, dropping her off for a history class. She disappeared into the revolving door.

"She moves like an emu," said Summer.

"Do you think I can sneak Peanut into Katie's room?"

"I'm not the best person to ask about appropriate behavior. But, no. You can't. This dog smells like pancakes and wet hair. Also, it might be truly illegal. Which I normally wouldn't care about, but this was a big trip. Let's not screw it up."

"You're oddly wise, Summer."

"Odd only because you're blocked about where wisdom comes from."

I couldn't argue with that; she was right. "Can you read my aura? Does it say I can go see Katie?"

"Your aura is already out the door. Go. I'll sit with the dogs and Utah. I'll be fine."

"I won't be long, my friend, and then you and I can go home, together."

———

The cool, humid Wisconsin air cleared my head. I moved on autopilot through the parking ramp and into the hospital, having done this trek so many times before. Inside, the security guard didn't bother to look up.

Outside Katie's room I steadied myself, and with a gentle push on the door, I saw my dearest friend sleeping, the green light of the IV shining in her hair. I sighed with initial relief. Somewhere on the unit a monitor dinged. I heard a groan from across the hall; a bed rustled as a body repositioned.

My Katie, with her long eyelashes and hair, her hand folded under her chin.

"Katie?" I said in the same tone I reserved for Maddie, a loving mixture of *I'm here* and *I love you.*

Nothing.

I ran my gaze over her forehead, smoothed my clothes, wept silently and deeply as adults learn to do. I wiped my face with the shoulder of my shirt. I said her name again.

She opened her eyes, reached for me. I crawled into bed with her. "I'm so happy you're here."

"I'm so happy I'm here." I inhaled. "You smell like Katie."

"You smell like McDonald's."

"Holly and Rosie had the baby!"

"Holly texted me. She sent a picture. So cute." I knew Katie was thrilled, but I saw her working to conserve her energy. My heart skipped a beat.

"How are you feeling?"

"Hand me my water." She pointed to the peach-colored water pitcher. "Tired. You know how it is."

I did know. All too well, and I let the feeling of seeing Katie and knowing the misery of *how it is* settle in my stomach. I sat up, tugged the rolling bedside table closer, lifted the damp Styrofoam cup.

"Where's Drew?" I glanced around, almost expecting to see his handsome face moving through the door of her room.

"He was here, but I sent him home." I understood now they were a couple and marveled at Katie taking care of Drew while he cared for her. *Lovely,* I thought.

She pushed herself to a sitting position, took a sip of water. "I want to hear about the trip."

"Holly and I are friends now." I blurted this like a second grader who had sat next to the cool girl on the bus to their museum field trip.

"Are you?" She rubbed her eyes, close fisted, keeping the IV port from scratching her cheek. A skill learned from spending too much time in the hospital. "Did she tell you about the letter?"

"You knew about the letter?" Shocked, I grabbed her fingers.

"I didn't until Rosie told me about it." She swallowed another sip of water. "I'd called Rosie to see what they needed for the baby. We got to talking. It was quite a conversation about our life partners," she said, winking at me.

I warmed at the term *life partner*; we used it lightly all the time, but it was true. We were each other's partners in life. Just as Maddie and I were, and I thought Holly and I would be again.

"Rosie is so great. She told me about the letter because she said Holly needed to get unstuck and you were the only person who could unstick her."

"She said that? That makes me feel so good."

"It's not like Holly was the first person in the world to have her heart broken."

"Did you tell Rosie that we didn't know anything about anything back in college? That I was a stupid kid with low self-esteem from a small town?"

"Yeah." She laughed. "That's exactly how I said it. I asked Rosie what she thought about you two going on a trip to get Peanut. And she was all for it."

"So this was a scheme." I laughed. I'd felt uneasy about meeting Rosie, sure she shared Holly's disdain for me. But, a scheme to put us together, work out our differences meant that Rosie was benevolent and complicated. Willing to keep an open mind about me. My anxiety dropped a notch.

"A scheme with a higher purpose," Katie said, fumbling for her robe. "Let's go visit them. Let's go see the baby."

———

It took a few wrong turns to find Rosie's room. We were a jangly parade, Katie pushing her wheeled IV stand, me steering Katie in a wheelchair. When we arrived, I heard Rosie's velvet voice saying something quietly, and I eased the door open.

"You guys!" Holly said from within.

We inched into the room and peeked at the tiny bundle cinched in a white wrap, a green knit cap perched on her head.

Katie hit the brake on the wheelchair and said, "She's so pink! Is her hair jet black? She's stunning!" Her face shone with excitement for Holly and Rosie. For my part, it was the white swaddling that reminded me of the heft and warmth of a newborn cradled close and snugged tight. Holly couldn't tear her eyes away from the baby, and we all sat in a quiet reverie for the infant.

Soon, Rosie lifted her gaze to mine and smiled. "It's so nice to meet you in person, Samantha," she said. "I've heard a lot about you."

"Look, Eleanor, this is such a wonderful day. I want you to meet your aunt Samantha and aunt Katie," said Holly, locking her gaze to mine.

And my head felt like it might burst with joy.

After a moment we all began talking at once. Katie leaned almost entirely out of her chair so she could whisper to Eleanor. I knew how thrilled Katie was for Holly and Rosie, but I also knew how hard this had to be on her. How Katie had always wanted a child. She seemed past it, but her gaze at Eleanor told a different story of longing. Glancing at Holly, I saw she understood what Katie was likely going through. She laid her hand on Katie's back. She flicked her eyes at me knowingly, and our friendship held its old supportive geometry of the triangle.

Rosie clasped her chest. "I think my milk just came in! They said if I put her to my breast it will come. They were right!" We all quieted at the miracle.

"Oh!" I realized suddenly. "Summer is in the car with the dogs! I left her."

Holly grinned. "Oh, you know she's giving herself a facial and making friends with the parking attendant." She turned to Rosie and said, "Wait until you meet her. She is a wonderful piece of work."

"Don't give her your car keys, though." And Holly and I smiled at our inside joke.

———

In Katie's room, after I untangled the IV tubing from the foot pedal, plugged in machinery, and got her to the bathroom, she touched my arm. "Can we figure out a way for me to see Peanut tomorrow?"

"Yes. He's so mad that I wouldn't bring him in here right now."

"He's never mad."

I pulled the blanket over her and said, "I have so much to tell you."

"I know." And despite her fatigue, she had a twinkle in her eye, and I knew she was about to tell me that she was in love with Drew. And that was okay. We got Peanut for Katie. I got Holly back. Griffin had been attracted to me. There would be others.

"Drew is crazy about you," said Katie.

"What?" I would have done a spit-take if I'd had water in my mouth.

She nodded vigorously. "Oh yes. He wanted to know everything about you. We'd be eating curry, which I think he brought just so we could chat about you, and he'd ask how we met, were you as fun as you seemed."

"You hate curry," I said dumbly.

"He said there was something about you. Like he knew you the minute he met you."

"I got him for you." Another stunned, dumb response, but the lobe in my brain that was made for delight was so swollen it seemed to be pushing on my speech center.

"Well, he wants you. And don't be mad. I texted him. He's in the hall."

"I don't think I can take any more surprises," I said, feeling instantly nervous like a teen seeing her crush notice her for the first time.

Katie pointed out the door.

———

Drew stood outside Katie's room rakishly leaning against the wall, gazing into the middle distance. I was able to view him before he saw me. Tall, lean, with a dark, full head of hair and a scruff of beard, his posture was that of a man who knew no one would ask him if he was lost. His blue scrub shirt was tucked into the front of his drawstring pants, no sign of extra weight anywhere. I'd heard what Katie said, but I wouldn't believe it, trust it, until I saw his interest firsthand.

"Drew," I said, a closed smile on my lips. The grin I used when I hoped there would be somewhere to go with my demonstration of glee. Joy to come, teeth to follow.

He turned his eyes to me, and *oh, his smile*. "Samantha."

"It me." I laughed and corrected myself. "It's me."

"It is you," he said, and touched his hair like he was nervous about how he looked.

"I can't thank you enough."

"I'm sorry it's over. But I'm glad you're back."

"Are you?"

He nodded and looked at his hands, wiped them on his pants. "I know I'm sort-of married. I mean. We are divorcing. Well, you know."

"Yes." I felt my mouth go dry.

"If you would be interested, I'd enjoy spending some time getting to know you."

I knew I would enjoy that too. I knew because Drew interested me instead of intimidating me. He was neither a tyrant nor untrustworthy. For once I felt curious and unafraid.

I straightened and said, "I'd enjoy that too." A formal reply, for an informal request.

We looked at each other, and I said, "Thank you." But, then I couldn't speak. I was so relieved to see him standing there, my support person during this stressful trip. "Can I hug you?" I said, feeling my throat tighten. He walked toward me, and I moved into him. My cheekbone slid into place just under the notch of his collarbone; if the dogs, with their supersonic hearing, had been present, they would have heard the two of us click together.

He held me lightly, and I heard him inhale. "You smell like fruit cup."

I didn't have a smart comment or a splashy rejoinder. Instead I said, "That's Summer," and he said, "Yes, like summer and sunshine," and I didn't correct him because I wanted him to think of me that way.

He leaned forward and whispered, "It's good to see you," and because I was close to him, and it seemed as natural as the scent of grapefruit between us, I kissed him. I kissed him on his smooth, beautiful lips, and, my friends, I knew it was a cliché, but my heart did indeed soar.

CHAPTER TWENTY-NINE

BOTTLE THIS

What I did at my house after waking and wriggling myself out from under Peanut, in my bed: I nudged Summer, who was asleep next to me, and I picked up my phone and texted Drew.

ME: What did you find out?

BDREW: The courtyard. Best place. No paperwork needed for an outside visit.

ME: Yes!

Summer, naked as always, grabbed my robe from the back of the door. "Making coffee," she said. "Strong coffee."

BDREW: Good seeing you last night.

Pleasure shot through me, and I rushed to the kitchen to show Summer his text.

"I think we use the lemongrass cologne today. We don't want to make any promises but want him to know you're very interested but not easy."

I kissed her temple. "You are a nut."

"Shaman Shamansky would be so proud. Your aura is clean today."

I made a move like I was poufing my bouffant hairdo, and she said, "No need for that. It's big."

I texted Maddie: We're bringing Peanut to see Katie in an hour!

MADDIE: Send Pics!!! Also, I miss you

I thought maybe my aura pulsed with delight.

ME: I miss you too.

I sent her a string of emojis: a syringe, a dog, and a red helmet with a white cross on it. Maddie sent me a thumbs-up.

"Okay, boys. Let's pee and finish sprucing up."

Back in the bedroom, I removed the grumbling Moose from under the comforter, where he'd spent the night at my feet. He yawned dramatically, stretching his back legs behind him one by one.

"Let's get moving, dude—we have a big day ahead."

I located Utah, wedged between my pillow and the headboard. After Summer and I had bathed the dogs and I'd told her everything, I'd placed the litter box in the bathroom, and by some miracle or mistake, Utah had done her business.

"Utah, nicely done. Mommy will be so proud."

I raced the dogs outside, hauled the cat and dog foods from the trunk of the Prius, and dropped my phone no less than thirty-seven times. I fed everyone, gave Peanut his insulin, and cleaned the gunk out of Moose's eyes. Eight a.m.

"Drink your coffee," Summer said, bringing me a mug. "I'm going to shower."

I took a sip; the hot liquid slipped down my throat, and like the lights on a pinball table, my brain came to life.

I left the bathroom to Summer, the dogs following at my heels, and looked at my favorite photograph: first day of kindergarten, Maddie and me kneeling, my tan knees poking out from an end-of-summer dress.

Next to that photo was one of Jeff, his brown hair and eyes so similar to Maddie's. I'd never put all his photos away, wanting Maddie to know her father even if she would never *know* her father.

I touched the frame. "It's time to say goodbye to you, my friend."

I picked up the picture and put it on Maddie's bedside table in her room. I'd make sure she packed it for school. His spirit wasn't hanging around me, but I hoped he was hanging around Maddie. A spirit father might be just the right thing for a girl's first semester at college.

Back in my room, I kicked off my pajama bottoms. I yanked on a pair of jeans and slid my feet into my go-to tennis shoes. Peanut knocked his head against my leg and slimed my thigh, and I patted his jug head.

Summer, wrapped in a white towel, led a cloud of steam out of the bathroom. There were black smudges of mascara under her eyes. "Do you want to pick something out of my closet to wear?" I offered. "It'll be too big, but it's clean."

"I won't stay long." She said this like someone who was often told, *The show's over; clear the set.*

In elementary school, I'd been cast as one of the princesses in the high school's rendition of *The King and I.* I had very little to do, no lines at all. Just a lot of scurrying across the stage between characters and occasionally moving a plant or two during set changes. Despite having the smallest of roles, there was something intoxicating about being among a troupe of people who spent weeks together reciting the same lines, singing the same songs. When it was all over, it was as if I'd been birthed back into a confusing social world without a squad and no script.

I looked at Summer. This was what her life was like. Weeks and months of pseudo-intimacy, working closely with the same people as if they were family. Everyone knowing all the inside jokes, everyone with all the same complaints, everyone knowing the score. The score being—we're not family; we're not friends; when this is over, it will be time to move on. Best of luck. To quote NSYNC from the year 2000, "Bye Bye Bye."

"Summer. I want you to stay as long as you want to."

"Oh no!" she said brightly. "I'll be out of here soon. I'll make flight reservations today."

I knew she was sensitive about her career, about the unpredictable nature of show business, so I didn't want to corner her, asking for too many details. Instead, I said, "Maddie's gone for the whole summer. You can stay in her room. Or stay in my room. Either way. I'm not used to being home alone."

Summer stood, her back straight, examining me. I almost saw her wheels turning, gauging my sincerity or maybe trying to figure out what I would be getting out of the deal. Peanut barked, and that seemed to rouse her.

"I won't stay in your room. Drew might be needing my side of the bed," she said and winked. Then she grabbed her two enormous bags and started toward the door. When she got to me, she said, "Yup, the lemongrass for today" and moved herself into Maddie's room, and I felt simultaneously bighearted and lucky.

In the bathroom, I glanced in the mirror. My skin looked, if I dared say so myself, good. I had the warm complexion of someone who'd been in the sun, taking care of something on her long and unfinished to-do list. Summer entered, and we looked at each other's reflections. The women in the mirror were clear eyed and capable.

Summer shucked off her daisy-girl visage and said, "You are not cotton. I have no business being proud of you, but I am."

I took a deep, cleansing breath, clasped her hand. "You are a good friend."

Summer squeezed my hand and said, "Too bad we can't bottle this feeling. Gwyneth would pay millions for it."

———

This drive to the hospital had all the makings of the first one. Was it only a week ago that we'd started this journey? Phone calls, rushing, anticipation, the obligatory Walgreens stop. I knew I shouldn't have been thinking about what to bring. I should have learned by now that my presence was enough. This time the stop wasn't for me or Katie.

Sweet Utah was curled in Summer's lap, both of them fully groomed and ready for a calendar photo shoot, if need be. But oh, the dogs. I glanced in the rearview mirror, and Peanut sat erect, scruffy-looking with his fat pink tongue hanging extravagantly. Not much was visible of Moose, but his wide eyes protruded possibly more than usual.

Something had to be done.

"I'll be right back," I said.

"Get me a Diet Pepsi and some Cheez-Its."

I must have looked shocked because she said, "Babe, we aren't in California anymore. When in Rome."

I glanced at the dogs, the car windows down, the breeze blowing through. Moose blinked as if one second away from an eight-hour nap. The bath we'd given them the night before had done little except create two startled dogs. Apparently a bit less of their natural oils made for an unhinged look. Peanut's Tinder profile would read, *For the stray-dog lover in you.*

I darted inside to the pet supplies aisle and found what I was looking for. I'd seen it the last time I was in the store. Two matching blue-and-white patterned bow ties, with a loop to fit their dog collars. Just the thing to tidy everybody up.

———

In the parking area of the hospital, I watched Summer brush orange powder off her fingers and take a final sip from her soda. "You know, there is something fantastic about the chemical high you get from artificial food. I can see why people are obsessed."

I'd been telling her about the many delights Wisconsin had to offer. "Wait till you try our Wisconsin cheese curds. They squeak when they're fresh. You can get them fried at a supper club with a brandy old fashioned."

She squinted at me and said, "I don't speak Wisconsin." She eased Utah into the inside pocket of her bag. The kitten was part floppy washcloth and part playful stuffed toy and seemed happy to not be in control of anything.

Leashes clipped into place, we paraded to the front of the hospital amid curious and indulgent smiles. A concrete path led to a patio with benches and permanent tables. We chose the seat with a metal plate screwed into the back and engraved with the words *For Loretta Larson*, and I felt so grateful to be alive.

I couldn't sit. I fussed with a patch of fur on the top of Peanut's head like a school mother before a class photo shoot. As a last-ditch effort to make everyone look less desperate and more sleek, I took a lint brush out of my bag and gave everybody, including me, the once-over.

"Oh! I almost forgot." Summer spritzed me with the lemongrass cologne and said, "You look pretty. Two o'clock." She pointed with her eyes.

We straightened. Both dogs twitched and rotated their ears to the tops of their heads before I saw the door ease open. Holly pushed Rosie in a wheelchair through the door, both women with enormous smiles and bleary eyes.

The dogs stood, wagged in unison, and tugged at their leashes.

"I'm so glad you're here," I gushed. "I'm so nervous and excited. I can't stand it."

"We would have been here before, but Eleanor had trouble latching on this morning."

Rosie had a red paisley pashmina around her shoulders, and her skin gleamed. "It's like trying to put a watermelon into a buttonhole, honestly."

Holly gestured for Summer to come forward. "Rosie, meet Summer."

"I hear you saved this trip," said Rosie. I watched the two of them like a nervous hostess hoping everyone had fun at her party.

Summer flushed. Lifted Utah for viewing. "It was an ensemble cast."

Rosie exclaimed, "Ohhhhh, I love her," and I was sure she meant Utah and Summer because who couldn't love them both? Nobody, that was who.

There was hardly time to wheel Rosie into position when the door swung wide. "Here comes Drew with Katie," I said and wanted to feel only joy, but my niggling fear for Katie elbowed in and sat down.

When Katie saw all of us, she said, "Oh my God, you guys!" with one hand covering her mouth, her eyes gleaming with tears.

If I hadn't seen her the night before, I'd have been shocked at how small Katie looked in the light of day. She wore a faded blue hospital gown that matched the bluish color around her eyes and a hospital-issue robe. I wanted to dodge it, to brush past it, and stay distracted by Peanut's unruly hair or Drew's lovely eyes, but I made myself take it in. Because as often as I let denial rise up in me and block out my feelings, I knew Katie was seriously ill. And denying that now was not going to help anyone.

The real reason we were gathered here lunged forward. Peanut tugged at the leash, and I let it go, but he didn't rush Katie; instead, he moved respectfully forward. Katie lowered her head, and the dog met her forehead with his. There was a collective moment for Holly, Summer, and me where it seemed we were the only ones present. Each of us observing the fruits of our time together, each holding the triumph of the moment like a red thread uniting us.

"Oh, love," Katie breathed. And every one of us was part of that inhale. Even Eleanor seemed to feel it as she nuzzled closer to Rosie. This was the comfort of love. It didn't cure cancer or reduce the pain of childbirth, but it cloaked lovers, friends, and family in an embrace that stretched far and wide and was supremely difficult to break, despite our best idiotic efforts.

Drew came from behind the wheelchair, silently crossed the grass, and I put my hand lightly between his shoulder blades. "I'm going to let you friends reconnect without me hovering."

I whispered, "Thank you for everything. I'll text you later." I spread my fingers against his back to feel the movement of air into, then out of him as we watched Katie together.

With one last look, he smiled and moved down the path and into the hospital. Katie wrapped her arms around Peanut while Moose sat quietly and waited to be noticed. Katie waved us in, and I bent to hug the dogs and Katie in one grateful hug. Her sharp shoulder blades told the story of a difficult week while we were gone. A story I didn't want to hear but was absolutely strong enough to.

CHAPTER THIRTY
I THOUGHT YOU SAID THIS
WOULD WORK

Eleanor made a gerbil noise, and Rosie smiled. "I already know that's her hunger sound." She glanced at Holly.

"We're going back to the room. Eventually we might be able to feed this baby discreetly, but right now it's a lot of skin and nipple," said Holly.

"It hurts more than I thought it would," Rosie said.

"I used lanolin to ease that pain," I said. Remembering how many surprises, how many tips and tricks went into motherhood.

"I have not passed out once." Holly winked at me.

"Come visit if you're up to it." Rosie took Katie's hand in hers, and they shared a warm smile.

I grabbed Summer's tiny wrist and pulled her in front of me. "Katie, this is Summer Silva. She made our trip more fun than it had any right to be."

"When I heard you joined Sam and Holly, I watched everything you've ever done on YouTube! It's so nice to meet you." Katie grabbed one of Summer's hands with both of hers.

Summer grinned and said, "Did you see the episode where that lady wanted a sex swing in her camper?"

"Yes, right on television she said, 'I like sex in motion, baby!' and all I could think of was what her mother would say when she watched that episode."

"Her mother is another story altogether. The leaf doesn't fall far from the tree, if you know what I mean."

"Fruit?"

"Yeah, she was a total fruitcake."

Katie darted a glance at me, and I shrugged like, *Yep, that's what the whole trip was like.*

Holly listened to our exchange with a delighted smile and turned Rosie's chair toward the hospital's entrance. "I'll drop Rosie and meet you two in Katie's room in twenty," she said.

"Samantha, hand me the keys," said Summer. "I'll take the dogs home. Do some laundry. Stop for groceries. You can't live on Cheez-Its alone."

"You hate Cheez-Its," I said, but Summer was already leading the dogs to the car.

Then it was just Katie and me. Together again, pushing her wheelchair through the hospital, picking up where we left off.

"Bradley and Bebe are here," she said. "At the hotel right now, but they are coming to my room later."

"They made it after all?"

"Mom had a panic attack, and Dad decided to drive her up here to give them both something to do."

"How does that feel?"

"I'm glad they came. Mom is a hard energy, but, you know, she's still my mom."

"Moms do their best," I said, thinking of my mom and her difficult lack of energy. "I can only imagine what Maddie says about me."

Katie lifted her phone and said, "She says you're the best mom in the world. I told her that I already knew that."

———

In Katie's room I repositioned an IV pole, two folding chairs, and an over-the-bed table. It was hospital-room Tetris, and I found it satisfying. We chatted as I backed Katie's chair next to the bed for an easy transfer. Holly arrived, and we all took our places.

"So, the trip," Katie said.

Holly rubbed her shoulder. "We'll fill you in later."

"Holly only barfed once. And she did it out the car window and not in a sink."

"To be fair, there was no sink available. I would have made it the whole trip, but dogs vomit constantly, and my gag reflex is always at the ready."

"You should have seen her when a cat gave birth. She was horrified but did not pass out."

"People can change." She laughed, and there was a gracefulness in that comment that hit all the right notes. No bitterness. No *I told you so*, just grace.

"The dogs will stay with me while we fill out all the paperwork for making Peanut a support dog." I explained what Holly and I had worked out on the trip. "I'm sure it's complicated, but we have Holly, our personal lawyer, who can explain all the things."

"I can't tell you how good it made me feel to see Peanut. He smells just like he always did. His own Peanutty scent," Katie said.

"We have to have his vet records, rabies shots, et cetera. Sam, can you call Griff for those?" said Holly. The mischievous grin she shot me made me roll my eyes.

"Who's Griff?"

"He's a supercute vet that took a liking to Samantha. He did not know about Drew."

"Neither did I. Know about Drew, I mean."

Katie nodded. "Drew's amazing. You guys. He was so nice to me. He was sneaky at first. Coming in. Asking how I was. But one night we got to talking, and he confessed he was keeping track and sending you updates."

"To be fair, we knew you wouldn't tell us the truth, and we didn't want you to be alone," I said. "It was a Hail Mary decision," I said.

"It's okay. It was kind of great having someone I didn't know helping out. Very freeing. Plus, he's professional."

"His updates were pretty lame. But it was good to know you were doing well. Not getting worse while we were gone," I said.

The air changed in the room, threaded between the three of us. Maybe it was my spirit animal, the quiet deer, galloping through space and time, pulling a new dimension along with her.

But then Katie broke the spell.

"You guys, listen. I'm pretty sick this time. Like, really sick."

I sat hard on the bed, everything fun slithering out of the room with the word.

I nodded. "That's okay. Peanut is here. He'll turn on your immunity, and it'll be like the last time. Tough but manageable." I cut my eyes at Holly. "Right? We've done this before. We know how to do this." I took Katie's impractically soft hand, felt the smooth knuckle, the cushy underbelly. "This time we have Peanut *and* Moose. The healing power of two dogs this time around."

Holly didn't speak, even though one of Katie's machines beeped and there was a thread of blood in the IV line taped to the back of Katie's arm.

I looked between the two women, my two best friends. I squinted at Holly's calm, knowing expression. No anger. No impatience or condescension. No disgust at the slow slog of my brain to get with the program. I saw only acceptance and patience. Support without sarcasm and love.

I shook my head with realization. "Oh, Katie."

I touched my sternum, tried to comfort my plucky, bruised heart, so worn out from this last week of jump and run, and beat, beat, beat. If only sleep would barge in and take over. Where was my get-out-of-life-free card?

People always said their heart was where they felt all emotions. But the heart was a survival organ and didn't have time for every quiver and quake. As strong and fearful, as complicated and sad as I felt in that moment, I realized that life was a cluster of love, fear, loss, and acceptance scattered between the heartbeats. That was what true survival was, keeping the heart beating while continuing to feel everything.

"Oh, Katie," I said again, instead of my usual *No!* of denial. I stood and crouched by Katie's side, my hands on her slight knees covered in a thick cotton blanket.

"I thought you said this would work," I whispered.

Holly placed her hand on my shoulder, her fingers finding the small hairs on my neck. She joined me on my knees, put her arm around me, touched her forehead to my temple the way she did all those years ago. During late nights studying, after boy drama, that one time they thought I had meningitis, but I'd just had a weird reaction to the flu shot. All those years, and her forehead felt just the same.

"You guys." The triplet emotions of pleasure, despair, and love competed in a kind of foot race through my nervous system. Katie dropped her hand on my head, like a priest or a kindly old lady who had lived ninety-seven years and had seen every single thing there was to see in life. Had the perspective of the ages and wanted to pass it on.

I was a child, now crying at her mother's knee, and through all of it, all I could do was mutter, "I thought you said this would work." I drew in a shuddering breath and clutched at my new, shaky acquaintance, courage, and met Katie's eyes.

And, like it was no big thing, like it wasn't one of the biggest things in my life, she flicked her gaze to Holly and back to me and said, "Oh, Samantha. It did."

ACKNOWLEDGMENTS

When I started writing this book, I thought maybe this time around I wouldn't need as much help from family, friends, and writing professionals. I was like a newlywed on a honeymoon thinking, *Marriage is not that hard—love is all you need.*

Then the universe laughed and laughed and laughed.

I loved this book at first blush, but I needed a lot more than a warm mushy feeling and a few jokes to finish it. I needed the support from the people in my life who never say, "Ann, shut up about your book." Christa Allen, Erin Celello, Tyler Fish, Karen Karbo, Jacquelyn Mitchard, Samantha Hoffman, and Lisa Roe were available for three a.m. texts like, "Do you think my protagonist should [insert bad idea here]?" And wisely, kindly, they told me to shut my phone off and go to sleep.

My nonwriting friends Tammy Scerpella, Linda Wick, Carolyn Bach, Teri Osgood, and Tyce Shirly fed me and listened endlessly as I talked about imaginary people while problem-solving an industry they knew nothing about.

I don't know how to even begin to thank my agents Jeff Kleinman and Rachel Ekstrom at Folio Literary Agency. I flailed around and they waited until I was finished and then they sold this book to Lake Union. I am so very grateful for them.

Look, I don't want to get ridiculous here, but my editor, Christopher Werner, seems to get me in the way I've always wanted to be gotten. With his and Tiffany Yates Martin's unparalleled enthusiasm and sharp insights, this book is far better than it would ever have been without them. I don't know what I did in the world to deserve them.

A huge thank-you to Erika Westby and the Best Friends Animal Sanctuary, where I spent several days touring, talking, and meeting animals. Who knew heaven was so close to earth?

The Tall Poppy Writers, my online writer family, has supported my dreams in so many ways. I can never thank them enough for caring about helping writers find readers as much as I do. Bloom, our online readers group, is the happiest place on the internet, and knowing there are readers is what keeps me loving what I do.

Finally, John, Julie, and Meghan: you all make everything work.

ABOUT THE AUTHOR

Ann Garvin, PhD, is the *USA Today* bestselling author of *I Like You Just Fine When You're Not Around*, *The Dog Year*, and *On Maggie's Watch*. Ann writes about women with a sense of humor who do too much in a world that asks too much from them. She teaches writing at the University of Wisconsin–Madison Continuing Studies and at the Drexel University master of fine arts program, and she has held positions at Miami University and Southern New Hampshire University in their master of fine arts programs. She is the founder of Tall Poppy Writers, where she is committed to helping writers succeed. She is a sought-after speaker on writing, leadership, and health and has taught extensively at conferences and festivals across the country. For more information on Ann and her work, visit www.anngarvin.net and www.tallpoppies.org.